I0730888

PATRICIA BOYER-WEISMAN
SERENITY
WORKBOOK PRESS
RECOMMENDED
LITERARY BOOK COMPETITION 2021

WORKBOOK PRESS LLC
187 E Warm Springs Rd,
Suite B285, Las Vegas, NV 89119, USA

Website: https://workbookpress.com/
Hotline: 1-888-818-4856
Email: admin@workbookpress.com

Ordering Information:
Quantity sales. Special discounts are available on quantity purchases by corporations, associations, and others.
For details, contact the publisher at the address above.

ISBN-13:   978-1-956876-90-1 (Paperback Version)

REV. DATE: 20/09/2021

Serenity

As I touched his little hand through the hole in the incubator, I thought, *Did I do something wrong?* He was so little; his chest was moving up and down as if it were difficult for him to breathe. He barely weighed four pounds. He was yellow—even his eyes were yellow. Doubts began to flood my mind. *What have I done to this little boy who did not ask to be brought into this world?* I was selfish and lost in my own pain. I had not taken care of myself. I ate little, drank more than I should, and hardly slept. But I had no idea I was pregnant. Foolish, impulsive behavior over my own need to feel loved.

I had fallen into deep despair after Joseph broke my heart, and all I wanted to do was to curl up in a ball. I allowed myself to enter the darkest part of my mind. No one could reach me. Not Saul, Rick, or Scott. Across from the incubator was the man who had rescued me. He was holding my baby by his other hand. Marcus, the man who would not take no for an answer. The man who came into my office, bypassed the secretary, and opened my door to find me in a total mess. He intervened even when I fought back in anger, asking him to leave me alone. How dare he come in and interrupt my self-pity party? With me, the only one in attendance. He, through his insistence, his charm, and his brutal truth, pulled me to my senses and said, "Yes, you are listening, and I am not leaving until you agree to have dinner with me."

My knight in shining armor. Always positive, always with a solution.

The man who had declared his love for me early on knew better than Saul, or even my closest friends. I could see the tears in his eyes as he rubbed each small finger. "Marcus," I said, "I cannot lose him. I am so sorry for the harm I brought upon him. Our son."

My head began to spin, an uncontrollable fear overcame me. I felt weak. I felt sick to my stomach, and my chest began to hurt. My legs began to crumble under me. I was shaking just as I passed out. I felt arms around me saying, "My love, I have you." The last thing I remembered was saying across the incubator, "I cannot breathe."

He had taken one look and had rushed around the incubator and caught me before I hit the hard tile floor. "Nurse!" he yelled, "We need some help here!" She quickly brought a gurney, and Marcus helped to place me gently on top of it and cover me up. "Get McCullough!" he barked at the nurse, who was already on the phone with the doctor. She got off the phone and started an IV.

"Dr. McCullough is in the hospital and on her way up. She said she was fairly sure she is having a panic attack and has asked me to start Adventum to calm her down." The nurse began to take my vitals. Except for a little high blood pressure and racing heart, everything looked okay.

I began to feel loose and felt a floating feeling, Dr. McCullough pulled off her stethoscope and listened to my chest.

"Panic attack? Right, Samantha?"

"Yes, the worst one I ever had."

"Marcus, Samantha has a history of panic attacks. Since she failed to tell you about them, I will a little later. In a few minutes, she will start to feel better, and she can discuss what trauma triggered this one."

"I said 'I cannot lose Jared.' And Marcus said, 'Darling, you did nothing to cause his condition.'"

"That's right," Dr. McCullough said. "This happens when we are dealing with rare and incompatible blood types. He was the smallest of the twins, and the foreign blood must have crossed over to him. Him being the weakest, he suffered the effects. His brother was six pounds. Much bigger and did not have any trouble throwing off the foreign antibodies. Jared is jaundiced and his blood-pressure is high. His breathing is shallow, but Dr. Wright has him under oxygen. We are waiting to get him typed and get a donor for a transfusion. Marcus, get tested so that we can cross-match you. Nurse, take Mrs. Matthew to her suite while I talk to Mr. Matthew."

Marcus leaned over the bed and kissed me passionately and whispered, "We will not lose our son. I will move heaven and earth. Rest. Let me take care of Jared." I reached up and placed my hand on his cheek.

"Thank you."

"There are no thanks needed, sweetheart. That's what dads do." The nurse took me away.

✳ ✳ ✳

Dr. McCullough said, "You know, I know you're not the biological father."

"Yes, I know," Marcus replied.

"But I am respecting your privacy. So, can you call him?" she asked.

"Yep, right now."

"But you call in the best doctor. I do not care where they are. And get them here at my expense. Whatever we have to do."

Marcus dialed Joseph's cell phone, "Hello, man. We need you. One of the babies needs a transfusion. How fast can you get here?"

"Two hours, Marcus. I will call and have them get my jet ready to go."

"Great, man. I'll have a car and driver pick you up and bring you straight to the hospital."

"Of course."

Both men hung up. Marcus called Mike, his head of security, and said, "Joseph Claiborne is flying in on his private jet. He should land in two hours. Have a car and driver there to pick him up and bring him to the hospital. Bring him in through the side door as we set up. I want discretion."

"Hey Marcus, I'm all over it. Get some rest, man. I got your back."

Mike and Marcus are dedicated friends and had known each other since college. Mike had always been a loner, so being the head of security for the Matthew family was a perfect job for him. Marcus started thinking back to when Samantha went into labor. She had been up for so long and must have been exhausted.

Samantha started contractions at nine p.m. at the reception. We left immediately for the hospital. Her water broke in the limo, and I was timing her contractions which were progressing rapidly. We arrived at the hospital twenty minutes later. She was fully dilated, so there was no chance for an epidural. Fortunately, Dr. McCullough was at the reception, and after receiving word from Mike, she was put in another limo and followed closely behind us. Very few people realized that we, the bride and groom, had left. Rick was instructed just to continue to host the affair. All the cutting of the cakes had been done. We were on the dance floor when I realized that she was in pain. I picked her up and rushed out. She arrived in her wedding dress, and me still in my tuxedo. Quickly we had to change into a hospital gown. The first baby was crowning as we got her into the delivery room.

Jacob had been born first, then Jared a minute later. I cut the umbilical cords and was handed my son, Jacob, and Samantha was handed Jared, whom they laid on her stomach. Both babies cried immediately. The nurses took the babies and cleaned them up and checked their vitals.

That's when they became aware of Jared's weakened disposition and jaundiced coloring. He was also having difficulties breathing. Jacob, however, was alert and active, ready to nurse. He was handed to me. I handed him to Samantha, and he immediately latched on to nurse. Delivery was at eleven p.m.

It was six o'clock in the morning. Joseph should be there no later than nine a.m. Dr. Wright had talked to a specialist at Johns Hopkins. They had phone conferences and were swapping information. Everything was on target for treatment. Marcus could tell Samantha was worn out and stressed. She had been up for twenty-four hours, and exhaustion had set in. Dr. McCullough gave her something to sleep.

"Sweetheart, rest. I will take care of our son. Joseph is on his way. Do not worry. I got it covered. I have a specialist working with Dr. Wright. This happens sometimes but he's not showing any severe complications, and they have him under light therapy. They are going to try and get him to drink from a bottle. They have a breast milk bank, so he will be okay. Rest, my darling. The boys need you, and so do I," Marcus said.

Dr. McCullough checked her bleeding and asked the nurse to page if there was any need to come back. Otherwise, Samantha was instructed to sleep.

"Marcus, will you come out in the hall with me?" Dr. McCullough asked.

"Sure." He kissed Sam's head and said, "I will be back." He could tell the sleep medication was taking hold.

"Marcus, Samantha has had many traumas in her life. She has told you about many of them. Over the years, these stresses and traumas have accumulated into her state of mind where she has panic attacks. Sometimes it's night terrors that she may not have shared with you. She can, at times, be fragile—emotionally. She clings to safety. That is why, when Saul came into her life, and Rick and Scott, they became the circle of protection and love that helped her to stabilize emotionally. It probably seems weird to you, who sees her as a tough, capable attorney, and then see her collapse emotionally."

"No, Dr. McCullough, I know my wife and her need for security and safety. Comfort and stability, that is what I offered her, and to love her for who she is." Marcus thought of the first night they were together, how she wanted to dominate him sexually. She had a plan from the time they sat down to dinner. But the sexual tension between them had caught her off guard. She had tried desperately to regain control of their conversation, but the attraction kept interrupting her plan. Yet, he saw a smart and fiercely independent woman that intrigued him the moment she sat down. At the end of their meeting, he wanted her sexually, and more. He wanted a relationship with her, on her terms. Her little tricks, such as drugging him, handcuffing him, and keeping him to the point of orgasm, and then pulling back, sort of her idea of torture, just intrigued him more. She confessed that she had judged him as a spoiled rich man but had changed her mind after spending time getting to know him. She, herself, could not fight the sexual tension between them and fell into a rhythm riding him, trying to satisfy her own desire. They ended up entwined together, making intense love. They were not careful and did not use protection, and he had a glorious orgasm inside her. That's why it made sense that he was the father. He had only good memories of that night, but he could see how men with no scruples could use her as a one-night stand. He knew Joseph had not treated her that way, his problem is that he simply did not know what he wanted for his life. But Marcus knew. He knew from that first dinner he wanted her for his wife. Marcus thought quietly to himself. *I never even thought of another woman, nor would I have put myself in the position of getting another pregnant. I am selective and when I find who I want, I go for her. I am no saint. In my younger days, there were a few trysts, but in my thirties, I was ready to settle down.*

"Dr. McCullough, do whatever needs to be done. We can talk more about this after we get Jared out of the woods," he said, looking back at the doctor.

"You're a good man. Most would have turned their back on her if they suspected that she was carrying another man's child."

"Those boys are ours. I will raise them and love them."

"Sam has a history of self-destructive behavior and when Joseph broke her heart, she went into a tailspin. Luckily, you were able to rescue her. But loving her, with all her faults, may become an issue without counseling, especially with the baby being ill."

"Dr. McCullough, my heart loved her before the rest of me was aware I loved her too. Whatever comes our way, we, or I, will handle it. She has an exceptionally large, loving family full of very stable people. So, we are all here."

"Try to rest, Marcus."

"I will. I'll settle down in her room until Mike, the head of my security team, tells me Joseph has arrived. Will you send word to her father and my parents to go home until visiting hours this afternoon? I'd like sometime to get Jared sorted out before they start visiting."

The nurse asked, "Do you mind if they come to the window of the nursery to see Jacob, or had you rather wait? I know you have blocked off the nursery for your children, for security concerns. They would be escorted by your security if that is what you want."

"No, tell them to go home and come back at six p.m. unless they hear from me. Reassure Saul, her father, that she is okay and asleep. Thank you."

Next, Marcus called Beth, his secretary, and asked her to call Melanie, their public relations person to tell her to be prepared to head off any gossip.

"Put out in the press that the Matthews are proud parents of twin boys. Mrs. Matthew is resting. Please allow us our privacy. The babies are doing well. The family just needs time to rest, etcetera, etcetera. However Melanie needs to phrase it is fine. Thanks, Beth. Oh, Joseph Claiborne is coming in, so make accommodations at the plaza. Thanks, Beth."

Beth had been with the Matthew's long enough to keep any speculation to herself. They were a very private family. After Marcus had assembled and organized his team, he went back into Samantha's room, set an alarm for nine on his phone, and laid down on the couch in the suite to rest. He had everything under control so far.

His alarm went off too soon. He had dozed off for about an hour. He looked at Samantha, who was still asleep. She needed the rest. *I hope to have good news when she awakes,* Marcus thought. His phone rang.

"Yes, Mike?"

"We picked up Mr. Claiborne and we should arrive in twenty minutes."

"Great. Show him up to the eighth floor and I'll meet him at the elevator." Marcus got up and went into the bathroom. A quick shower and a change of clothes would help revive him. He still had on parts of his tuxedo. Mike had brought him fresh clothes as soon as he saw that they were going to be leaving from the reception. *Mike, he thinks of everything,* Marcus thought. He had gotten Samantha's bag, that she had packed several days ago, as well. Also, having the suite was so much better than a regular room. He could stay with her as much as he wanted and still be comfortable. There are only three of these suites at this hospital, and each one was financially supported by wealthy families in New York. Money always makes a difference, and when it came to his family, there was no expense spared. But he also tried to make sure there were accommodations for those less fortunate than he was.

He let the warm water trickle down his face. It felt so refreshing. After he showered and dressed, he thought about shaving and was looking in the mirror. *The boys could look like me. They are darker complexioned, like me, and have blue eyes and black curly hair.* But when Joseph shows up, there would be no question who their biological father is. Either way, no one would question the Mathews Family or the daughter of Saul Weinstein. Power and money make everything right.

Marcus stepped out in the hall to meet with Joseph. Mike had brought Joseph up the back elevators to avoid any reporters or curiosity seekers. The men shook hands and Marcus thanked him for coming, Joseph answered in return.

Marcus said, "I'm not going in to all the details, but bottom line, you are the biological father of twins. From your attorney's letters, you suspected that you could be the father. To be honest with you, so could I. We had a one-time sexual encounter the night before she left for Boca. Samantha is looking for someone to love her for her. So, I think until you called, she had given up on you. But you called and off she went. None of that is important now. The smallest twin, Jared, needs a transfusion, preferably from his biological father. The doctor can explain exactly what it's called and the effects it will have on him."

A nurse appeared in the doorway. "Is this the

father?" "Yes, the biological father."

"Please come with me so we can get you typed and get your blood. We need to get the transfusion going."

"How is he?" Joseph asked.

"He is a fighter and doing better. This transfusion will put him in the position to fight the foreign antibodies that crossed over during birth." Joseph followed the nurse into the lab and rolled up his sleeve.

"So, how's the other twin?" Joseph asked.

"He is fine. A real character, very demanding and always hungry. He was six pounds, and his brother was four, so he took valuable nutrients from his brother. And the mother, Mrs. Matthew, is sleeping right now. She had a rough delivery. Then with the news about the baby, she had a major panic attack. That's it, we will get this to him immediately," the nurse said finishing.

"Can I see them?"

"Um, maybe you should talk to Mr. Matthew. He has a lot of security posted around the nursery where the boys are."

"I gotcha. I do not want to push your rules. I'll find Marcus."

Joseph went back down the hall where he knew Samantha's room was. Mike was standing at the door.

"Hey Joseph. You'd like to see Samantha?"

"Yes."

"Marcus is telling her you are here. Let's knock." Marcus answered the door.

"Come in, Joseph. Give me a minute to wake her up. Samantha, darling." He touched her cheek tenderly.

"Sweetheart, Joseph is here. Do you want to see him?"

"Yes. Yes. I had an awful dream. I could hear a child's voice calling me, but I could not find the child."

"Baby, it's a dream. Jared is doing well, and Joseph just gave blood to get the transfusion going."

"Samantha," Joseph said. "Darling, I'm here for you," he whispered.

Samantha replied, "Please, come closer." Joseph sat down on the bed bedside her. She put both arms around his neck and stated sobbing.

"I am so sorry I kept this from you. I felt spiteful. I know it was childish, but I want my life to be complete, with no issues. I'm tired of complication. Marcus has offered me this life. And he loves me, faults and all. No expectations, no plans I must follow to please others. I can be me. I can have my family and my peace. Joseph, I'm tired of struggling with doubt. You may not understand. The love I have for you is a complicated one. I do not want to compete for your love. I want to be first in my husband's life. Marcus gave me his heart and I love him for that. Can you understand?" she finished.

"I understand, and now is not the time to talk about what should or could have been. Let's focus on our son."

She removed her hands and reached for Marcus's hand. "Yes, let's focus on my son."

"May I see the boys, please?"

"Yes, sure, man. Follow me," Marcus said. "We will be back, love. Rest, sweetheart. You need it."

The two men left the suite and Marcus allowed Joseph into the nursery. Because of security problems, both boys were isolated in a separate nursery. Being the sons of multi-billionaire parents makes them vulnerable. Joseph went first to Jared's bed. He was under a light to help raise his bilirubin levels. He was jaundiced and still lethargic. Joseph said, "He's so little."

"Yes, but he is a fighter, and he looks so much better. The doctor said it's all about time now. He needs about three days of light therapy, nutrients, and a few blood transfusions, and he will get back to normal. He needs to gain weight, but we nurse him with breast milk. He has physical therapy each day to get him active."

Joseph reached for his hand, and Jared curled his little fingers around Joseph's fingers. A tear ran down Joseph's face.

"What mistakes I made, Marcus. Here is my son and I cannot claim him without disrupting so many lives, including his."

"Hey, we will work something out," Marcus said. "We all want what is best for our children and our family. Sometimes we must sacrifice a little, to savor what we have. Let me introduce you to Jacob." Marcus picked up Jacob and handed the bundle to Joseph. He was squirming, flapping, and kicking his feet. Then he began to cry. Marcus said, "Hang on to him; he is a lively one. Let me get the nurse to give you a bottle so you can sit down and feed him. He's always hungry, but healthy." The nurse brought a bottle and handed it to Joseph. He placed the bottle to Jacob's lips, and he immediately latched on and began to suck vigorously.

"You have to pull the bottle away from him from time to time or he will suck it all down and then throw it back up on you. Just use the burping cloth on your shoulder and pat him on the back. He settles down in a few minutes. He is already showing signs of being aggressive. After that, you can feed Jared. He tries to sleep through his feedings, so you just have to keep waking him up," Marcus said.

"Joseph, I'm going to clear your entrance into the nursery. Spend as much time as you like with the boys. We are going to be here for the next seven days. The doctor wants Jared to gain a pound and make sure his liver is functioning correctly and the jaundice is gone. I think my secretary has been in touch with you and has made arrangements for you at the Plaza. Mike has arranged a driver and car downstairs. Here are the cards with both their numbers. If you need anything, just let them know. And thanks, man, for coming."

"Of course," Joseph said. "These are my sons, even if I cannot publicly acknowledge them."

"Well," Marcus said. "We will work something out. I have an idea, but I want to run it by Sam first. It's clear to the eye that these children are mixed genetically. No one will question their paternity if they are a Matthew. They look enough like me, dark features, and all. My mother is full-blood Spanish. My public relations firm will keep a lid on everything. Let's just focus on them getting well."

Joseph smiled, "And maybe we want to get a diaper change? There something rotten in Denmark."

"Man, you are on your own with Jacob. The nurses will help you out. I am going back to check on Sam."

❉ ❉ ❉

The nurses reached for a diaper and said, "Mr. Claiborne, do you want help?" Joseph laid him down on the changing table.

"I'd like to try and change him with your help. Will you pull the diaper down first and grab a handful of wipes?" Joseph did as he was instructed and looking at his son, he thought, *I will never be able to show my son how to be a responsible young man. There must be a way.*

"Mr. Claiborne you want to act fast. He has a habit of peeing just as the chilly air hits his penis." Sure enough, Jacob began to pee on Joseph's hand. The nurse put a clean diaper over the stream of urine.

"Thanks, I'll remember that next time."

The nurse said, "This one is a little rascal."

Joseph smiled and said, "He's a lot like his father." The comment had already registered with them, but they knew to not speculate or say anything further. They were there because they were loyal to the Matthew family. Marcus Matthew had helped their family many times and they would never betray his trust.

Marcus entered Samantha's room just as she was getting out of the shower. She was embarrassed for him to see the changes in her body. Her breasts were twice as large as they had been, and she still had a small belly. She was hard on herself; she said she had never felt beautiful like the blond-haired women that always demanded a man's attention. Marcus could tell her confidence was waning. In the baby books he purchased, he read that women who are very sexually inclined may feel different about their ability to attract men, especially after their body had changed by pregnancy.

"Sorry darling, I should have knocked. But when I did not see you in the bed, I was concerned where you were. Anyway, what a treat. Wow, you are so beautiful."

Marcus went toward me, pulling me to him. He kissed me passionately and kissed each breast. "I am jealous of my sons. These jewels used to belong to me." He pinched each nipple, and the pain made my vagina ache. I could feel the tension in my body responding. It had only been two days and already I wanted to feel him inside me again. His erection was pressing against his jeans. He began to pull my butt up to crotch level.

"Baby, if I do not stop now, I'm going to put you against the shower wall and have you right now." I pushed him back, "Now, you know that doc said twelve weeks."

"Sam, I will be lucky to last six weeks. My hand is going to be tired. There are other ways to satisfy me, and I am going to take advantage of you, my dear." I laughed.

"Get out of here and let me get dressed." He left and went into the bedroom to wait. I dressed in the gown that Isabella had given me. It was soft, blue, and exceptionally low-cut with a matching robe. I took my time to put on makeup and spray some perfume. I always did the best I could with my hair. It was curly and had a mind of its own. I walked into the room where Marcus was waiting.

"Wow." He stood up and went to embrace me. He leaned down and smelled my hair, then nuzzled my neck.

"You smell so good, and you look beautiful. Is this for me?" I laughed again, "No, it is for me. But I appreciate you noticing."

"Sweetheart, I'm going to need to unzip my pants in a few minutes."

I came over and sat down on his lap and put my arms around his neck, "Thank you. It is all going to work out. I am so ready to go home."

"I know, darling. But if we leave before Jared's ready, then we will leave him by himself. I think we all want to go home together."

"Yes, sweetheart. I agree," I said.

"Samantha, I wanted to talk to you about Joseph. He is suffering. Those are his boys, even though I'm going to be their father and raise them, he needs a role. So, I was thinking about him being the godfather. Then at some point, when they get old enough, we tell them the truth about their paternity. I believe they will need his input along their lives. They are biracial, and they will need advice along the way. I will have all that time with them and legally be their father. They will be Matthews. I will have established my role as their father, spending that much time with them, raising them. I am confident that my relationship will be solid. But I think, at some point, they should have choices."

I listened quietly, "I think you're right, darling. Let's talk to him. I guess he's still here?" Marcus called Joseph's cell.

"Hello, Marcus. What's up?"

"Well, I am hoping you are still here."

"Yes, just gave Jared his bottle and changed his diaper. He is asleep again and seems to be doing better."

"Joseph, do you mind coming down to Samantha's suite? To talk with us about the boys?"

"Sure, I'll be right there."

Then there was a knock at the door.

"Come in, Joseph." He looked tired but just as handsome as always. I knew I looked attractive, and I was glad he could see what he lost. I know that was a selfish thought. Always afraid that if I did not work hard enough, look good enough, please the person I was with, then he would not love me. Marcus loved me for who I am. He was the better man for me, but I was still a flirt. I wanted to look good and be recognized for it.

Marcus started, "Joseph, I understand your heart is conflicted. You're married, you have a daughter, and now you have found out you have two boys. I know sons hold a special place in their father's heart. So, we talked about it. About you being the boys' godfather. You can spend time with them and help shape them into men. Then when they get old enough to understand this situation, *we* tell them that you are the biological father. They will need input from you along the way. They are bi-racial, and I know there are somethings, that as black men, they will need to know."

Joseph was quiet for a few minutes. "I'd like that."

"Samantha said the bris will be in six days. Saul is handling the ceremony, so I'll tell him what we decided. I'd like to meet Emily and Sophia. Let's try to be families together. Raise our children knowing each other."

Joseph reached out and shook Marcus' hand and came to hug me.

"Samantha, you look beautiful." He put his arms around me and kissed me on top of my head. "Thank you," I spoke.

"You look tired. Why don't you go to the hotel and rest? If anything changes, I'll call you," Marcus said.

"Thanks, man. I could use a good meal, a drink, a shower, and a good sleep. I learned something about our boy," Joseph continued. "He's quite a little character already, once the air hits that missile of his, you better have a shield ready unless you want to get wet." He smiled.

"Yep." Marcus laughed, "He got me a time or two."

"Well, I will be going. Goodnight."

"Samantha, let's order a steak dinner this evening and eat together after you nurse the babies. I feel like celebrating tonight."

"Sounds good, Marcus." He left the room to let the nurses know to bring in the boys at feeding time, then called down and had a steak dinner delivered to the suite. I called Saul.

"Everything alright, Samantha?" he asked.

"Yes, dad. We decided today concerning the boys' bris. I'd like Joseph, Rick, and Scott to be their godfathers. So, in six days, you have to have it all set up." I listened while he talked a bit about the bris, then he asked about the boys.

"Yes, Jared is doing a lot better. He had a transfusion, and we had a long talk with Joseph about his role in the boy's life. Dad, it was Marcus's idea. He is confident in his role as their father. Anyway, we will see you tomorrow at visiting time. Love you."

Tomorrow came and Saul and Margaret were the first to arrive. The nurses had brought the babies in for early feedings in hopes that they would be settled and sleepy when the grandparents arrived. The grandparents had only been able to see them through the nursery window, so they were going to be excited to see them in person. Breakfast had gone well, and Marcus had to go out and check on the new house's progress; all ten houses had been sold. There were quite a few questions that Marcus had to answer for the project manager. There were two doctors who had purchased in our neighborhood. One was Dr. McCullough, who had loved the concept of being just out of the city with a gated community and so many amenities. She had teenage boys and thought that an equestrian community would be exciting for them and keep them occupied during the times she spent at work. Her husband was a law professor at NYU. Marcus thought having attorneys would make good neighbors. The second doctor was a heart surgeon, whose wife was a socialite. They had three children, all teenage girls. Another couple was an international banker and his stay-at-home wife expecting their fourth child. Then there was an import/export couple—very Jewish, which added more diversity to the group. One couple owned a health food restaurant, as well as several health foods stores. Then there was an entertainer and his wife having their first child. They wanted the privacy and the seclusion that the new development offered. They liked the idea of the security and the gated entrance. An accountant and his wife, who was also an accountant, were a lovely African-American couple with no children yet. The banker who had brought the project to Marcus in the first place, and his wife, who was a local designer, were childless, but liked the idea of being a part of this new development. A local artist and her spouse were the only lesbian couple that had applied and been accepted. They were in the process of adopting two children from Venezuela and were just so happy to find such a group of culturally diverse future neighbors. The last couple was building the only ranch home, as it was to be their last home. Retired, they wanted the land and liked the idea of the wooded areas and the lake. They, too, found the diversity of the new owners appealing, as they liked to go to parties and wanted to be around people. Their children were all grown, but they had five grandchildren who visited quite often. It was their house that Marcus was making the exception on because it was only going to be 4,000 square feet, the smallest in the neighborhood. Marcus wanted the design to include stone wings on the side that gave the appearance of a larger home. They had been botanists and loved the idea of all the outdoor space. They wanted a solar house and a greenhouse.

All the homes were high-tech, which was good and bad, as there were varying degrees of understanding amongst the group about how it would work. There would be a board governing the association with a property management firm to work toward enforcing the community standards. Marcus was building what they hoped would be their forever home to raise their children. Their home was the second largest with thirty acres and 25,000 square feet. It had been pushed back several times to accommodate the other homes' progresses. The young pregnant couple was due in late November, so Marcus had promised to finish their home first in time for the baby. The artist and her wife wanted to get settled with their new home so that it would be ready for their children when the adoption was complete.

Our home was going to be the largest, and Marcus wanted it finished by the boys' second Christmas, which was fine with me. We had the penthouse and that had plenty of space until our new home was finished. Today he would be meeting with the retired couple for the final approval of their plans. Billie, his architect, was having issues getting the solar panels placed, along with the trees that the couple did not want to remove, to fit the lot so that all worked in harmony. An attorney from my office would be on hand to finalize the contract. Marcus, at this point, had the final say on every modification, as he had not turned the association over to the board yet. He was incredibly good with people and was confident that he could get it worked out in time for the grandparents' visit. He approached life with his laid-back disposition, which made one think that Jared was his biologically.

Margaret and Saul would be the first to arrive for visitation, which would help me out if he were not back before his parents arrived. Margaret would be there for support. She had a way of taking charge and creating order, which is needed with Isabella and dad.

Jared was doing much better. The second transfusion and the light therapy were turning him around. He no longer acted so lethargic and had started gaining weight. His jaundiced skin had almost disappeared. It had been three days since his birth, and his liver tests were perfect. He had shown no signs of respiratory failure. Rest had helped me, as had my new anxiety medication. I was now looking over some work that Rick had sent over and occasionally took interest in the house plans. We talked about taking a honeymoon trip to Wyoming to see our new ranch. There was a new colt that was training as our first racehorse.

Life seemed to be going our way. Joseph was here at the hospital every day to visit the boys and made himself scarce during family time. He accepted his role as godfather. Marcus was now back in the suite, although his phone never stopped ringing.

"Hi, Mr. Matthew. The West family is looking over the plans I had drawn up for the third time. For them to be accommodated for the moving of the solar panels, my solution was going to cost an extra thirty thousand. They had already agreed to a 2.5-million-dollar price. So, they had wanted to stay under three million, and could, if there were no more changes," I heard Billie say over the phone. Marcus thought going in, they hit the three million mark as their house centered around being self-sustaining and environmentally friendly. He waited to be patched through to them and began a short negotiation. Marcus was charming and so good with people; I knew he could resolve this quickly.

"So, Mr. and Mrs. West, what do you think of the new modification and the cost associated with them?" Marcus asked.

"We are pleased." said Mr. West, "And the repositioning of the greenhouse should provide better sun that is needed for the plants. It's priced well, and we are still under budget. Now, how's your wife and sons?" they asked.

"Good, ready to come home," Marcus replied.

"Mrs. West said for you to tell Mrs. Matthew 'Not to hurry getting home too quickly, take her time and get plenty of rest,'" he said with a chuckle.

She had sent over two large packages and I opened them while they were still on the phone. "Now, here are quilts I made for the boys. I made them twin-sized, as I suspect they will be sharing their room. And here is a jar of honey from our beehives. We are so grateful that you and your wife are supporting the building concepts of our home.”

“My wife is all about it, Mrs. West. She will be the first one to approve a goat if you decide on one.” Marcus laughed and continued, “She’s been reading on how good goat milk is over cow’s milk. I’m sure she will have many questions for you since these are our first children. Sam is open to the help.”

“She’s a good one,” said Mr. West. “Reminds me of my mine.” I could hear his delicate kiss to his wife over the phone. I loved knowing that two people could stay in love after fifty years together.

“The change orders you need to sign will be handled by my attorney. I need to be getting back to my wife and boys,” Marcus said as they wrapped up their conversation and said goodbye. Margaret and Saul had gotten to the hospital. Margaret had made some homemade vegetable soup. She poured me a bowl and placed it next to a plate of crackers. Marcus came in and gave Margaret a kiss on the cheek.

“Wow, that smells good. Sam, how about a bite?”

“Nope. No, sir. I did the work; I get the rewards.” Margaret laughed, “Now, kids, there is plenty of soup. Marcus would you like a bowl?”

“Yes, ma’am. I would and some of those crackers.”

“I brought hot sauce. I thought you may be a hot sauce man.”

“You know it. Man, this is good!” Marcus said as he was spooning the soup into his mouth. Saul reached for Marcus’ hand and then pulled him into an embrace.

"You and Samantha have made me so happy. I never thought I'd see grandchildren before I was pushing up daisies."

"Sir, I am happy, also. I love your daughter with all my heart."

There was a knock at the door and in came John Marcus and Isabella. "Dad, Mom is fashionably late as usual."

"Your mom, son, did not know what to wear to meet her grandsons."

"Oh, come here and give your mother a kiss. I am so proud of you. More twins! I love it." John Marcus gave his son a big bear hug.

"I'm so glad you decided to settle down. The company, marriage, and now kids. When you decide to settle down, you do it in a big way."

"Dad, it took the right woman."

"Samantha," said John Marcus, "How are you feeling? We viewed the boys through the glass in the nursery. I cannot wait to get my hands on them."

"Yes," said Isabella, "I want to smother them with kisses!" Isabella kissed me on both cheeks. "I brought you a present. It belonged to my mother." It was a pearl rosary with a gold diamond cross. She placed it in my hands. It was beautiful.

"Thank you," I whispered.

"Well, I want to let you know, I started a trust fund for their education. A hundred thousand for each of them. How about it, Saul? You think you can match the amount?" he said teasing.

"That's not a problem." He got on the phone and dialed his banker. "Transfer two-hundred thousand dollars into the educational trust that John Marcus Matthew set up for my grandchildren." He hung up. In came the nurses with the babies. You could already tell them apart. Jacob was much bigger and was always fussing to be fed. Jared, on the other hand, was smaller but catching up quickly. John Marcus reached for Jacob and took a bottle from the nurse. Saul took Jared and sat down in the rocking chair.

"This is my boy. I can already tell he is smart," John Marcus said.

"Dad, are you just a little prejudiced?"

"No, he has the look of a very smart and studious soul," said John Marcus. "This boy is a born developer; see how he squirms and cannot be still? We will have a tough time keeping this one in line. Anyway, it will be so much fun watching these two grow into men." Isabella was sitting on the arm of the chair.

"I could just pinch those sweet cheeks. The boys are certainly looking like the Spanish side of the family. They have that dark complexion like Marcus. And the blue eyes are Samantha's," said Isabella.

"Okay guys, visiting hours are over. Time to go, we want to get these boys to bed and get some sleep ourselves." Both sets of grandparents reluctantly left.

"I hope to see you home soon. Oh, dad, do you have the bris all ready?"

"Yes, sweetie. Now that I know who the godfathers are. I have lined up the mohel and have yarmulkes for the little ones.

Isabella interrupted, "And, of course, there will be a Catholic christening in about six months. We can use the girls' christening gowns. We had to buy an extra one when the girls were born. We used Marcus' gown for one and then a new one for the other one. Samantha, I'll take care of all those details. I guess you will be using the same godfathers'?"

"Yes," Samantha said. "And the girls, I'd like them to be the godmothers."

"Well, goodbye, kids. The nurses are telling us to go. Love you!" Margaret said.

"Goodnight, Dad. Sleep well." Saul came over and gave me one more kiss.

"Thank you, sweetheart."

"Oh, darling, remember the girls are coming tomorrow. They bought everything in the store with your dad's American Express. Anyway, good night," said Isabella as they walked out, shutting the door behind them.

"Sweetheart, you look tired. Go home," I said to Marcus. "Sleep in our bed and get a good night's sleep. Jared's doing well and you're a phone call away. Carol left me a sleeping pill and I am going to bed after I nurse the boys."

"I think I will help you with the boys, then go home and sleep in our bed, even though I will miss you."

Jared came in first, he began to latch on my nipple as quick as Jacob would. After he had nursed for about twenty minutes, I handed him to Marcus to change his diaper. He swaddled him with his blanket and handed him back to the nurse. Jacob was sucking so hard that I was wincing in pain. "Darling, I'm not sure I can nurse for three months. My nipples are so sore."

"What about more pumping of your breast? Let's talk to Carol tomorrow." I handed Jacob to Marcus, and he changed his diaper and swaddled him. The nurse took him back to the nursery.

"Let me rub the cream on your nipples before I leave. I'd enjoy that." Marcus grinned. He rubbed the cream on my nipples and kissed me passionately, thrusting his tongue in my mouth. I began to feel the tension in my core.

"Marcus, do you really think I am going to be able to sleep tonight, after all this?"

"That's the idea. Goodnight, my love."

I was thinking of Marcus, and his naked body, when the phone rang.

"Hello, Marcus, sweetheart. Missing me already?"

"It's not Marcus. Could I see you in the morning? Just to talk, just the two of us?" Joseph asked.

"Yes. I think that will be fine. Come around seven, when the boys need feeding. You can help with that."

"I'd like that."

After we hung up, I dialed Marcus. He sounded sleepy, "Sam, is everything okay?"

"Yes. Joseph called and he wants to come by to talk, just the two of us. I wanted you to know and be okay with that."

"Yes, love. I love you. And will you marry

me?" "Yes, goodnight." I smiled and hung up.

The next morning, at seven a.m., I got up and showered, put on one of my linen jumpsuits, and made sure my makeup was perfect. My hair, well, it always does what it wants, so I left it down. I was going to a lot of effort for Joseph. But that is who I am: Flirtatious and always wanting attention. I had asked the nurses to bring the babies in when he arrived, along with bottles of milk. I had also planned to breastfeed while Joseph was there. I wanted him to get a feel of our family, even though it would be from a distance. I ate a poached egg and toast and drink a cup of chai tea. Now, I was ready to say goodbye to the person who I had wanted to spend the rest of my life with. There was a knock at the door. Joseph walked in wearing jeans and white linen shirt. A beautiful man. Together, our children will be beautiful.

"Joseph, how are you?" He walked over and sat down beside me on the couch.

"I had better thoughts, but you know that. I have not seen our boys yet this morning, but I understand Jared is basically recovered?"

"Yes, he is doing well. He gained a pound and a half. He has not caught up to his brother yet, but he will. Jacob will always be the active one. He is always fussing until he gets what he wants."

There was a knock at the door, and two nurses brought in both boys with bottles.

"Mrs. Matthew, we just changed their diapers." The boys were cute in their diapers and little shirts. Jacob in blue and Jared in light green. Marcus and I had decided to dress them differently, to respect their individuality.

"Joseph, will you take Jacob and start bottle feeding him? That will give me a chance to breastfeed Jared." The nurse handed Jacob to Joseph and Jared to me. We looked like a perfect family. Joseph put the bottle to Jacob's lips, and he grabbed it with his little hands and directed it to his mouth. I laughed, "Well, that's new. He is strong for three days old."

Joseph kissed his head. I unbuttoned my jumpsuit blouse, exposing one breast and held Jared up to my nipple. He immediately latched on and began to suck.

"So, Samantha, if we were together, this is what it would look if we were a family."

"Remember, darling, this is what I always thought...we would be together."

"I so regret my foolishness. Now I have three children and can only claim one. Don't forget, Samantha, how good we were together. You could always finish my thoughts. Our sex was like no other I have ever had with any other woman. Intense, freaky, and fun. Remember our camping trips? And sneaking into vacant classrooms to steal some sex? How many times did we almost get caught?"

"Yes, I remember, but we cannot go back to that time. We were kids, enjoying each other's bodies. Carefree, but with no plans for a future together. I know what I want. I want security and stability. Marcus offers me that. You now have a family, not by choice, but by an impulsive act. But look at it as a chance to get some direction in your life. Figure out what you want and go for it."

"But Samantha, I can never love another the way I love you."

"Love your daughter. Make her the new love of your life, and love her mother, because she gave you Sophia." Jacob had finished his bottle and Joseph had him on his shoulder to burp him. Jared had drifted off to sleep, so I moved him to my shoulder to burp him.

"Let's switch boys. I like to breastfeed Jacob some so he can feel my touch and smell me." We switched babies, and Joseph tried to get Jared to drink from the new bottle of breast milk. He sucked a little and then would drift back to sleep. On the other hand, his brother latched on to my nipple and sucked with force. Joseph saw me wince. "Painful, yes. He makes my nipples sore. Marcus and I are going to breastfeed for a month and then use breast milk in bottles. I want to get my body back in shape," I sai,d answering him before he asked his question.

"Samantha, motherhood becomes you. You're more beautiful

than ever. I just wish it were me and you making these decisions, not you and Marcus."

"Joseph, you have a wife. And I have a husband. I thought at one time it was meant to be, but not anymore."

"I know. I have decided to go ahead and run for office. First state representative, then senator. And who knows where the next office might be? I've been thinking I might like to be a judge. I will figure it out. Emily will make a great political wife. She will be wrapped up in Sophia and okay being in second place to my career. Not you. You will have to be first in everything. Marcus, I believe, knows that. I have to say, he is a confident man. No jealousy with him."

"No, Marcus said he loves me enough to let me go, but he said he'd love me so much I would never want to go." There was a knock at the door and two nurses came in for the sleeping babies. To the nurses, it looked like a happy family. They knew what was going on, but there would never be any mention of it.

"I am leaving today. My wife called to remind me that I have a daughter waiting for me and she misses those nighttime stories."

"Go, Joseph. Go to your family. I am going to close my eyes and you walk away." Joseph took my face in his hands and kissed me passionately on the lips.

"Please remember me." And he closed the door and was gone. I opened my eyes and tears began to flow down my cheeks. I would remember, but I had to look forward to the serenity of a love that made me feel complete and whole. A few minutes later,

Marcus came in the door and took me in his arms, "I love you darling, will you be my wife?"

"Forever. You're my friend, my lover, my husband, and the father of my boys. I now have the serenity of a family. The complete circle of love." He hugged me tightly.

"Sweetie, I just wanted to let you know, maybe you forgot, but my sisters will be here in an hour."

The driver and car were waiting downstairs in front of the building. "Good morning. I am here to take you to the airport."

"Yes," I said. "Take me directly to the airport. I have already called my pilot and he will have the plane ready." The driver closed the door. He got in the front of the car and raised the glass between the front and the back of the car. He seemed to know I needed the privacy. I remembered our first sexual encounter. We had climbed and repelled a rock cliff in Virginia. One of my favorite places to hike. Samantha was unafraid and was determined to keep up with me. I just wanted to keep her safe and when she came down behind me, I got a pleasant view of her butt. I wanted her to be safe, but I wanted that ass too. I had loved her for a while, but I had wanted to give her plenty of time to accept me. It would be a mixed-race relationship, and one that would always come with issues, especially from my own family. But all I could think about was that cute little butt coming down to me and expecting me to keep her safe. Then having her naked in my sleeping bag, the heat from our bodies keeping us warmer than the fire. Kissing her passionately and the first plunge, deep inside her. My cock was so hard that I was not sure I could hold my own pleasure back before she reached her climax. Then splashing naked in the chilly water. *This memory is burned in my mind.* She was a unique woman: smart, beautiful, compassionate. There would never be enough words to describe her and my love for her. And now we have boys together. I will never be able to give my heart to another. I just cannot do that again. I reached for my phone.

"Emily, sweetheart, I am on my way home. Yes, the boys are better, healthy. We have a lot to talk about, but it is all good. How is Sophia? Tell her daddy is on his way and will be there to tuck her in. Emily, I hope you and I can seriously think about our family. Let's put the past behind us and try. Make an appointment with a marriage counselor. Please, for Sophia's sake, let's try."

"Joseph, it is important to make a family out of this mess for Sophia. We have been friends and playmates for years. Yes, I am willing to try. See you when you get home. Goodbye, husband."

The room was filled with balloons and flowers, and there were gifts everywhere. Marcus' twin sisters had outdone themselves once again.

"Open this one," Penelope said. She was the most outspoken. "I picked out these little western outfits with matching booties that looks like boots. And these little hats. Where are the boys?

Can we hold them?" Marcus took over from there.

"Sis, you two need to calm down. And I'll have the nurses bring them in." Marcus went into the nursery and asked that the babies to be brought in.

"Oh, let me have one, which is which?"

"Jared is in green, and Jacob is in blue."

Penelope took Jacob and Paige took Jared.

"Brother, I cannot believe you are a part of such beautiful babies. Samantha I can see, but not you, Marcus," she teased.

"Thanks, sis. I did my best." Paige took pictures of the boys and I continued to open their gifts. It looked as if they had bought out the whole baby store.

"I hope we get a lot of free babysitting after you take a first aid course."

"Yep. Mom has already signed us up," Penelope said.

"How about your first crash course?" Marcus said. "Why don't you take them to the nursery? The nurses will show you how to bathe them and get them ready for bed." They giggled.

"I'd love to."

"Sam, is that okay with you?" Marcus asked.

"Darling, this experiment is on you," I replied. Marcus led the girls to the nursery and asked the nurses to let the girls help them get the boys ready for bed. Marcus was barely in the room when the phone rang. "Yes, Mike, what is up? What?" All the color drained from Marcus' face.

"What happened?" He listened intently, then said, "Mike, find out what happened. Put extra security on the family."

"Already done. I know the girls are with you, but we have a team outside the hospital to take them home. We beefed up security at all the construction sites. The brake lines were cut. I am thinking someone was trying to send you a message, Marcus. Lisa and her husband would not have had any enemies." I heard Mike say over the phone's speaker. Marcus asked about their girls.

"I checked on them. They are with a sitter, and I put security at their house. She agreed to keep them a couple of days to see if there is any family."

"Mike, you can look, but Lisa had made me their guardian. She swore that her biological mother, who gave her up for adoption, could never get her hands on them. So, give me time to talk to Sam."

I watched as Marcus got to work. His first concern was for his family; he wanted to know who was out to harm them. That was how Marcus handled everything. Then he would take a moment to deal with his emotions.

"Darling, what is it?" He came to my bed and sat down beside me.

"Lisa and her husband were killed in a car wreck. Their brake lines were cut." He had tears in his eyes. I pulled him close to me. "I know how close you and Lisa were. I am so sorry, darling.

How can I help?"

"Samantha, she made me guardian of her two children. She wants to make sure her drunk of a mother does not take her girls. Lisa went from foster home to foster home until she came to work for me. She busted her ass. I put her through college, and she went on to graduate school and got her MBA. She was loyal. I counted on her to run the office. No matter what I asked, she was always available. Then she met one of the supervisors that worked at another construction company. They dated for two years and got married, then had two girls. She had pulled herself out of the gutter and made something of her life. Lisa was smart, and I loved her." His tears started flowing down his face.

"Where are the girls?" I asked.

"Mike was close to Lisa; they even dated for a while. But she wanted a family, and well, Mike is a loner. He does not want children, but he was like an uncle to her girls." He wiped his face with the arm sleeve of his shirt. "The girls are with a sitter. Lisa and her husband were going out for their weekly date night. Mike said they did not have security with them. Lisa did not want security always with them. She felt like she wanted as much normalcy for her children as possible. She used to bring them to the office and let them hang out. They have blonde hair with big blue eyes. She was with me since she was eighteen and was thirty-two when she died. They had bought a house in one of our smaller developments. I had given her a large bonus one year, and she put it down on a house. Hell, I'd have given her a house, but Lisa worked for everything she got." Marcus began to cry harder. I pulled a tissue from the box next to my bed. I held him and just listened to him talk and sob. I knew he needed to release his tears and then go back to his plan of action. The phone rang.

"The ambulance took them to the hospital." I could tell Mike was having a tough time talking. "I had the bodies taken to Cone funeral home. Do you want me to handle the arrangements?"

"Yes, you know the only family she had was you and me," Marcus said.

"Her husband, I think, had a grandmother who raised him. She is about eighty. I will see her and break the news to her. I think she is in an independent living facility. What about the girls, Marcus?"

"Mike, take care of the funeral at my expense. Have Pete pay off her house and create a trust for the girls. Once they have death certificates, send them to Robert. Have him find Lisa's mother and pay her for her rights to the children. Tell him to see how Lisa's husband's grandmother is financially. Tell him to set up a trust and put all of Lisa's assets in it for the girls. I will take care of everything." Marcus turned to me, "The girls, Sam, I am their guardian. Lisa made me the guardian of her children long before I met you. Honey, we just had twins, and it is a lot to ask of you, but I'd like to adopt them. I can hire plenty of help. We have a big house. Sam, what do you think?"

"I think we will adopt them and make it work. Lisa wanted you to have them, and if that is her wish, I am supporting that. She sounded like an incredible woman, and you know I was in a comparable situation growing up, and then came Saul."

"Yes, sweetheart. Let's adopt them."

"How old are they?" I asked.

"Mike, I'll call you back. They are two and four. The youngest is Ester, and the older one is Matilda. They are like two peas in a pod."

"I'll call Margaret. She will help with all the arrangements, and so will dad. Darling, we are quickly building a large family."

"Sam, I know this is probably not the time to talk about this, but I have to say it. You know I love the boys like they are my own. They will bear the Matthew name. And the girls will bear the name Matthew."

"But," Samantha interrupted, "Do you want some Matthews that are biologically yours? I think we can do that. Just give us a couple of years to get the boys up and walking and we will try for another. This time, with my husband. I'll be thirty and you will be thirty-five."

"I think that is a solid plan."

"Hell, I can probably keep having kids until I am forty. You just have to promise to love me through all the body changes."

"Barefoot and pregnant, I love it."

"Marcus, remember, I also want to work."

"Honey, we can afford plenty of help. I want you to work if you want to work. I want an adventurous life."

"Well, looks like you have a really good start." He got into the bed with me. "Only because I found the right woman. Will you marry me?"

"Yes, my sweet man. Always."

"I'd like to stay with you tonight. I want to feel the warmth of your body."

"Of course, just remember we cannot make love yet, even though we both want to."

"Yes, but we can play around." I called the nurse on the monitor. "I'd like you to take all the late-night feedings of the boys. Mr. Matthew will be spending the night. Please have breakfast for two sent up. Bring the boys in after breakfast for nursing. We just got some tragic news."

Greta, the nurse in charge said, "I am so sorry. Do not worry about the boys; they are sleeping soundly. Their aunts wore them out. Even Jacob is sleeping soundly. You and Mr. Matthew get some rest and let me know if there anything else I can do."

"Thank you, Greta." Marcus began to remove his clothes. "I feel like a quick shower."

"Okay, while you're doing that, I'd like to call Margaret," I said picking up my phone. "Hello, may I speak to Margaret? Dad, no. There is nothing wrong with me or the boys, just put me on speaker phone, please. Lisa, Marcus' assistant, was killed in a car cash tonight with her husband. Her brake lines appeared to be cut. Marcus does not know if it was someone trying to send him a message or what the reason is. Mike is investigating it. Anyway, he has put extra security on all the family, including your house. There will be a car out front of your house, just as a precaution. However, Margaret, the reason I am calling, is they had two small girls, and there is no next of kin. Marcus is now their guardian. We decided we are going to adopt them. I am supposed to stay one more day before I can be released. Margaret, could you call Mary, our decorator, and work with her to turn one of the rooms into a girl's room? Call Mike and ask him to move their clothes and toys, and set them up at our place. Buy clothes, dresses, toys, everything. Make their room into a princess room. Will you visit them and see if they are open to coming with you overnight? The sitter is there, but she is a student and needs to get back to classes, so she will do what she can."

"Of course, Samantha, what great fun. I never had a girl, now we have two granddaughters and two grandsons." Saul said, "I am delighted. Yes, you can count on us, my darling girl. Always something unusual going on with you, my girl. How old are they and what are their names?"

"The two-year-old's name is Ester and the four-year-old is Matilda."

"We got you, sweetheart. Rest up," said Margaret.

"I will. And dad? Will you hire another au pair? I think we will need two with four children."

"On it. Goodnight. Sweet dreams, my darling daughter."

Marcus came from the dressing room. He was bare-chested and had on pajama bottoms. I opened the covers to invite him in. The bed was smaller than we were used to. He took me in his arms and began to kiss me passionately. He opened my mouth with his tongue and began to explore. At the same time he pressed his hard dick into my leg. He cupped my butt and started rubbing my breasts. I knew that the sensations in my body were signaling my brain that this tension was going to make my milk begin to flow. An ache between my thighs began to tingle, signaling that I was wet and ready for him.

"Marcus, sweetheart. We are treading on dangerous

ground." "I know, but I want you. I need you."

"Sweetheart, it's only been three days."

"I will pull out before I come." I was limp with desire. The passion he was showing me had made me give in to his desire. He moved my legs apart and slowly began to enter me.

"Please, tell me if I am hurting you."

"Just make love to me. I want you. It's been too long since I had you inside me. Just pull-out, Marcus, before you cum. I trust you to take care of me." With my body signaling his, I was ready. He entered me, and with one thrust, I came. My breast was wet with milk. He took his tongue and licked at my nipples. He pushed twice and then pulled out. His hot sticky release went all over my legs. I heard him groan with relief.

"I am sorry, darling. That was selfish of me and risky for you."

"I agreed, sweetheart. I could have said 'no'."

"Just let me get up and take a quick shower."

"I will join you." The two of us showered most of the evidence off. We both put on pajamas and looked forward to what the next day would bring. Sliding into bed, he said, "Breast milk does not taste that bad." He laughed, "But that is reserved for the boys."

"Goodnight. I love you," he said as he rolled over. I knew his mind was racing.

"Goodnight, husband." I was tired and drowsy. It been quite a day. I knew the man next to me would take care of all his responsibilities, no matter what came.

***

We were both up early. I wanted to be dressed before the boys came in to nurse. Dr. Wright was coming in to talk with us about the boys. Marcus was a little sheepish this morning. We both felt like children who had stolen the cookies out of grandma's cookie jar. He grabbed me and pulled me to him. "Sweetheart, last night will not happen again until you are released by the doctor."

"Are you going to kiss and tell?" I giggled and kissed him on the lips. "I love you so much and wanted you as much as you wanted me."

"Sam, I needed you last night. I was, and am, so fucked up over Lisa's accident." The phone rang. Perfect timing. "Good morning, Mike. Any news?"

"Yes, it seems that Phillip, Lisa's husband was a gambler and was in deep with a not-so-nice group of gamblers. He owed over a hundred thousand, maybe more. He was also caught cheating, and I am fairly sure the brakes were cut to send a message. They were not thinking that it would end up an accident that would kill them both. I set up the funeral arrangements and Robert is handling all the legal stuff. Margaret came early this morning to have breakfast with the kids. She made them chocolate chip pancakes and plans to spend the day with them. The designer, Mary, will have the room ready late this afternoon. Saul is interviewing au pairs. We have everything under control. Lisa did not know how deep in debt he was. My guess? She never knew he was a compulsive gambler. She would have never put up with that behavior, or the risk to her kids. The service will be tomorrow, then the cremation. I called a child psychologist, and I am meeting with her today. I have no idea how to tell the children."

"I will be there. Mike, track down everyone he owed and pay them. I do not want any more risk to the family. Pay in such a way, or have Robert pay, so they know that that's all they get. Hire some of the best thugs and card sharks and let them play in that group. Have them beat the shit out of them. I am angry, and I really do not know how to deal with my anger. I need some time to process this. However, keep the extra security for a while. Thanks, man. The doctor's here. Got to go."

Dr. Wright had come into the room with a file folder in hand. "Parents, both boys are doing well. Jacob has been ready to release from the start. Jared had a few manageable issues, but all his testing looks good. I'd like to see him in three weeks. Continue to feed him on his schedule and watch for any signs of jaundice. The two blood transfusions did the trick. The antibodies in the transfusion, which is Jared's blood type, were able to fight off his mother's antibodies that somehow crossed over in birth. He was so much smaller and a little underdeveloped. He is good now, so both boys are okay to go home today. I am going to discharge them."

I looked at Marcus, "We can take them home

today?" "Yes, today. Unless Carol does not release

you?" "Yep, today."

"Thank you, Doctor." Marcus reached for his hand. "You're very welcome. I have a lot of respect for your quick actions. And your very generous donations. With the grant, we are going to be able to start a community health care screening for anyone that needs prenatal care. With Carol and I on the board, we are starting a community clinic. The donations are flooding in. We have already found a financial director, and the hospital board has approved a plan to designate a wing for the free clinic. We were hoping one of you would sit on the board."

"Sam, would you like to do the honor? You understand how important identifying blood incompatibility is better than I would. But if you think it's too much...?" Marcus said.

"No, darling, I'd loved to. It will let me get more involved with the community. Thank you. It's an honor." Carol came bustling in, frazzled as usual. Dr. Wright excused himself.

"So, Samantha, how do you feel?"

"Great," I said, as if I had been caught slipping outside to meet a boy.

"Well, one last pelvic examination and a program shot, and you can go home today. Your boys are ready, and I am fairly sure you are, too. Please get up on the table and assume the position. Marcus, would you like to step out?"

"No, ma'am. I think I'd better stay." Carol used her gloved fingers, pushed them up into my vagina, and pressed on my stomach. She then pulled them out and took the glove off.

"Okay, you two. Confess up. It's all over your faces. You have had sex, four days after delivery. I hope protected. Samantha can easily get pregnant again." Marcus started stumbling over his words, "I had some tragic news last night and I needed Sam so badly that I sort of..." he stammered.

"I know, Carol. I could have said no, but I wanted him just as bad as he wanted me."

"Kids, let's get serious. She needs at least six weeks to properly heal. Then you can resume what is an abnormal amount of sex. Samantha, I recommend the depo shot, as you have a habit of forgetting your pills and your shot. You get pregnant easily, so stick to the plan. Marcus, I know you love your wife, and I know you're Catholic, but pregnancy is hard on a woman's body. So lay off the sex for six weeks. There are several other things you two can do without penetration."

"Carol, you have my word. I will be busy finishing your house, and mine, along with the two boys. Last night, I do not know if you heard about my secretary, but we are going to have two little girls added to our family."

"Yes, I heard. I am so sorry. Just Samantha, rest a lot. I know you will have lots of help. Use it. These boys and those little girls are going to be exhausting if you do not put yourself first."

"Carol, I will see to her health. She's my life. Without her, we would not have our family."

"So, I am discharging you today."

"Thank you, Dr. McCullough."

"Thank you, Marcus, for all you have done for the clinic. With your generous donation, and your call for others to donate, this made our clinic free to all who need it. There is going to be a move to call it the Matthew Free Clinic." The nurse came in and gave me a shot of B12, a program shot, and a depo shot. Marcus had called our housekeeper and let her know we were coming home late this afternoon. He asked to have everything ready, including the girl's room, and to have a family dinner prepared.

Mike had made sure everyone was aware of the changes that were going to happen. Marcus called Mike and let him know to get the plan ready that he had developed from the beginning. The nurses would be leaving with the boys from the side entrance, and we would be leaving from the front. Our publicist would be out front to answer questions. Security would be around both cars to make sure nothing went wrong. I called Margaret and asked her and Saul to meet us at the penthouse around five that afternoon. Saul said he had found an au pair and Margaret said everything was in place. She said they had been picking out toys; that was their favorite part. They had had fun putting them in boxes.

She said they were too young to understand anything other than Uncle Mike was taking them to see two baby boys to play with. They had not asked for their parents yet.

That afternoon, around three p.m., both me and the boys were released. Marcus wanted Mike to lead the security that would take the boys down to the second floor and leave through that exit. The van was already equipped with two car seats. Next to the boys was room for the nurse. Mike would drive the van. James, the other security man, was behind the van and ready to follow Mike with the boys to the penthouse. Marcus and the other security team, along with the publicist, would leave out of the front, that way the boys would not be photographed. It took me a while to get used to having so much security around all the time. I get it, though—when you are a Matthew and worth billions, anything can happen. Marcus' great fear is that one of his children or family members would be kidnapped and held for ransom.

"Are you ready, darling? You know we just have to get through the cameras and let Melanie handle the questions."

"I am ready, sweetheart." He took my arm, and we rode the elevator to the first floor. There were three security men waiting at the bottom as we stepped off the elevator. As we walked to the van, they deflected the cameramen. I got into the van and Marcus was behind me. He had his hand on my back to guide me into the van. The driver was ready to pull out. Marcus fastened my seat belt and then his.

"Go, man. Go." He pulled out, and the other van pulled out behind us. The publicist was answering the questions, "Where are the babies? We heard one died!"

"They are both healthy little boys,"she answered.

"We heard that Marcus is not their father. How did an unknown woman catch the most eligible bachelor?"

Melanie, very calmly, said, "The Matthew family is happy to have two healthy baby boys. What they ask is for some privacy. After a while, Mr. Matthew will give a complete story. His close friend was killed in a car wreck a few days ago. The family is mourning her loss. She had two small girls that the Matthews have agreed to adopt. They now have four children, all under the age of four. Thank you. That will be all." Melanie left in another car with security driving.

Home. It sounded great. It was so great to get home. Marcus and I walked into more turbulence than we had expected. The girls were playing on the floor with Saul, and Margaret was helping the cook with dinner. Mike was sitting in a chair holding Jacob. "Man, this kid is demanding. It took me a while to quiet him down. Marcus, you are going to have your hands full with this one!"

The nanny had Jared, and the nurse was in the nursery putting things away that had been left at the hospital. Our housekeeper was working with Mary, the designer, to finish the girl's room. Our houseman, Peter, was putting my business things in the library, including my desk. It seems my office was now the playroom and was decorated with carousels, ponies, and shelves for all kinds of toys. They each had their own desk, and there was a princess castle in the middle of the room. Inside the princess castle was a child-sized table and chairs for the girls to sit on. Saul was treated to tea, along with a couple of the dolls. The two-year-old was playing in a corner filled with stuffed animals and looking at picture books. They had no care in the world, and it'd be up to me, Marcus, and Mike to tell them their lives were going to be forever changed. Marcus said, "I guess the mail can wait." Peter, our houseman, said, "Sir, I took the liberty to look through it, and nothing seemed urgent. Your desk and files and books are now in the library. We did not touch the music room and the extra bedrooms, as we figured you needed them for guests."

"Sorry, Peter. I know you did not sign on for all this extra work."

"No problem, sir. We are glad to see this new generation make the household lively. We will, however, be glad when the new house is finished. We are running out of space." This is a five-bedroom penthouse, nine thousand square feet, and it seemed to be brimming with activity.

"Sam, do you want to lie down before dinner?"

"I'd like to meet our girls, Ester and Matilda. Dad, do you have room at the tea table?"

"Actually, my darling daughter, I have had all the make-believe tea I can hold. Be my guest."

"Hi, Matilda, my name is Sam. May I join your tea party?" She moved one of her dolls and said, "You can sit there. Would you like a cookie?" Margaret had provided cookies for the tea party.

"Ester, join us," I said to the two-year-old in the

corner. "I don't want to. I do not like tea."

"Okay, that's simply fine with me. Maybe later you will show me your picture books?"

Mike handed Jacob to Saul, "Take your grandson for a while. Ester likes books. She's quiet but she speaks her mind." I was glad to have Mike there; he knew the girls well. The doorbell rang and Peter announced the new au pair. Her name was Kelly. She was around twenty-five and came to America to work as a nanny and to attend classes in child psychology, especially trauma.

Marcus said, "Mike, could we talk?"

"I talked to a psychologist, and she said the best thing to do is tell them in a kind, but straightforward way, that their parents will not be coming back. She said that the two-year-old will not remember them in time. She will initially miss her mother's warmth and gentle touch, and the four-year-old will be the one most affected. But with counseling, and with a strong circle of love and support, she too, will have some memories but will forget. They both will remember what you and I tell them about their mother. I talked to the grandmother, and she wants to see them occasionally, as they are her only grandchildren. She can tell them about their dad. As far as Lisa's mother? Robert gave her a hundred thousand dollars and she was glad to sign over her rights. He offered her rehab, but she did not want it and said she was going to move to Florida. Robert set her up in a retirement community and all we can do is just know her whereabouts.

So, when do you want to tell the girls? And do you want them to attend the service tomorrow?" Mike asked.

"Wow, man this is a lot to analyze. Give me time to talk to Sam. I guess the new au pair will take one of the guest rooms until we work this out, and the nurse will take the other room until we get the new house. But she will be on call during the night. Instead of you staying in the condominium upstairs, will you sleep on a couch somewhere? Just in case we need you. And I guess Peter, and the cook, Hilda, will leave after dinner and be back in the morning."

"One thing you got going for you, man, is Margaret. Your new mother-in-law has everything and everyone under control."

"That's good, man. I never have seen Saul so happy. He's lost ten years off his age. He's been crawling around the floor, playing horsey." Marcus laughed, "But he'll pay for it tomorrow when he can't get out of bed."

Margaret announced, "It's time for dinner. Marcus, will you take the girls and show them where to wash their hands? Both boys are being nursed, so Sam is about finished," I heard her say as I was giving the boys over to the nurse and the nanny. "Please bring their infant seats so they can sit at the table with us," Margaret asked the nanny.

"Girls, you have seats next to Mike. Mike, will you put Ester in her seat please?" We all sat down to the table where there was plenty of childlike food; macaroni and cheese, fruit, applesauce, chicken nuggets with several sauces, three casseroles, a hearty salad, and vegetable sticks.

"Marcus, will you say the prayer for us?"

"Yes, ma'am. Would everyone hold hands?" Even Jared and Jacob's hands were held. "I am so proud to have all of you as a part of my family tonight." He bowed his head and said he was thankful for the kindness shown today, and the goodwill of all. He pledged before this gathering and God to be the head of this family, to see that it was safe and taken care of. He thanked the providers of the food and said, "Amen." The little girls said, "Amen," too.

"Marcus, will you serve the children? I will pass the salad., Margaret said.

"Margaret, should I put a little of everything on their plates?"

"Yes, let them pick through what they want for now."

Mike spoke up, "Girls, napkins in your laps." Marcus took on the role as father and I was attending to the boys who were asleep. Then, it was time for them to get ready for bed. Mike, Marcus, and I were going to talk to the girls about their parents. Dinner was lively. We only had a couple of spilled milk cups and a few food items dropped on the floor. The nannies attended to the spills. They would all eat later in the kitchen. Hilda had food set for the nannies and nurses in the kitchen. She and the housekeeper would wash up the dishes while we put the girls to bed. Margaret and Saul took the sleeping boys ,placed them in their cribs and sat with them. The girls room looked like a fairy room. There were fairies and friendly dragons and princesses stenciled on the walls. The decorator had used their furniture to furnish the room. She thought it would make them feel more at home. There were books and stuffed animals everywhere. Next to a rocking chair, she had put a picture of their parents. For the time she was given, she had made everything perfect. It was a little girl's dream room—even their bathroom reflected the bedroom. After baths, teeth brushed, and pajamas on, Mike suggested a story, instead of reading a book.

"Mike, Sam and I think you should take lead on this," Marcus said. So, Mike began, "Matilda, remember when your mommy said her and your dad were going on a date?"

"Yes, Uncle Mike. Are they back yet?"

"No, sweetheart. They decided to go to heaven and be angels. You see, they were in a car wreck, and they did not survive the wreck."

I asked them, "Do you know what that means?"

"Like our goldfish that died, and we flushed it down the toilet because Mommy said that's where goldfish heaven was?" Matilda said, "Ester, do you remember the goldfish?"

"Yes." She was barely awake and was too young to understand. But Matilda did. "So, Mommy and Daddy will not come back for us." Tears began to well in her eyes. Marcus went over and sat on her bed. "That's right, but your Mommy had asked me and Sam and Mike to take care of you."

"So, Uncle Mike, you still come to see us?"

"You bet, my sweet girl."

"And we will live here, with Sam and Marcus?"

"Will they be our new daddy and mommy?"

"Yes, and they will love you. We will tell you about your mom and dad and how much they loved you."

"Marcus, will you sleep in here tonight? With Uncle Mike? Sometimes I have bad dreams, and daddy or mommy would stay until we fell asleep."

"Sure, I think we can do this tonight. And tomorrow, we can talk more." I went over to Matilda, "May I hug you and kiss you good night?"

"I'd like that." Ester was already asleep, so I pulled up her covers, tucked her in, and kissed her good night. "I will bring you guys a pillow and blanket. I guess you can make do on the floor."

"Mike, I want to tuck my boys in and kiss my wife goodnight."

"I think, so far, it went well. But like the psychologist said, they are so young it will take time for them to process this," Mike said. Marcus and I left the room, the boys were having their final feeding. I took Jacob and Marcus took Jared. We finished giving them their bottles and burped them. We handed them off to the nanny to change their diapers.

"Marcus, I'm going to stay in here awhile. I'd like to sing to them and rock them."

"Goodnight, my sweet wife and mother of my children. I'll go back and help Mike with the girls." Margaret and Saul had already left, as well as the help. Tomorrow would be a new day, but a sad day. Lisa's service would be tomorrow.

The next morning, I was up at six a.m. and dressed. I was ready and nursing the babies. Jacob was content for the moment. He had his tummy full, and Jared was eating and gaining more weight. He was healthy and normal. He was a few pounds lighter than Jacob, but Jared was physically more like his father. His biological father. Jacob, on the other hand, was more like Joseph's grandfather. Jared had finished nursing and I was about to change his dirty diaper when Marcus came in with Esther on his shoulder. "Good morning, and from the smell in here, I think we will go to breakfast."

"Not so fast, mister. I have already changed one. I think it's your turn." Ester was pinching her nose and saying, "It stinks in here."

"Right? Ester, let's let these two get cleaned up. See you at breakfast, sweetheart." I gave Marcus a kiss and gave him the diaper. Marcus looked like I had hit one of his fingers with a hammer. I left with Ester in my arms. I loved having her in my arms. It just seemed right. The nannies were not due until eight, and the nurse was asleep. She had been up all night. Breakfast was served, buffet style, in the dining room. Mike was fixing a plate for Matilda. "Good morning, Matilda. Mike, how was your night?"

"Great. Matilda, how did you sleep?"

"I slept all night, with no nightmares. Uncle Mike said it was because of all the good fairies and dragons on the wall." He put a plate in front of her with a pancake and scrambled eggs.

"No bacon?" I asked curiously.

"Today, Matilda told me she is a vegetarian and cannot eat meat. So, today we are a vegetarian. Who knows what she will be eating tomorrow? So, Ester how about a pancake?"

"Yes, please. And bacon. I like bacon." "Mike,

is Ester closer to three than two?" "Yes.

Actually, her birthday is next month."

"Wonderful! We'll have a party. What day?"

"July 7th. Matilda will be five in August."

"So, just in time for kindergarten. I'll investigate some schools here. And a preschool for Miss Smarty-Pants." I put Ester in her chair and put her plate in front of her. Mike said, "Girls, napkins, please."

"Yes, Uncle Mike."

"Are you eating, Samantha?"

"Yes, a little. Trying to get my figure back."

"You have just given birth. You look damn well to me."

"Uncle Mike, you said a bad word. You are not supposed to talk like that. You owe a quarter to the swear jar," Matilda said.

"Yes," said Mike, between bites of pancakes. "Where is Marcus?"

"Dirty diaper duty," I replied.

"So sorry for him!"

"Yeah, well it was his turn." Speaking of the new dad, Marcus entered the room. "I'm ready for a large plate of pancakes to get that ordeal out of my mind." I laughed, "So, where are the boys?"

"Both are taking a nap. Life is hard when you're a baby. Eat, sleep, and shit."

"Um. Marcus said a bad word. He has to put a quarter in the swear jar."

"Swear jar?"

"Yes, darling. The girls monitor the language around them and every time they hear a bad word, you owe a quarter to the swear jar." Matilda, with syrup on her face, said, "And Uncle Mike owes a quarter also."

"Wow, I guess I better start watching my words."

"Yes, darling. Dads need to make concessions, and proper language is one of them."

"Use your napkin, sweetie," I spoke. Marcus sat down, "Darling, would you pour me a cup of coffee?"

"Yes, sweetheart."

"I want to tell Hilda to hire at least one more maid. We are going to need it," Marcus said, taking a sip of coffee. The doorbell rang and Peter answered the door. "Hi, ladies! Have you eaten?"

"Yes, sir. It's time we get to work," Kelly said. "Are you girls finished?" Ester said, "I just want to finish my milk."

"I'm finished," Matilda said.

"Okay, let's see how your bedroom looks and let's learn to make your bed. What time is the service, Mr. Matthew?"

"It's at one p.m. If you could have the girls ready by 12:30, that would be great.

"I want to help pick out their clothes for the service, please," I spoke.

"Of course," Kelly responded. The girls and the nanny went to the girls' bedroom. Ester grabbed a piece of bacon and was stuffing it in her mouth as they left the room. Marcus leaned over and kissed me on the cheek, "Our first day as a family. I had no idea it would be this busy. I'm glad we can afford the help. So, Mike, have the cars ready at 12:30. I'm going to take look at what is piling up on my desk."

"Gotcha, boss," Mike said as he grabbed a pancake to go. I was having one last chai tea before I called Rick at the house. "Hey, girl! Missing me already? You are supposed to be off at least three months."

"I know. I just wanted to check and see if I needed to help with anything."

"No, I gotcha girl. All is good. I know you have the service today. Wow, what a mess. But you now have four kids! Uncle Rick and Uncle Scott will see you next week when things calm down." We talked for a few more minutes before eventually hanging up. I went to the girls' room and their new dresses had arrived. I had a navy dress sent over for Matilda, and a black skirt and white short-sleeved blouse for Ester. They had matching white sweaters, lace socks, and black shoes. "If you need help, Kelly, let me know. I'm just going to check on the boys."

"Mrs. Matthew, we were going to make a scrapbook if that's okay?"

"Sure, that is a really clever idea. There will be roses for the girls to present at the ceremony. We will stay a few minutes at the reception, and then we are leaving."

"That's a good idea, Mrs. Matthew. We can go for pizza, and just have time to talk." "Good idea. I'll talk to Mr. Matthew and Mike. Thank you, Kelly. See you at 12:30." I had laid out a black dress for myself and a black hat with a small vail in front. Marcus would dress himself, no doubt. He had plenty of black suits. I went to the boys' room; they were ready to eat again. We were going to do bottles this time since we have the ceremony today. Jared was watching his mobile in his bed. The nurse had Jacob in her lap.

"Thanks, Teresa. You have everything under control and if you need help, just ask Hilda, she runs the house," I said kissing the boys goodbye.

"The car is downstairs, Marcus," Mike called up. We were all ready and looked like the perfect family. Marcus was holding Ester. She seemed to be clinging to him. Matilda, however, was just not talking at all. The psychologist said that may happen.

Matilda looked nice in her black dress. Ester was clinging to Mike. The funeral was at St. Paul's, which was the small chapel that Lisa's family belonged to. There would be a short ceremony and Marcus would say something, and so would Mike. There would be pictures of the girls, their dad, and their mom. The girls would each place a rose in front of the urn that held their parent's ashes. We would stay shortly at the reception and then leave for a pizza place close by. Mike had rented out the party room for privacy. It was not going to be a party, just family time together. Hopefully, they will want to talk about the funeral. Our cars arrived exactly at 12:30 p.m.

Everyone had seated, and the little chapel was full of construction workers, company vendors, and many other employees of the Matthews firm, as well as Lisa's husband's grandmother and close friends. Rick and Scott were there in the family section, with John Marcus, Isabella, Margaret, Saul, Matilda, Ester, and their great-grandmother. Marcus had sent a driver to make sure she arrived all right. The priest called for a prayer, then the organist played and the choir sang. The girls were quiet but pointed to the pictures of their mother and father. Ester started kicking her feet and getting restless. She was seated next to Marcus, and it was his turn to speak. He took Ester with him and said such sweet, memorable things about Lisa. There wasn't a dry eye in the chapel. When it was Mike's turn, Matilda grabbed his hand. She was understanding some of what was going on. He took her little hand in his and went up to the podium. He lifted her up in his arms and talked about being Uncle Mike; about how much fun it was and what a wonderful family life they had together. Then Marcus brought Ester and joined Mike and Matilda at the urn that held their parents' ashes. Together, they laid their white roses down in front of the urn. The priest said a prayer and the congregation left to go downstairs to the reception. We all went down to the reception area and thanked all the guests. After some time, we loaded everyone into the car and headed for the pizza place. Marcus, Mike, Kelly, and I were riding in the limo with the girls. Marcus had invited the great-grandmother, but she was too broken up to go. She said she would like to stay in touch with the girls. Kelly had mentioned that the girls wanted to make a scrapbook together and had hoped she would help with it. She said she would love to see them, and they set up a time for next week. Ester did not want to stay in her seat. She was getting very impatient. "Sweetie, you have to stay in the seat. We are almost there."

"Daddy, I want out." She flung her foot, and one shoe flew off. Marcus looked at me. Kelly spoke up, "This is normal behavior. Children want stability, so now she wants a daddy, and she has bonded with you. She is so young that her memories will fade fast, replacing them with new thoughts." She texted us this from her phone so that they children had no clue what was being said. Matilda still had little to say. It was going to be a wait-and-see with her. It was going to be important to keep a schedule and create stability surrounding the girls. Once the owner led us over to our table, and the server brought us menus, Matilda spoke up. "I want a vegetarian pizza, please." Kelly said, "Nice words."

"Okay, what does everyone want?"

Mike said, "Marcus, want to split a large meat lover?"

"Daddy," said Ester. "I want some of your pizza."

"Honey, that's fine. Saul?"

"Cheese, with Canadian bacon and pineapple."

"Mom and dad, what do you want?" Marcus asked his parents.

"Sweetie, you order. I'm going to join Matilda with a vegetarian."

"Kelly, sorry. What would you

like?" "Pepperoni," she replied.

"Beer for the men. The girls will have apple juice. Mom, Margaret, and Kelly? What do you want?"

"I think a glass of sweet tea for me," Margaret said.

"White wine for me," said Isabella.

"Kelly?" Marcus prompted. "Water, sir." A buzzing from my pocket told me I had a text message. *Sweet ceremony. I'm back at the house. If you need anything, call. -Rick*

Marcus picked up the phone and called Teresa to make sure the boys were okay, which they were. She was playing with them and reading to them. "Kiss them for me," he said before hanging up. Our pizzas had just arrived when Matilda spoke, "Mommy liked vegetarian pizza. And my dad drank beer." Those was the first words she had started to say about her mother and father. Kelly was the first to respond, "That is an excellent choice. Your mom must have liked to take care of herself."

"Yes, mom was always careful with our diet. She only let

us have fruit and juice and things like vegetables. But dad and mom argued a lot. I heard it when they thought we were asleep. I did not like the arguing. That's when the bad dreams came. Last night, I didn't have a bad dream." She reached for my hand, "Can I call you Mommy? And will you and my new dad never argue?" I answered, "If Marcus and I ever disagree, I promise we will not argue. We are a family. You even have uncles and two aunts you have not met. Grandparents and all kinds of people who will love you."

"Mommy said Marcus was rich. Is that true?" Marcus answered, "Why do you ask?"

"Because mommy and daddy fought over money."

"Yes, sweetheart. We have plenty of money and I cannot wait to show you our business. And Sam is a lawyer." She took a long draw on her apple juice and asked, "Can we have a puppy? I always wanted a puppy."

"Mommy?" Marcus looked at me, "Can we have a puppy?" I kicked him under the table, "Yes, Matilda. Let's eat our pizza before it gets cold." Kelly texted me, "*Excellent job. She will mention other demands, just do not fall into all of them. A puppy, I am guessing, will be a responsibility that will fall on me and the girls.*" I texted back, "*And Marcus.*" She laughed.

We all dug into our pizza. The talk was fun and interesting. The children had a lot of questions. They had pizza all over their faces. Ester went around to Margaret and held her arms out to be picked up. She was getting tired. Margaret wiped her hands and face then kissed her little fingers. How could anyone not love

These girls?

"Are you my grandmother now?"

"Yes, darling. And this man beside me is your grandfather. And that beautiful lady across the table is your other grandmother, and her husband next to you, is your grandfather," Margaret replied. She snuggled down in Margaret's lap, getting sleepy. Matilda spoke up, "So what do we call you? We have never had grandparents."

Isabella spoke next, "How about calling us grandmother and grandfather?" Matilda said, "You look like a grandmother and grandfather. But you two look more like Papa and Mama," she said turning back to Margaret.

"That would be fine with me," Margaret replied. "You have four grandparents." I said, "And I think those names will work. Dad, I never thought of you as Papa."

"Samantha, they can call me whatever they want. I am so proud to have them in our family."

Isabella said, "And your daddy has two younger sisters that will be your aunts. You have cousins and great aunts and great uncles. So many people to love you. You will meet your Uncle Rick and Uncle Scott next week. But for now, let's get you girls to the bathroom and cleaned up. We'll use the bathroom and head home to check on your brothers."

"We never had baby brothers. Are they stinky?"

"Yes. they can be stinky, and sweet," Marcus said. I lead them to the restroom and showed them how to wash their hands after they use the bathroom.

"Honey, let's go please," I said to Marcus as we made our way back.

"Mike, will you have the driver pull up front with all the cars? Make sure security gets everyone in the cars."

"Don't forget to call Hilda and tell her no one will be hungry. And Kelly, if you can, get them ready for bed. Marcus and I would like to spend some time with the boys," I spoke. Everyone hugged and kissed each other. The grandfathers were in a competition already with the girls and promised play dates soon. Isabella wanted to do a shopping date. Margaret said she'd be over tomorrow for a cookie baking class. Margaret had also investigated piano and dance classes. And Isabella would talk to the priest about getting them enrolled in school and their upcoming christening. Isabella wanted them to have Spanish classes, too.

Getting home late meant that the boys were already having a bottle. I picked up Jared and said, "My love, I missed you today." Jared smiled. "Marcus. Jared smiled at me."

"Well, my son is happy to see his mother. But darling, I read it might be gas." He shrugged.

"No, you are silly. It was a smile."

"A smile it is," he responded. Teresa spoke up in my defense, "I am fairly sure it is a smile, because if you tickle Jacob, he will laugh aloud. They have advanced verbal skills."

"Takes after their mother," Marcus said. After bottles, bath, and a story, we put the boys to bed, then the nurse took over.

"Goodnight, Teresa. See you tomorrow."

"Yes, sir," she whispered, closing the door.

"Now, let's go see what the girls are doing." Kelly had given them baths and put their PJs on. "Looks like you're ready for a book. Did they eat?"

"No, they had some milk. So, after the books, I suggest one more trip to the bathroom."

"Thank you, Kelly."

"You are doing well as parents. You two are going to get it."

"Goodnight, Kelly. See you in the morning," I called out as she left the room. "Okay, girls, whom do you want to read to you? Mommy or daddy?" I asked the girls.

"Daddy. We like his voice." Ester curled up next to Marcus, and I laid on the bed with Matilda. Ester is going to be a daddy's girl. Matilda was choosing me. She was older. Marcus began to read "Green Eggs and Ham". Esther yawned and was almost asleep. Finally, the story ended. We tucked them in, turned on the night light, and set the monitor so that the nurse could hear them, just in case they needed someone during the night.

"Boy, am I exhausted, darling. Who said two was no different than four?"

"Sweetie, they are all so young. I'll let you sleep in tomorrow morning. I can handle the kids along with Hilda. I'm sure we can handle it until the nannies get here," I yawned. "Excuse me.

Four children are a great deterrent to sex."

"Oh no, my darling, I'll take you in the broom closet if I have to." He began to kiss me passionately. I felt the tingle between my legs, and suddenly, I was awake and ready for more. We fooled around until an alarm went off in my head.

"Darling, remember what Carol said?"

"So, what am I supposed to do with this bulge in my pants?"

"Well, let me help you out. Turnover, on your back." I began to kiss his chest and move down close to his navel, then licked his groin area. Marcus began to moan. I wrapped my tongue around his cock then took him deep into my mouth. I sucked hard until I knew he was about to come. Once he was close, I let go and watched as he came all over his hard cock. I rubbed his warm release up and down his hard dick until he came again. He groaned in pleasure, then pulled me up on him. He started kissing me passionately. Kissed me down my neck and lifted my gown. He kissed down toward my stomach and my delicate area between my thighs. He licked my clitoris. I started pulling his hair, "Oh God. Shit. Fuck me!" I moaned. He began to lick me harder, and I pulled his hair harder. I quivered from the orgasm. He moved back up to my mouth and kissed me again. I could taste my juices on his lips. We fell asleep in each other arms. He rolled over and said, "I love you. Will you marry me again?"

"Yes, my darling. Always."

The next morning, the door to the bedroom flung open. Marcus yelled, "What the heck?!" Ester and Matilda jumped on the bed with us.

"Wake up, mommy and daddy! Let's get a puppy!" Marcus reached for the girls and started tickling them. They were giggling and thrashing around the bed. "Do you two wild hyenas know how to knock?" There was a knock on the open door, "Sorry sir. I tried to stop them, but they move fast."

"It's okay. Girls, go with Hilda and have breakfast with her in the kitchen. Mommy is sleeping in. We will talk about a dog after you have done a little research. When Kelly gets here and you get dressed, then your job is to research the type of dog you want. Make me a report. Include how big they get, how much you need to walk them, and how they are cared for. Things like that. Go with Hilda, that's the plan. Tell Mommy you love her. Let her sleep. You two get out of here." Both girls jumped off the bed and went with Hilda.

"Sir, do you want breakfast in the dining room?"

"No, Hilda, I will eat with the girls. In a couple of hours, fix my wife a tray. She needs to rest." Everyone left the room and closed the door.

"Sweetheart, thank you for last night. I love you. Sleep in and I will see you later. I will check on the boys and have already handled the girls. My darling, this afternoon, we may be buying a dog if they produce their report. I need to go out to the housing neighborhood I am building, if you want to go with me. We can take the girls." He got up and put his pajamas pants back on, then closed the door. I turned over, pulled the covers up, and went back to sleep. *I'm married to a wonderful man,* I thought. I really could not sleep, so I decided to get up, shower, and dress.

My phone rang, "Hi dad. Are you calling about the Brit Milah?"

"Yes, it will be at the synagogue at ten with the boys. I have a mohel, and the rabbi is going to give the baby to the mohel. Then, he will give the boys to me. The godfathers will be there to help hold the boys. Marcus will be there, also. You know this will last about twenty minutes, at the most, with prayers and all. I will do all the Hebrew prayers. I also thought about doing Brit Shalom, a naming ceremony, for the girls. I thought you could ask Marcus' sisters to be godmothers. Mike will be their godfather. Margaret got the caterers to do the Jewish festival meal. So, all is set up. Just wanted you to know the schedule."

"Okay, dad. I will talk to Marcus. Thank you. Oh, dad, do you have the yarmulkes?"

"Yes, I have all of them, plus two special blue velvet ones for the boys. Samantha, I really want to do a Brit Shalom for the girls. It is a naming ceremony, just like we did for you. I know you agreed to bring them up Catholic, but I'd like them to know something about Judaism. You are Jewish and their mother; that makes them Jewish. I want them to learn Hebrew and attend some Jewish classes. I will pay for everything. Margaret converted, and she has two beautiful shawls for them. This will be a blessing ceremony, welcoming them into our life. The festival is already set up. The candles in the synagogue will be lit. The godparents will be a part of the ceremony. They will also bless the wine with the knife. So, will you do this for me?"

"Yes, dad. I'm sure Marcus will be okay with it since we will already be there."

"Oh, and the wedding tent will be the reception room. Thanks, darling."

"Thank you, dad."

When I left the room, it was about eight a.m., so Teresa was with the boys. I peeked in and they were asleep. I said quietly, "I'll be back in an hour." I went to the kitchen, "Oh, Mrs. Matthew. It has been bedlam in here. I have your breakfast ready though."

"Mommy, we were going to bring you breakfast in bed." Kelly had arrived and she was trying to usher the girls to their room to dress. The maids were helping clean the kitchen. Marcus was still in his pajama bottoms, "How can two little girls cause so much craziness?"

"Because their daddy is letting them get away with murder." He pulled me to him and nuzzled my ear.

"I have some things to learn. Maybe I need to take a parenting class."

"That is a good idea. I checked on the boys, and they are asleep. I want to be there when they wake up to nurse. Will you join me?"

"Yes, my darling." He reached and stole a piece of my bacon and said, "I'm going to take a shower and get dressed. Kelly is going to work with the girls on researching the dog. I suggested a Labrador. They are good with kids and easy to train."

"That's on you, buddy." He laughed, slapped my butt, and went to shower. I placed a call to Marcus' sisters and got Paige on the phone.

"Hi Paige, you heard about the girls? We are having a ceremony at ten at the synagogue. My dad wants to include the girls in a welcoming ceremony. Bottom line is, will you and Penelope be their godmothers? We will have another Catholic ceremony for the children when the boys are six months old, and we want you, of course, to be their godmothers. I know it seems strange, but my dad really wants to introduce them to Judaism. Marcus is fine with it."

"Samantha, I'd love to, and I am sure Penelope will, too. Dad and mom told us about it, and I totally understand."

"Thanks. See you tomorrow morning." Now, all I must do is get Mike on board and my work is done. Marcus came back downstairs, "Are the boys up yet?"

"Let's go look. Dad wants to do a welcoming ceremony for the girls along with the boys' circumcision."

"I'll call Mike." He dialed his cell. "Hey, man, we need you to be godfather to the girls at a ceremony after the boy's circumcision."

"Sure, man. I guess Saul will tell us what we're doing?"

"Yep, he has all the hats. Suit is good. See you later around three. I need to go out to look at the development and I want to take the girls with me. Sam is going. And Kelly will be with us."

"I'll pick you up in the van with a driver at three," Mike said before hanging up. Marcus finally joined me in the nursery where I was breast feeding Jared. Teresa was changing Jacob. "Teresa, let me do that, please," Marcus said.

"Sure."

Marcus put his hand on Jacob and made sure he was strapped down to the changing table. He opened the diaper to only find that it was wet. He took a wipe and gently cleaned Jacob up. "Son, tomorrow is going to be a big day. I hope you do not remember what is about to happen to your little sword." He picked him up and sat down in a chair, then tried to get him to hold a rattle. Jacob was strong and he was already able to curl his hand around the rattle. I had insisted that they always listen to classical music. I had read so many books on increasing a child's brain power during infancy. "Let's swap boys, sweetheart. Jared has on a dirty diaper and Jacob needs to nurse."

"So that's the deal? That's what a dad's role is? They get the dirty jobs." I threw a diaper at him. "That is the least you can do." Teresa said, "Mr. Matthew, I can do it."

"No, I am going to clean my son's butt and remind him some day that he owes me." Marcus strapped Jared to the changing table and opened the diaper. The smell was overwhelming. "Sam, when does it stop being like green slime?"

"When they start eating food, Mr. Matthew," said Teresa.

"That is going to be awhile. Boy, I need to get you a steak so that we change the slime situation." He finished with the dirty diaper, wrapped it up, and put it in the Diaper Genie. Teresa said, "I'm going to go empty the pail, while I have both of you with the boys." Jacob had finished feeding and I was burping him. Jared was listening to his dad read to him. In ran the girls, "We did our report, daddy. Now what?"

"First, see your brothers and say hello. Pretty soon they will be old enough for you to play with them." Ester was holding Jared's hand. "His fingers are so little."

"Yes, your fingers were that small once upon a time," I spoke.

"Girls, we'd like to spend some more time with the boys. But I want you two girls and Kelly to locate a rescue and contact them. Also, draw me some pictures of this dog. Kelly, have the girls ready at three. We are going to look at our new house. I have some details to take care of. Sam, are you going?" "No, sweetheart. The house is still mostly unrecognizable to me. I want to stay with the boys, and I'd like to check up on my office and maybe take a nap later."

"Okay, as long as Kelly is with us. And Mike."

"Mr. Matthew, after today, I'd suggest that the girls start resting, at least before dinner. They are still young enough to need a nap."

"Gotcha."

The next day, Hilda had breakfast ready at eight and the girls were moving slow. I had already breastfed the boys and Teresa was getting them ready for the bris. The girls had a fun time with Marcus. They had already picked out their room. And they talked about the couple who were expecting a child. "And daddy said he had to get their house finished before the baby was born," Matilda added. They went to the horse barn and rode a horse that was there. Marcus had gotten them home late and had brought in a Labrador puppy. They were all showing signs of being tired. They picked at their food. Kelly was trying to urge them to eat so they could get ready for the ceremony. They just were not excited about the festivities.

"Okay, girls. Let's get ready. I think your mother has laid out some clothes for you."

"Mrs. Matthew, we need to get them on a schedule."

"I agree. My husband has no idea about being a parent. He is just having fun, not realizing what advantages the girls will take. So, Peter will watch the dog until we get through the ceremony today. I am doing this for my dad."

"I understand. We can talk about getting a stricter schedule after the ceremony."

"That sounds good. Let's focus on the ceremony and then we will talk about the schedule."

Marcus said, "Honey, what would you like me to do to get things going for the ceremony?"

"Marcus, would you please make sure the girls get ready? Sweetheart, you mean well, but we must get these girls on a schedule."

"Gotcha, I am sorry. I'm just not thinking."

"I know. It's not that I am criticizing you, it's just you have yet to know how manipulative little girls can be, especially Ester. She has bonded to you. So, I will handle the boys and you handle the girls." Marcus went to the girls' room and found Kelly trying to coax Ester into her dress. She was in her slip, laying on the bed. Ester said, "Marcus, why are you not dressed? I do not want to wear that dress. I want to wear the red one, but Kelly said I have to wear the blue one."

"Well, did mommy pick that blue dress out?" "Yes,

mommy did. But I do not want to wear it." "Let me

ask you, have you ever been to a bris?" "No, daddy. I

do not even know why we are going."

"Okay, that's fair. Kelly, will you look up what a bris is and what a naming ceremony is. Also, Ester, your grandfather really wants this ceremony, so we are doing this to make him happy. Sometimes you do things you do not want to do for other people. Especially people who love you. Kelly, have you told the girls all the treats that they will get to eat after the ceremony?"

"No, but that is a good thought. The food, cakes, and pies. I cannot wait." Ester was listening carefully now. "Okay, daddy. I will wear the blue dress. Will you help me put it on?"

"I think I can." Marcus helped Ester put her dress on. He brushed her hair and put in the barrette. Matilda was already dressed. There was such a difference between the two girls. Matilda was easygoing. Ester was stubborn and strong-willed. That was a difference between the girls, and we will just have to work on that. At nine, everyone was ready to go to the synagogue. Marcus' sisters and Mike had gotten there early to find out what was expected of them. Joseph, Rick, and Scott were there early to find out their role in the ceremony. The synagogue was beautifully decorated. Everyone was there and ready to get started. The boys would be first, then the girls. Jacob was first. He was handed to the mohel by Saul, and after the circumcision, he was passed to Joseph. He was having a fit. I am sure the drops of red wine did nothing to block the pain. Joseph held him close and was soothing him by talking to him. Jacob settled down. Then it was Jared's turn. Dad passed him to the mohel who put the wine into his mouth. The circumcision lasted about five minutes. He put the foreskin in a jar to be buried. Jared whimpered a little and was handed to Rick.

Now, it was the girls' turn. Matilda was up first and was blessed. Ester was brought up to the Rabbi and received her blessing. Saul prayed for them in Hebrew, then it was over. The food was in the reception hall, so everyone gathered there. The girls were interested in the sweets. Jared was given a bottle by Rick. Scott was there for support. I went to talk to Joseph, who still had Jacob. "This boy has a temper or is strong-willed."

"Thank you, Joseph," I spoke. "Would you introduce me to Emily?" Emily was talking to Margaret, who was holding Sophia. "Samantha, have you noticed how much Sophia looks like the boys? Especially Jared."

"Yes, they look like their biological father. But Marcus is the man who will raise them, and he will be their daddy." Joseph took me over to meet Emily. "I wanted to meet you," I said. "Sophia is so beautiful. Thank you for coming."

"Samantha, I understand that to make this work, we will have to be some sort of family, regardless of if we want to or not. So, thank you for inviting me. I can see the resemblance between the boys and Sophia." Marcus joined the conversation. He had Jared, who was asleep. "Thanks for coming, man. Emily, thanks for bringing Sophia. In time, we will figure all this out."

The festivities ended and the limos were parked in front of the synagogue. The boys were strapped in their seats, the girls were buckled in, and Marcus and I went in his car. Everyone was going to their homes. The nannies and the children were being brought home by Mike. It was getting close to one and everyone was tired. At home, I was going to suggest that everyone rest or nap, but when we got home, Peter met us at the door with Buddy, the lab puppy. "Sir, I hope I can relinquish the dog to you and the girls."

"Yes, let's put him in the girls' room and see if he will take a nap with them. If not, we will put him in a crate. Tomorrow, I will have a trainer to teach him some manners."

"Very good, sir. I walked him several times and took a doggie bag and picked up his messes."

"Thanks, Peter. I'll take over now," Marcus said. I went to the kitchen. "Hilda, please have dinner ready by six. Everyone is tired and ready to relax." Kelly and the girls change clothes and Teresa changed the boys. Marcus handled the dog, which seemed to want to lay down with the girls. Kelly was playing them music and Ester drifted off to sleep. Teresa swaddled the boys, and they also went to sleep. Marcus and I changed clothes, then laid down. "Sweetheart, we are getting there as a family. There was a server there who approached me, and he said his name was Phillipe Matthew. He said wanted to talk to me. I told him to call my office and make an appointment."

"I did not see him, darling. I just want to rest for a while," I responded. Marcus left the room and called Mike.

✳ ✳ ✳

"Did you see the man hanging around the reception? He was a server; introduced himself as Phillipe Matthew. He asked me for an appointment to talk. I told him to call my office for an appointment."

"Yep, I saw him talking to you. Want me to check him out?"

"Yes, please. He looks familiar to me. Anyway, how's the office doing?" Marcus asked.

"Samantha sent over one of her paralegals, said she would be perfect for the job. Just let her handle the office. She has great organizational skills and could review a lot of the legal stuff. So far, she hired a receptionist and your own private secretary. She did an organizational chart, and we all have our place. I am still head of security."

Marcus laughed, "Do I still work there?"

"Oh yes, you're at the top. I think you're the designated bill payer and the final approval of all projects. She wants the office redone and asked our designer to modernize the office. So, they are working on the design plans. They say it will be finished in thirty days. She is also putting in a nursery area for when you bring the kids. Said that Samantha had put one in her office. They had built a daycare in her office building to offer her employees a place to feel comfortable leaving their kids. Samantha also has a cafeteria that offers sandwiches, coffee, tea, salads, and things like that. She said this makes their employees more productive. She said we have room to build the same thing and it builds morale. She is looking over benefits and all the liability issues you may have. Marcus, I would not cross this woman; it'd be like crossing Samantha. She's good. She wants a meeting with you this week to go over the changes and her salary. Marcus, this is a good move for you, with a family and a wife."

"Maybe that is what happened to Lisa. She spent all her time working and maybe her husband turned to gambling because he was lonely," Marcus said.

"I do not know, and we cannot go back. My friend, I want you to be careful about that revenge trait you have. I get it, but you have a lot at risk now: a wife you love insanely and four children. Just saying. I've known you for most your life. Hell, we went to grade school together, then high school and college. Then your dad sent me to follow you around Europe. I saw the women that chased you—I usually got the leftovers. Your very good friend Elton would tell you the same thing. Watch that temper. You bankrupted that Kenneth guy. And I get it, what he did to Samantha was wrong. Saul took care of her father and stepmother. Let's put all of that in the past. We raked the tables by putting in our card counters; we got them for 300 thousand. So that's done. As far as his bookies, leave them alone. Take out the horse and put in that money is gone."

"I just wished Lisa had come to me or you, and let us help.

But I guess she was embarrassed or tried to handle it herself," Marcus replied.

"Man, let's go forward."

"Mike, you're right. Just keep reminding me. I appreciate our friendship. You are family. I will call Denise and see when she wants to see me. Find out what you can about Phillipe Matthew. Something is up with that. If he was younger, I might think he was one of my responsibilities, just showing up like this. Thanks, man."

Marcus called Denise next. "I have time this afternoon. Mike is impressed with what you have done so far. I can't wait to see it all. So, how about five?"

"That is perfect, Mr. Matthew. I'll have everything outlined and ready for your review to be signed off." Marcus opened the door to the bedroom. Sam was asleep. He went to check on the boys. Teresa and the other nurse were changing diapers and putting salve on the newly circumcised penises.

"Everything good with the boys?"

"Yes, sir. They are a little fussy, but that is to be expected. But their penises look perfect."

"Good. I must go to the office. My wife is asleep, so if you will, let her know? Thanks." He went to Hilda and requested a simple dinner. "I have to step out to the office, so go ahead and prepare everything to be served in the dining room." Next was Peter, "Will you call a trainer to have him pick the dog up and lay out a training plan around the girls? We are making it their responsibility to care for this puppy."

"Right, sir. I'll get that done today." The next stop was the girls.
Ester was still asleep; Matilda was on the computer.

"Sir, I have developed what I think would be a good schedule for the girls. I'd like yours and Mrs. Matthew's input."

"Okay. Let's set an appointment for tomorrow, say ten?"

"Sounds good, sir."

"I have to go into my office, and Sam is asleep. If you'd let her know. I'll be back here for dinner." Take out with Hilda, leave in he kissed Matilda and left the room.

He went to the garage. There sat his Harley. He had not ridden it in months and decided to put on the helmet and tear out for the office. It felt good, the wind hitting his face. No thoughts in his head; riding through the streets, clearing his mind.

By the time he reached the office, he was relaxed and ready to talk with Denise. He opened the door to the office. There was a lot of activity going on.

"Mr. Matthew, let's go back to my office and you can review my proposals. How is Mrs. Matthew?"

"She's tired. I hope she takes all her maternity leave."

"Your wife has a mind that has to be challenged with work. Rick is trying to send her over simple things to work on. No court appearances until your adoption order is signed by the judge, and her father is handling that, which should happen next week.

No next of kin that can claim the children. Now, I have some plans: an organizational chart, a proposal for structural changes, and an employment agreement. So, if you'd like we can go over everything and offer any changes?"

"No, Denise. I'm going to let you run with it. You worked with my wife, that is all the reference I need. Salary is $150,000, a company car, and an apartment in one of our buildings—all the typical benefits. Run it through human resources. Your title will be office manager and assistant to me. So, meet with all the other employees. Everyone is expected to be loyal, no drugs, excessive drinking, or domestic violence."

"Sir, I am single and not dating anyone."

"Call me, Marcus. Let's sign these papers." Marcus signed all the papers, met the receptionist, and his personal secretary. His receptionist's name was Jenny, "Will you order flowers for yourself, my secretary, Rita, and Denise? Welcoming them to the company."

Marcus went over to Rita, "And Rita, if a Phillipe Matthew calls, send him to my secretary and tell her to make him an appointment right away. Also, ask Mike to be there."

"I will, sir." Marcus got back on his motorcycle and spun out of the parking lot. Hopefully, these changes will lighten his load at the office. He was going to be late for dinner, but in time to put the kids to bed. A call was coming in through on his motorcycle. "Yes, Mike?"

"Well, it's not good. Phillipe Matthew is an illegitimate son of your father. His mother is Italian and dated John before he went to Spain and met Isabella. He never knew of Phillipe, but his mother has cancer and finally told him who his father is. There is a birth certificate naming John Marcus as the father."

"No chance it could be someone else?"

"First, she was not that type of woman. She found out she was pregnant right after he left for Spain. He never had anything more to do with her once he met Isabella. He broke her heart, and she has worked in the restaurant industry until she got sick. They do not have a lot of choices. You are two years apart. There needs to be a DNA test and a conversation with your father. He is your half-brother. So, that is the story." Mike paused for a moment and continued his findings. "He has worked in the restaurant industry, mostly as a cook. Seems he's good, even with no formal training." By now, Marcus had pulled his bike over. "Shit, Mike. I guess bring everything to the office tomorrow afternoon. I'll call dad and tell him to get his butt to the office. Then we will call Phillipe in. I am already late getting home."

"Call your wife, dummy. Tell her you're going to be late."

"Right. See you tomorrow. I signed all the papers with Denise. I like her. But you're right. We better not piss her off." Mike laughed. "Go home," he said hanging up.

Marcus called Sam. "Darling, I'm sorry. Got tied up at the office. I'm on my way to help put the kids to bed."

"Darling, I got your back. Love you." And she hung up. He rode his motorcycle through the streets of Manhattan. It was a joy; he had not done that since the twins were born. He had refused to give up these small pleasures just because he was now a father. *I must take Sam out this weekend. Things are going to change as far as priorities. Sam and I are not going to be that stale couple with all the kids. A new plan was going to be laid out tomorrow morning,* he thought to himself.

He did not get home until eight. The girls were already in bed and Sam was reading them a book. When he came into the room there was a chorus of voices saying, "Daddy, Daddy!" He went over first to Sam and kissed her on the lips. "Sorry, I am late. How can I help?"

"Well, do you want daddy to finish the book, or mommy?" Of course, it was daddy. "Do you mind Sam?"

"No, sweetheart. Hilda put your dinner in the warmer. You missed a lesson on eating spaghetti. I videoed it for you. I'm going to check on the boys; they have been fussy all day."

"Of course, sweetheart. I'm glad I cannot remember the day I was circumcised."

"Anyway, I want to nurse them before they go to bed. I hope you will join us?"

"Absolutely, let me get these monkeys in bed and settled down. Kelly, you can leave if you like. Hopefully, when the house is finished, home won't be so far away." Marcus read the books to the girls; they chose another Dr. Seuss book. He tucked them in, heard their prayers, and kissed them goodnight.

When he went into the boy's nursery, Teresa was changing Jacob's diaper and Sam was nursing Jared. Betty, another nurse was there and said, "Mr. Matthew, sometimes the feel of your skin next to them will calm them down. That's why they calm down when Mrs. Matthew nurses them."

"Honey, Jared could use a diaper change."

"So, my punishment for being late is to change a dirty diaper?"

"Well, you can look at is as one of the joys to remember of fatherhood."

"So, Mr. Matthew, be very thorough when cleaning the end of their penis. There is a salve to put on." *I will be glad when it just us boys,* he thought. "Mr. Matthew, we are also putting alcohol on their navel cord. It helps it heal." The boys went down easily, and Marcus went to the kitchen to get his dinner out of the warmer. "Have a glass of wine with me and keep me company, darling," he said to Sam as he ducked out of the nursery.

✳✳✳

"One of the things I want us to promise each other," Marcus said as he was pouring each of us a glass of red wine. "I want us first and the kids second. That may sound selfish, but I do not want to miss my wife. So tomorrow, I'd like to establish some plans with the girls. And this Saturday, I'd like to take you out on the motorcycle and on a picnic. It's like the children are dividing and conquering. I do not want to miss you, and what we were before them. They make us better, but I miss the sex like we had before. I want date nights. And weekends away. We can afford an army of help. Let's plan at least two major family trips and make after church 'family day.' We both love our jobs, and we can take them with us when we can." He swallowed the last of his wine.

"Well, what brought all this on?"

"Riding my Harley and thinking of the time I took you to the best place to see the sunset."

"Darling, I am so glad you feel this way. I also want exercise time for us, and me-time, as well. I still have my apartment. We can slip away there."

"Denise is incredible. She has the office under control. And I found out today, I might have a half-brother. I'm too tired to talk about it right now. Let's just go to bed." We went to bed. He kissed me passionately and said, "I want three weeks with you on the honeymoon. We have not had one yet. Maybe when the twins are three months old? The girls will be in school by then. I miss you, the way we were."

"Is being a father too much?"

"No, but I want to have it all. My mother did not work, but she and dad spent many times alone together. And it was just me. But I was so busy, it was not like I missed them like you'd think I would. We had family trips and my parents had date nights. Then the twins were born, and we still managed to be a family, but mom and dad were still this romantic couple. I want romance."

"Marcus, I know what you want," I giggled. "You want to hold me up against the shower wall and thrust yourself deep inside me, as hard as possible."

"You're right."

"Now, what about this half-brother?" I asked, not letting that one go.

"I will know more tomorrow afternoon when I meet dad."

"Well, I hope no kid comes knocking on our door claiming to be one of your long-lost children." "Not a chance, but I know you'd love them."

"Yes, I would. Now hold me next to you and try to sleep."

The next morning after breakfast, Marcus called a family meeting with the girls. He put two twenties on the table and said to the girls, "Kelly, will you take notes so you can draw up their contract please?"

"What do you mean?" Matilda asked.

"Well, if you live up to the terms of your contract, you will get twenty dollars a week for your payment."

Ester asked, "What's a contract?"

"Kelly, have them look up what a contract is and what it means to sign one. Here are the terms: If mommy and daddy's door is shut, knock before entering, and we will do the same with you. What that means is that everyone is entitled to privacy."

"What if we have a nightmare?"

"Then that will be an exception and you may come in. Or call us on the monitor and, of course, we will be there. After breakfast, you are to take your plate to the kitchen and give it to whoever is cleaning up. Then you are to make your beds, make sure your toys are put away, and your dirty clothes in your hampers. Kelly will determine the order of the contract. Before breakfast, you are to take Buddy for a walk. And yes, you must clean up his poop. You wanted a dog. And, like we must take care of you, you must take care of Buddy. He will need fresh water and food in the morning and in the evening. You will also need to walk him again after dinner. You need to play with him at least twenty minutes each day—ball, or fetch, something. You will work with the trainer twice a week, so Buddy learns manners. You will take piano and dance classes twice a week, as well as read a book once a week and write a one-page report on it. Kelly will guide you. I'd like to see some science projects. Kelly, feel free to order any supplies or educational materials you feel that they might enjoy. I would suggest art supplies and cooking. You have two sets of grandparents and one great-grandmother; weekly phone calls will be necessary. And I'd like you to keep a diary. At first, you will not be able to write much about your day, thoughts, and dreams, but you can draw pictures. Twenty minutes a day with your brothers helping and teaching them in anyway Kelly or Teresa suggests."

Matilda spoke up, "Even changing dirty diapers?"

"Yep, you have to help. We will have family day after church, all day. Mom and I will have date nights every Friday. Every other Saturday we will have fun together as a family. But every other Saturday belongs to mom and dad. When school starts, I expect you to join a sport, in addition to this list, and your schoolwork. So, any questions?"

Ester said, "We need to know what a contract is first. Does this mean you will spend time with us and read and sing and play with us?"

"Of course, my darlings. And some days, we will take you to work with us," I said.

"We want our family to be adventurous, but really understand how privileged you are," Marcus chimed in. "I'd like to see some volunteer work in there somewhere," I added.

"Now, Kelly, will help them put all this together? Make a calendar and help them understand?"

"Yes, Mr. Matthew. All of this is a good idea."

"And girls, you will have free time, an hour every day, just to do what you want," Marcus added.

"Mom said we call this 'me-time,'" Matilda said.

"Also, the twins are only a few days old, when they are three months old, mommy and daddy are going on a honeymoon. Can you figure out how many days that will be? And we are going for three weeks. So, figure that out, too. At breakfast, I plan to have a math problem ready. There will be some days that dad or mom may have to miss breakfast with you, but we will be there for dinner. So, get to it. See you after dinner to see what you two want to negotiate on."

"Ester," Matilda said, "You just need to look it up. That's what Dad will say, so don't ask."

"Let's go girls, we have a lot to do," Kelly said leading them back to their room.

"Sweetheart, I need to meet with my dad and Mike at the office to figure out this half-brother situation. Do you mind?"

"No, kiss the boys goodbye once I nurse them. I'm going to exercise some. I am ready."

"Maybe later I can hit the gym. I want to keep more of our lifestyle, like I said," Marcus replied.

"I think you did a fantastic job. Let's see what happens." We went into the nursery together. Teresa was bathing Jacob. Marcus kissed both boys. Teresa said, "Mr. Matthew. Look at Jacob's navel cord, it came off today. Now he has a beautiful belly button."

"Did Jared's?" I asked.

"Not yet, but soon."

"Thanks, Teresa," Marcus said, "I got to run."

✳ ✳ ✳

When Marcus got to the office, John Marcus was already there with Mike, drinking coffee. "Well, dad let's get started." Mike laid the folder in front of John. "Dad, do you remember Francesca De Rosa?"

"Well yes, son. I dated her for a while, then I went to Spain for that development. I met your mother, who took my heart away. Married her, brought her back to the States, and a couple years later, you were born."

"Dad, did you ever stay in touch with her?"

"No, son. Just told her I was madly in love with your mom. I told her I was sorry. She cared a lot for me. I'm fairly sure I broke her heat. Proud woman. Beautiful. She was about thirty-five when I met her. She worked in a diner in Brooklyn, and I stopped by every morning for breakfast. She was a great cook. And then I asked her out. And son, you know how it is. I was reckless, never thought much of what I might be to her emotionally. I figured she'd find another man to love her like she should be loved. Your mother, well you know, Marcus, when the right woman comes along, you'll give your left nut to have her son." He took another drink of his coffee. Mike sat quietlyHe knew from experience when you marry the wrong woman, it just does not work. He was married once, and he was having nothing to do with marriage ever again.

"Well, dad," said Marcus. "Do you think you may have broken her heart?"

"Maybe. But Isabella, well, she was twenty years younger than me, a very polished woman, a model. I just fell hard."

"Dad, in addition to breaking her heart, you left her pregnant. Francesca had a son. Yes, nine months after you left her for Spain. She did not tell you she had a boy. He's two years older than me and his name is Phillipe. He is asking for a meeting with me. She named you on the birth certificate. He said his mother is sick, and all these years she was too proud to ask for help. Dad, he looks like you. But we're scheduling a DNA test. He could be your son."

"If Francesca says he is, he is. She was devoted to me."

"Then I assuming that after the DNA test, you will want to meet with him and see how we can help?"

"He will be family, son. I am responsible for them, it seems."

"He is a really good cook, even with no formal training."

"Marcus, set up the meeting. Mike, find out where she is and if it's medical treatment that is needed, get the best. I'm just going to have to tell Isabella."

"Mom will understand, dad. We all have pasts as men." John Marcus left, and from his demeanor, it was apparent that he dreaded telling Isabella. She had a fierce temper, but when it came to children, she was a softy. She always said men were pigs when it came to sex. "Marcus, do not be a pig," he remembered his mother saying. "Do not let a woman believe you love her just to get in her panties," she told him once. He was thirteen when she started having 'the talk' with him. "Use protection. And if you get a woman pregnant, do the right thing. Or else, see this butcher knife?" She'd always pull it out of the drawer. "I cut your penis off and feed it to the dogs." My mother was 100 percent Spanish culture, and she spoke her mind.

"Well, that went well," said Mike, "However, I would not want to be the one telling your mom." "Well, here's how it will go. Dad will have his driver stop and let him go in and buy red roses, then he will stop at Cartier and he'll buy a hundred thousand dollars' worth of diamonds. Then he will go back home, give her the flowers, and pour mom a glass of her favorite red wine. He will take her to her Florida room, her favorite room in the house, and then he will say, 'Isabella, I have something to tell you, my love. And I am hoping for your forgiveness.' Mom will already know he's about to tell information that he has kept from her and that he is trying to get out of the 'doggie house,' as she says. It was sometimes hard to get out of the doghouse, but you better not lie. Own up to what you have done, and you were less likely to get her Spanish temper going. So, if dad is just truthful and explains, then she will understand. Oh, she will call him a pig. And hopefully, she won't throw the wine glass. It may cost more than the roses and diamonds. But she will say, 'You do the right thing. Where is this woman and her son? You must find her, and I want to meet her.' He will feel like a dog, but my mom and dad love each other deeply, so I doubt the marriage is in jeopardy."

Marcus paused, and then continued. "He may be sleeping in a guest room for a week or so."

"Let's hope that's how it goes," Mike said. "That's why I'm staying single. Work is my girlfriend. My left hand does fine."

"Mike, until I met Samantha, I said the same thing. But, when you meet the one—well, man, your legs go Jell-O and your heart feels like it will burst. Life changes, you change, and you will do anything to have her in your life."

"My friend," Mike said, "I know that from your reaction to Samantha. Most the time, you acted like a damn fool. And I know firsthand what you accepted to be a part of her life. So, as mama Isabella says, 'Do not be a pig,' and as I said yesterday, 'Do not be a dummy.' Your wife is one you better not take for granted."

"You know, there is a man who did and lost her," Marcus replied.

"But he is still waiting in the wings, so to speak," Mike said.

"Man, I know that. That's why this morning, I got the kids in order and told them how it was going to be. Mom comes first. So, Friday we are having a date night, and Saturday, I am taking her motorcycle riding for the day."

"Well, that's a start." Mike's phone rang, "Yes, Isabella. I have all the information. Yes, I can come right over. I checked and she is in the general hospital in Brooklyn. They are not sure yet, she has a mass in her stomach. I can arrange to move her to one of the Matthew suites. And yes, I can call. Or yes, ma'am, you call and get a specialist involved. You want to speak to Marcus?"

"Yes, mom?"

"Get a meeting with the son right away and let's see how we can help them. Son, how long have you known?"

"Since yesterday evening. Phillipe, that's his name. He approached me at the bris and asked for an appointment. He did not say anything else. I knew there was something familiar about him, so I had Mike get right on it."

"'Your father's a pig, but an old pig. And since he did not know about the child, he will stay in the doggie house a week. And my new diamond bracelet is exquisite. So, let's as a family, make this right. But, as I told John Marcus, you are our son, and you are the head of the company. He agreed. We trust you, we raised you, and know your heart and mind.”

“Well, thanks, mother.”

“Love you, son. Arrange the meeting soon. Love you.” And then she hung up. Mike said, “I better get over there, so I do not end up in the doggie house. On my way I’ll get her transferred to Manhattan. Here is Phillipe’s number. Here is the lab that will do the testing and expedite the results in a day. I assigned another security person to you since you’re on that BMW bike.”

“Mike, I will be fine.”

“Nope, I’m not answering to Samantha.”

“Well, I am going out to the development to see if the first three houses are ready for the designer, then I’ll get on the other seven homes, plus mine.” Denise knocked on the door, “I’d like to have your schedules on my desk today before you leave. Please see Rita and she will type it up. Would you like coffee? I’ll have Christi bring it in.”

“That’d be great.”

“In your office or in the conference room?”

“In my office, please. Mike, man, we had better get used to women telling us what to do. I think there may be a doggie house here, too.”

“Yep, I agree. But I like Denise’s style.”

“You be careful. She’s tough.” Mike smiled. Marcus left and

called Sam, "The meeting went well. Looks like I do, indeed, have a half-brother from an old flame that dad had before he went to Spain and met my mother. Mom took the news better than I thought—only took a hundred-thousand-dollar bracelet and a week in the doggie house, but he is forgiven. Remind me to start talking to our boys as soon as they know what their thing between their legs is for, besides peeing."

"And our girls?" Sam responded.

"Forget it. They are never dating."

"Honey, when those urges hit, all we can hope for is that what we taught them well enough to override those urges."

"Or we can have security sit in on all their dates."

"Or maybe you can be a shot gun dad."

"It has made me think, sweetheart, that men are pigs, as my mother says, when it comes to sex."

"Yes, sweetheart. Some are, but your mother instilled in you a sense of responsibility."

"Sam, she scared the shit out of me with a butcher knife saying that if I did not do the right thing, she would cut *it* off." Sam giggled, "I love your mom. Maybe we will let her give the boys and the girls 'the talk.'"

"Oh, and my sisters managed to get out without security riding in the same car on their dates. Getting dad to let them go to Europe for a month was a big family decision, as you know. I am getting it. It's not all baby clothes, sweet smells, and hugs. This is serious stuff."

"Sweetheart, you did a good thing when you laid down the contract terms and the scheduling. Once we get an agreement, then enforcing is part of the deal. Even when they bat those big, blue eyes at you and shed a little tear."

"Yep. Let's see what they come up with."

"Well, Kelly and the girls have been working all morning, so please get in before dinner so we can have a family discussion."

"I will. I'm just running out to the development and making sure they are ready for design work. I only have a month on that one house because of the baby being born. But we will make it in two weeks, and the other two will be two weeks later. Then I should have each of the seven other homes ready every other month. It is ours that is going to take the most time. At least all the amenities are in. That was a help. I never heard from the developer. It was too hard to lose his project, even though I paid him a fair deal."

"Marcus, I know you did."

"Will you tell Hilda to do Chinese food? I'd like to do chop sticks lessons tonight. That'll be fun."

"By the why, Jared lost his navel cord. He has a perfect, sweet navel. I cannot decide if I want to save them for their baby books."

"Honey, that's on you. See you later, baby. Hey, have I asked you to marry me lately?"

"Not since the other night."

"Well, will you marry me?"

"Yes, darling. Always."

"So, we are in our what, twelfth day? And the doctor said six weeks?"

"Do you think she likes punishing

me?" "I can call and ask."

Marcus was serious about keeping things alive as a couple. His passion for her ran deep. All the memories in shower stall, where he lifted her up and pounded her until they both came. The way they were always naked all over the house. The times on the grand piano and the floor. Even on bike rides, as hot and sweaty as they both were, they always found a secluded spot. Sam was always up for anything. Security had to keep their distance; it was clear that privacy was paramount. Then the dinner when she had told him she was pregnant, and he had insisted that she wear nothing under the gown he bought her. When they went maternity shopping and he told her he liked her barefoot and pregnant. That first night together, when she was trying so hard to be in control but lost herself in her own passion. The fear that he would reject her because of Joseph. *No, I am having her for my wife. I am going to make it impossible for her to say no,* he told himself since their first meeting. Marcus swerved on his bike. "Sir." Security came through the speaker in his, "Are you okay?"

"Yes, James. Just need to get my mind back on my driving."

"Yes, sir. Of course."

Marcus pulled into the gate house and the security man stepped out to greet him. "Good morning, Mr. Matthew. I am assuming security is behind you?"

"Yes, Frank. About two blocks behind, but I am going in and starting work. James will catch up."

"Yes, sir." He opened the gate and Marcus drove through. The last two ten acre lots belonged to the expectant parents and the adopting parents. The design team was already there. Landscaping was putting in the final plants and flowers. The supervisor for these two projects was ready to walk the house. Marcus took off his helmet and placed it on his bike. The families would be here in an hour. Marcus wanted to have a handle on the punch list before they arrived. James finally pulled up.

"Where have you been, old man?" Marcus smirked.

"I am not a mad man like you are, sir. Can you at least let me know if we take an alternate route, sir?"

"Sorry, James I just have a tight schedule, and well, have you had a BMW motorcycle between your legs?"

"Well, no, sir." Roger, the superintendent, said, "Mr. Matthew, I am ready on the first one." They went into the house. The columns were just big enough to look stately, but not ostentatious. The foyer had a twenty-foot ceiling with a very ornate crystal chandelier. It was large enough to impress the guests before they even entered the house. To the left was an office/library combination. On the right was a dining room with double crown molding at the top, along with another ornate chandelier—this one was bronze. The room was square, perfect for a round table. "Roger, do you have a flashlight?"

"Yes, sir, right here." Marcus turned the flashlight on and shined it on the walls, "That's the only way to find imperfections. Paint drips, runs etcetera," he explained. Not in a Matthew house. The open floor plan of the den and kitchen made the family room feel cozy and facilitated communication with who was in the kitchen. There was a nook for planning dinners, enough storage space to store pots, pans, and dishes, and a large, walk-in pantry. Through the mud room was the laundry room, a pull-down ironing board, and folding tables. Marcus went into the downstairs master suite, complete with an on-suite bathroom. Perfect, another large Asian chandelier. This couple was adopting their baby from an international agency. Four bedrooms upstairs, each with their own private bath. Also, a large playroom, a study for the children, a game room, and a movie room. They had already picked out the nursery and there was an intercom system throughout the house. Every inch was designed for the safety of a child. "Looks good. Bring the design team in and have them set up in the kitchen, then pop some champagne. I approve." Marty, head of design said, "Hello Mr. Matthew."

"Hello, Marty." Marcus had gone out with her once, and she adored him. But no chemistry, no fire. "This house has to be finished in two weeks. They are expediting the closing with an extra hundred thousand to make it happen."

"Yes, sir, Mr. Matthew." The next house was another two-story, this time a Georgian, with big balconies. Same procedure, walk through to make sure it was up to the Matthew standards, then bring in the design team. Perfection. "Marty, same deal. Two weeks turn around," Marcus said, continuing to walk. The pool installers were finishing the pools and landscapers were putting in last of the landscaping. This one had a large screened in porch. "Marty, did you schedule the families at least a couple hours apart?"

"Yes, it's all handled." The third house was a contemporary style. It had lots of steel, a balcony, and stairs that were like a swinging bridge. Marcus' only concern was, because it was suspended, if it would be safe or not. His engineer had added extra stability to make sure it was stable. It was ready to turn over to the designer, who would follow the same procedure with the couple. The attorney would be there to explain the extra fifty thousand over budget because of the suspension of the stairs and balcony.

"Thanks, got to go." He passed Roger on the cobblestone drive, "Excellent job. Please make sure whatever Marty needs, she gets. I want these three closed in three weeks."

"Yes, sir. It'll be tight."

"How about I throw in one of these babies as a bonus?" Marcus said pointing to his own motorcycle.

"Sir, that's a man dream."

"Well, if that is what it takes, then it's yours."

He revved his motorcycle, "James, I will see you at the office." "Sir, can we please stay at least on the same route?"

"Yes, I promise. Call my office and make sure my dad, Mike, and Phillipe Matthew are there." Through the headphones on his helmet he heard, "Yes, sir, they are all there."

As he arrived at the office and removed his helmet, there was an old car sitting in front of the office, along with John Marcus' car and Mike's SUV. He ran up the stairs and passed the reception. They were in the conference room. "Please, bring in fresh coffee for all."

"Yes, sir."

"And I have not eaten. Order in some sandwiches, roast beef."

"Already done. Denise said to make sure lunch was served."

"Well, that is thinking ahead." I opened the conference room door. *Of course, I am in jeans and a biker jacket,* he thought. "Dad, Mike, and Phillipe?" He walked toward him and shook his hand. Mike slid the DNA report. "So, it says here, you are my dad's son and my half-brother?"

"Yes. Thank you for helping my mother."

"You will find out that my dad takes care of his family. Since now we know we are family. And your mother, well, she's family too. Your mother will get better. I have her medical report. She does have cancer, but with an operation that will remove the tumor and part of her stomach, she will recover. As soon as she can move, we'd like to move her into a nicer house. I am assuming she will want to stay in Brooklyn. She can retire or work part-time or whatever she wants. She will have around the clock care and whatever she needs. Dad wants to set her up on a monthly check and will take care of all her expenses. What can we do for you, Phillipe?"

"Nothing, I came for my mom."

"Now, that's not going to work. You're the son of a multi-billionaire. We must be press conscious. So, let's say the first thing you do is go with Mike and choose whatever kind of car you want. And for God's sake, burn that junk outside. Also, I understand you like to cook. So do I. But not professionally. How about Dad sending you to cooking schools in Europe?"

"Is this to get me away?"

"No, man, it's so you can achieve what you want. At least figure out what you want. But know dad also wants to spend time with you. I understand this must be overwhelming, but I have an important meeting with my family."

"Dad, will you take it from here? Denise, make sure Phillipe and his mom have security."

"I am on it, Marcus."

"Go home, son. We are good here. I want to get to know my son," John Marcus said.

"Philippe, welcome to the family," Marcus said.

✻ ✻ ✻

"Daddy's home! Time to start the meeting." Ester went running into the foyer just as he entered the door. Marcus picked her up, "Slow down little girl. Where is Mom?"

"She's upstairs, getting ready for the meeting, I think."

"Well, you and Matilda tell Kelly to meet us in my office in an hour. I going to check on mom." She crossed her arms and stuck out her bottom lip. "Now little girl, that's not how you look at the person who you're going to sit down and negotiate an important contract with. Nor is that the way you look at your daddy." She put her arms around his neck and kissed his cheek, "Sorry, daddy."

"That's better. Now scoot and set our meeting up in an hour. Daddy has been riding his bike all day and I need a shower." Instead of taking the elevator up to the bedroom, he took the stairs two at a time. He went into the bathroom to find Sam, still in the shower with her back to shower door. Marcus quickly tore off his clothes and shoes, stripped off his underwear and got in the shower. He reached out to Sam and pulled her back against his hard dick.

"Well, welcome home, darling. You better make it quick; my husband will be home soon."

"Is that right, little lady? What I have for you will only take a few minutes." Marcus lifted Sam up and began to kiss her passionately, kneading each breast while holding her upright in the shower. She pulled his head under the water. "Sir, I am a poor woman. And as you can see, I have no valuables."

"Ma'am, these two nipples that I am about to bite, look like gems to me. And that triangle between your legs? Pure gold. He inserted his fingers deep inside her. She began to moan. He rubbed his hardness up to her patch of gold and she opened her legs.

"Samantha, do not tempt me. You are so tempting right now," he groaned.

"So, what are you waiting for? My husband, I told you, will be home in about fifteen minutes. He had an important meeting with his family, and I am sure he would not approve of his wife fooling around. And who did you say you are?" she moaned.

"I am the help. I repair those expensive cars and motorcycles in the garage."

"Well, my engine is running hot. What do you think you can do for it?" Marcus slapped Samantha's butt, "How about an oil check?"

"Marcus," she said as she lowered her legs from around his waist. "The boys are not even a month old, if you get me pregnant..."

"I promise, I will marry you."

"Okay, then," she said. "Fuck me. And be careful. I am not ready for another baby yet. But I am so intensely hot for this mechanic that claims he can fix my engine that, well, I will take the risk. As long as my husband does not find out."

"So, a little role playing?"

"No, sweetie. Just a little fantasy."

"Well, let me wipe that fantasy out of your head." With that, he picked her up against the shower wall, braced himself, and entered her to like what felt like all the way to her backbone. Two thrusts later, she leaned forward and moaned loudly. The sound, he knew, meant she had reached peak. He thrust once more and pulled out.

"Damn, this pulling it out is going to have to end soon," he whispered in her ear, "You know, this is the old Catholic birth control. Not really that effective, but it's all we have until your doctor has mercy on me."

"Well, I called her today and she said next week I will get a follow up examination to make sure all has healed. But she still cautioned that no birth control was 100 percent. It would also take time for the depo shot to become effective in preventing pregnancy. So, raincoats are a suggestion, until at least three months had passed."

"Hell, yeah." With that he grabbed a towel and began to dry her off and then himself. "Sweetheart, we have twenty minutes to show up for our appointment or I am afraid we will forfeit our rights as parents." Sam took the towel and popped him on the ass.

"Get dressed. My husband's home."

Samantha put on jeans and a silk shirt with tennis shoes and Marcus put on jeans and a t-shirt. She reached into the closet and pulled out a tie. "I am thinking a tie should be worn at this important family meeting." He hung the tie around his neck, pulled on his socks and shoes, and they both headed downstairs.

We walked into Marcus' office, which once was the library, and all four children were there with their nannies. There were copies of the contract in folders for each of us. Matilda spoke up and said, "I will be representing my brothers and sister." We sat down and began to read their version of what Marcus had outlined this morning. Marcus got three highlighted pens out of the desk drawer and gave one to Matilda, one to me, and kept one for himself.

"Matilda, we must go through the points of the contract that we may have to negotiate. The pens are to highlight those areas," I explained.

"Do you have your written report on the definition of a contract and negation?"

"Yes, sir. It is in the back of your folder." Marcus flipped to the back of the folder and read their report.

"Mom, do you agree with their definition of contract?" he asked looking at me.

"Yes, Marcus," I replied.

"And Matilda?"

"Yes, daddy."

"Kelly, will you be so kind as to mark this as addendum A to the contract?"

"Yes, sir."

"And Kelly, will you take the notes on any revisions that have to be made?"

"Yes, sir."

"Okay, well the first disagreement is what time you walk Buddy in the morning. You say you want to move the time to eight a.m., but breakfast is at seven. When school starts, there will be no time to delay breakfast, nor can Buddy last the entire night without going to the bathroom first thing. Do you children wait to go to the bathroom?"

"No, sir," said Matilda.

"And you will also have to have an adult walk Buddy with you until you are old enough to walk him alone. So, it will be your assigned security person. And it is a city ordinance that animal poop must be picked up and disposed in the trash cans along the dog walk path. This is part of being respectful to other people. It is like flushing your toilet or disposing of the boys' diapers."

"So, Mom, if you agree, I am going to strike that."

"I agree."

"So, we have to get up earlier to walk Buddy?"

"Mom, do we have to get up earlier to feed and walk Buddy?"

"Yes, sweetheart. Your choice is to wake up earlier or give

Buddy to a more responsible home and owner." Ester chimed in, "Dad, Buddy's family."

"Well then, it's non-negotiable. Playing with the boys, it says twenty minutes."

"Marcus, I'd like to define what playing with the boys means. It's reading, singing, games, and feeding. I agree that we can take out diaper changing for now."

"I agree, darling. Free time," Marcus read, "You want to move it to an hour and a half? With the prevision that your chores, homework, and extracurricular activities are finished?"

"Agree, mom?" I nodded my head.

"Matilda, only as long as you use your free time as 'me-time.' Do you know what that means? That needs to be another addendum to the contract. Do you agree, Dad?"

"Yes, that sounds fair. Three family vacations a year. I think that's fair, but let's reword that to 'at least three family vacations'. Oh, I see another point on Buddy, in addition to you giving him one bath a week and brushing him, he is to get professional grooming at your parent's expense. His water bowl and food bowl are to be cleaned daily, taken up, and stored after he eats. When you meet with the trainer, you are to follow his instructions and recommendations. No resistances to them at all. Modifications can be made, but only with his approval. When parents and children are not at home, Buddy is to be crated. He may sleep in the girls' room until the boys are old enough to share in the responsibility of care. Let's see...next, picking out your own clothes, within reason. Daddy will have some final approval.

Mommy will also be able to pick out items that are essential to certain occasions. Let's see, you like to serve your parents breakfast in bed occasionally. Knocking is still required. Where are the math questions I asked for? And the calendar of events?"

Matilda brought them forward, "The answers are the boys, as of today, are ten days. There are twenty-nine more days in this month and then five more months until they are six months old. So, there are 175 more days until you go on your honeymoon."

"I'd like to shorten this to three months, as long as Mom feels comfortable with this?" I nodded. Marcus continued.

"I see you penciled in the dates you are doing extra activities, vacations, family days, and weekends. Add subjects to school schedule and mom and dad's work schedule. Make sure you check with anyone else and get their agreement if staff or nannies are to participate with carrying out the terms of your contract. Unless anyone has any more to say?"

"Kelly, if you will make the revisions and provide signature pages? One more thing, I would like the girls to understand the contract is the enforceable instrument, not the parents. The breach is the forfeiture of their twenty dollars allowance each week."

"Also, I think that they should be required to create a budget, with a savings plan as an attachment. So, if there are items that the parents decide, at their sole discretion, that we are not paying for, then the girls, and later the boys, will have to pay for it themselves," I added.

"Good point, counselor. Glad to have you on the team. And if we get into a dispute, then we go to mediation by Saul, the other attorney in the family."

Matilda spoke up, "This was fun."

"Well Matilda, this is what your mommy went to law school for. So, one of the first things you want to read about and do a report on is being an attorney. Now, if there are no further questions or discussions—let's eat Chinese food." The girls scrambled from their seats. Kelly picked up the copies to add the revisions, and Teresa took the boys into the nursery to get ready to sit in their infant seats at the dinner table. Marcus reached over and kissed me on the cheek. "Maybe this will work," I spoke. "If daddy does not give in to an occasional tear or hug or 'I'll do it tomorrow please, daddy.'"

"Well, if daddy does, then mommy gets to extract any sort of punishment on daddy that mommy wants to."

"Like spanking and handcuffs?" I reached over and kissed him passionately on the lips, then left the desk.

"Hey!" Marcus said, "I was not finished with you."

"Like I said, any form of female manipulation." Marcus got up and I ran into the dining room. The doorbell rang, and Mike was shown in by Peter to the dining room.

"So, what's up?"

"Well, man I just got a tough lesson on feminine wiles."

"I told you, man. They have all the power, that's why I am not

Married," Mike said. "So, where is this Chinese food?"

The Chinese dinner was comical. Hilda had gone all out. Lo mien noodles, sweet and sour chicken, beef and broccoli, mixed vegetables, rice, pork lo mien, stirred eggs and tomatoes, egg drop soup, small tangerines, Mao-tofu, shredded pork with garlic sauce, and even fortune cookies with green ice cream. We had green tea, Sake, and water for drinks. The girls were overwhelmed with choices. Hilda had it served in the dining room and strung Chinese lanterns on the chandelier. A red tablecloth was placed on the table and paper dragons were hanging from the ceiling. Red drapes hung for the backdrop to the buffet. And, of course, there were chop sticks. The girl's where squealing with delight. We all had place cards and each nanny was positioned between the boys and the girls. Mike was sitting next to Matilda at the end of the table, and Marcus was at the other head of the table next to Ester. Teresa and the boys were on my side with bottles ready for them.

"Okay, line up, girls. Mike, will you help Matilda? I got Ester. Kelly, just help with both girls." Teresa and I took the easy route; we had the boys and bottles. Hilda had hired two Chinese entertainers. They came out dressed in their traditional clothing and gave us all a brief lesson on their country and what it means to be Chinese. They spoke about traditional Chinese art and dance and taught us all a few words in Mandarin. After this lesson, they finished by showing us how to make a proper cup of herbal tea. Everyone applauded them.

"Hilda," I said. "This was extraordinary, and Marcus only told you this morning."

"I have lots of friends who cook for many culturally diverse families. When they want German or Swedish? They call me."

"Okay," Marcus said, "First lesson, no sticking or cutting with your chop sticks." The girls were watching Marcus demonstrate. "Take your top, long finger, and place it along the top chop stick, with your bottom long finger, hold the bottom stick and you use it like tweezers." Ester said, "What's a tweezer?"

Mike said, "Forget the Tweezer. It's better to watch me." And he demonstrated how to pick up a piece of pork. "Now the key," said Marcus, "is to get it to your mouth, so take your time." He picked up some noodles and showed them how he got it to his mouth. It was so much fun trying to help the girls learn to enjoy a new experience. This dinner went on for two hours.

"When all else fails, use your fork. It better than being hungry," I spoke. Lots of food went on the floor, but the extra servers Hilda had hired for this event picked it up quickly with small dust pans and brushes. The green tea was not a favorite with the girls. Mike and Marcus had Sake and I had tea and water. The nannies also enjoyed the tea. The fortune cookies and the green ice cream was the favorite of the evening. The boys began to fall asleep in their chairs, so Teresa and I took them to the nursery. Teresa said, in her Swedish accent, "You have a beautiful family."

"Thank you," I responded.

At about 8:30, Marcus said, "It's time to sign that contract and get ready for bed." Kelly had the changes made and all parties to the contract signed, with Matilda signing on behalf of Ester and the boys. Uncle Mike witnessed the signatures. Both girls hugged their dad, "You are the best dad." Then they hugged their Uncle Mike, "You said we would like it here, and we do." He kissed both girls. Kelly helped them get ready for bed and then they wanted to thank me with goodnight kisses. Both brothers even got a kiss goodnight. Kelly was reading tonight. Mike and Marcus were going to the den to have some Sake and beer. Mike lived in the building and had to only go up one floor to his apartment. After putting the boys to bed, the nurse came on duty and the nannies left for home. I could tell Mike and Marcus were getting lit. It was eleven p.m., and I was heading to bed. I went by the den and to say goodnight. "Boys, please keep it down. And Mike, if you cannot master the elevator, the couch is yours."

"Good night, Samantha," Mike said.

"Good night, my love. See you soon," Marcus said with a kiss.

As I was going upstairs, my cell phone began to ring. "Joseph, it's eleven. You're still up?"

"Yes, I just was working, and thought I might catch up with you. I wanted to check on everyone."

"It's going well. We had a Chinese dinner tonight; Marcus' idea. He wants these girls to learn other cultures and we were celebrating a family contract. It was his idea to set some boundaries with these girls."

Joseph laughed. "Yes, Emily says I'm going to have a tough time if I do not stop catering to Sophia's every whimper. So, maybe email me a copy?"

"I sure will."

"How are the boys, about two weeks old now?"

"They're good, growing, with no health issues. Shots will be due in a month. They sleep all night. The nurse just mainly sits and reads and listens to them breathe. That has been a hel. Marcus and I are not so exhausted. The girls are two and four, soon to be three and five, and very much a handful. So, we are trying different things to set boundaries, but you know, a tear or a hug gets a man every time. The boys are laughing. I mean laughing aloud. Very observant, so smart."

"Well, look whose genes they

have." "How are you, Joseph?"

"Well Samantha, I think of you a lot. I guess I'm still not ready to let my heart open that way. The way we were. I mean, I love Emily, but not like you. I must work up to sex with her, with you— never. I could just think of you and I got hard."

"Joseph, maybe it's a different love. A more solid

love." "It's not what I want. I want fire and passion."

"Joseph, you made your choice. I hate to say it, but you broke my heart."

"I was a dick. I get it, but it's in the past. So, let's not go there. Emily is a missionary, vanilla-type, rolls over and that's it. I'm not even sure she gets off. Men like to think that they can at least get their partner off."

"Joseph, I'm not sure I am the one you should talk to about

sex.”

“I mean. I took one look at you and...”

“Same way with Marcus. Joseph, you’re not beating off while I am on the phone with you, are you?”

“See, Emily would never say something like that. She’s so shy.”

“Well, maybe you have to teach her or go to a sex therapist.”

“Samantha, I am a United States Senator. Do you realize what would happen if that got out?”

“Yea, I can see your point. Go to Europe. Find one there.”

“I don’t know...”

“She was raised conservative, right?” I asked.

“Yes, very.”

“Then maybe get her drunk. That’s how you ended up conceiving Sophia.”

“She’s still breast feeding, will not touch booze.”

“Well, my doctor thinks that a little booze helps the milk flow easier. So, how long is she going to breastfeed?”

“She said a year.”

“A year? Not me. Well, I supplement with an organization of lactating mothers that donate milk. In a month, I’ll stop breastfeeding. Have you had sex since Sophia has been born?”

"No, Emily is usually too tired after a day with Sophia. And Emily is more about Sophia's needs than mine."

"Joseph, love, Marcus and I have already had sex three times, and my doctor knows it. Now we use Catholic birth control, which sucks, but next week she's releasing me. We still must be careful, since I get pregnant so easily, at least for a while. My doctor knew we would not last six weeks. Anyway, I feel weird talking to you about your sex issues, but being your best friend, and a person who loves you, maybe when we get the families together, we could have a woman talk."

"Samantha, she likes being in the background, second place, in the support role."

"Hey, it's late. I hear my drunk husband coming up the stairs to bed. Probably could not find the elevator button. Mike and Marcus had a boys night."

"And now you are going to reap the benefit of it?" "I'm sorry, but I have to go. Anyway, when we go on our honeymoon, come down and spend a week with the boys. Hey, how about a honeymoon? Take her on a fucking romantic honeymoon. Let your mom and her mom watch Sophia. And get a nanny. Love you." And I hung up.

Marcus entered the bedroom at about 12:30. He went into the bathroom to brush his teeth and take a shower. It was as if he was trying to be quiet, but I knew from the noises he was making, he and Mike had gotten tipsy. I'm glad the children's bedroom was on the bottom floor of the penthouse. At least he had not awakened the children. Just me, and I was already awake. He pulled the covers back and said, "I know you're awake. Come here, beautiful."

"First, did Mike get home okay?"

"Yes, what a lightweight. I took him up to his apartment and threw him on top of his bed. Pulled his shoes off and threw a cover over him."

"Well, I'm surprised you could find the elevator."

"Sam, remember, I have twenty-four-hour security."

"Yes, that's right. So, I guess security has picked you and Mike up before?"

"Are you angry?"

"No, sir, I am not. I spent an hour on the phone with my ex-lover. He was telling me how much he missed me and what a dick he was for letting me get away."

"What? Joseph called you to talk about his love life?"

"Yep, misses me. I told him I did not think I was the person he should be talking to."

"Damn right. How about his wife?"

"He said he tried, but she's the good Catholic type."

"Sam, that is his problem." He pulled me close to him and said, "What did you tell him about our sex life?"

"Kiss and tell? Not me," I replied.

"Yea, I bet. You said good things, I hope."

"It is not a competition, but you men always think it is."

"No, sweetheart. I'm just teasing you."

"Our love life is our business," I replied.

"Speaking of love life…"

"No, Marcus not tonight."

"You're thinking of sloppy, irresponsible sex," he groaned.

"My love, here is all you get tonight." I pulled his face to mine and kissed him passionately on the lips.

"That'll do, Sam. You're right, but you have never turned me down."

"And you never tried to have sex with me while you're drunk."

"Now, Sam, I do remember one time. Almost a year ago."

"Yes, well, that was my doing. If I am going to have sloppy sex, it's going to have to be a day when we do not have a schedule we must adhere to. Now, if we were on our honeymoon, or our weekend that we could sleep in, I'd go for it. But today is Wednesday, so work and kids."

"Bachelor days. Those were the days," said Marcus.

"If you really mean that, then the oven can be closed forever."

"My sweetheart, I'm just kidding."

"Goodnight," I spoke. Marcus put his arm around me as if to keep me from going anywhere. *Yep, Isabella said all men were pigs.*

Next morning, I got up at six. Marcus was still sound asleep, his naked ass hanging out from under the covers. I walked over and sat on the bed, then gave his beautiful naked ass a hard slap.

"Hey, what the hell?" Then I kissed it where my red handprint showed. He reached up and grabbed me and said, exposing his fully erect penis, as always, "Now here is something you can kiss."

He pulled me into his lap and began to explore my mouth with his tongue. I lingered there just long enough to tantalize him into believing that there would be more to come.

"Sorry, buster. I'm on my way to the gym before the babies need us. I can use a spotter this morning, weight training. Unless you want me to find one at the gym?"

"You, sassy devil, come here."

"Nope! See you at the gym!"

✵✵✵

When Sam left the room, he headed for the shower, even though his head felt like hell. She had left two Tylenol and a sparkling water on the vanity with a note, "Boys should not play a man's game." He smiled. *Wait till Friday. I'll show her a man's game.* He threw on his workout shorts and a tee, grabbed his tennis shoes and headed for the front door. Security was there waiting for him. "Sir, your wife said you might need some help finding the elevator."

"Funny, James. Let's go." The gym was down on the building's first floor with other retail shops. As they got on the elevator, Mike was dressed to work out. "Man, I'm never again getting drunk on Sake again. And that beer made me sick. I've been chugging water since five this morning."

"Yeah, you passed out and I dumped your ass on the

bed." "Well, are you in the doghouse?"

"No, Sam's cool. She said for us boys not to play a man's game. Slapped my bare ass and said she needed a spotter this morning. Either I could come, or she finds one at the gym."

Mike said to James, "Do you think Marcus is pussy whipped?"

"No. I think Marcus found a one in a million and he knows he better keep his eyes on the prize." They opened the door and went into the gym, and sure enough, there was Sam with a guy who was acting as her spotter.

"Hey, man. I can take over for you. I got her." Mike and James laughed.

"What you got is his wife," Mike added.

"Well in that case, my name is Chad. And your name?"

"Marcus, and these tag-alongs are Mike and James."

"Are you the Matthew that owns the building?"

"Actually, my dad."

"Well, great to meet you. Good gym."

✳ ✳ ✳

Me and Marcus rode the elevator back up with James and Mike. Mike got off, "We have a one-on-one with your dad and new brother. He wants you there, and me."

"Okay, I'll see you there, but I have to check on the three houses today. We are closing them."

"See you later," Mike said getting off on his floor. James went up to the penthouse and then went back to his place to grab a shower. He was expected to drive Marcus to the development at ten a.m., then back to the house for the closing, then to the meeting with Mr. Matthew. When he got off at 5:00 today, he would drive Marcus home. He had to pick up the girls this morning at 7:30. He almost forgot the dog walking they had to do. He had to rush. The house was starting to wake up. From the nursery, I could hear that the boys were already up and wanting a bottle. Marcus and I went into their room, picked each boy up, and kissed them good morning. "I'll run up and get a shower and be back to feed them."

The nurse said, "Take your time. They are learning to self-sooth." Matilda, Ester, Kelly, and Buddy were on their way out for a walk, bag in hand. James was meeting them out front in the dog park. Hilda had breakfast going. Soon, Teresa would be there to take over for the night nurse. As I was getting on the penthouse elevator with Marcus, I said, "Oh, what was that comment about being a bachelor?"

"You know, I cannot remember. Sounds like something like a drunk would say." He swatted me on the butt, "Shower, my lady."

"Yes, your highness, but no monkey business."

"Who, me?" He grinned.

"Yes, you."

"Remember, you're saving yourself for our date night." He gave me a little push to the wall and cupped one of my butt cheeks. "Just a sample…" and then turned the shower on. Breakfast was quick: cup of coffee, toast, and fruit for Marcus. I would get something later; I just wanted time with the boys. Teresa had gotten there and was bathing the boys. The girls were having breakfast with Kelly in the kitchen. Marcus came in, "Thank you, girls, for walking Buddy this morning. Dad has got to get to work."

He took one of Ester's pancakes, stuck it in his mouth, and kissed both girls on the cheek. "I'm off to work. See you at dinner."

"Good morning, Kelly. Hilda, great breakfast. Thanks."

"You're welcome, Mr. Matthew. And may I say, it is a joy to have a family here to care for."

"I guess it was pretty boring when it was just me."

"Well, sir, calm would be more like it." "See you

all later."

James was standing by the new Mercedes. "Shall we try this baby out this morning?"

"Sure thing," Marcus replied. He programmed the directions to the job site and off they went. Marcus opened the newspaper to find an article on the illegitimate son of John Marcus Matthew. Must be one of the things dad wants to talk about. Then there was a wedding picture of him and Sam. Then a caption saying, "Who is the mystery man seen at the hospital the day after their twins were born? It looks like the new senator from Virginia."

"Call Denise and have her tell the publicist handle the society gossip," he told James. Marcus pulled out his phone. "Hello, Joseph."

"Marcus, what's going on?"

"Just a heads up. You probably heard about my dad's illegitimate son contacting us?"

"Yes, your family news reaches Virginia."

"Well, of course, dad stepped up to the plate. But, in this article there is a statement about a new senator who spent a lot of time at the hospital when Samantha Matthew gave birth. I have my publicist working on that, just wanted to give you a heads up. We do not want to cause any issues for you, but we are not ready to go public with the news that you're the biological father of the twins. So, you are best friends with Sam, and you did graduate law school together, and you are their godfather. That is what we are going to say for now."

"Thanks, man. Yes, that'll be tough on both families right

now. But it will come out at some point. It always does."

"And that's okay. We just want to be prepared."

"I agree. Hey, sorry for calling your wife so late."

"Hey, that's what friends do. But here are my two cents, you cannot go back. You can only change yourself. So, give it some time. Can you see Sam being a senator's wife? You'd never get elected. Let's keep the family together, if possible, and not compare them. My wife is who she is and yours is who she is. Focus on what you can change about yourself. My dad always said, 'Grab life and go for it. If something needs changing, then change it.'"

"I get it, man. And I am blessed with a wife and a beautiful daughter."

"Joseph, you are blessed with a beautiful wife who gave you that daughter you adore."

"Oh, Marcus, Sam sent me the family contract."

"Yea, the girls were about to drive us nuts."

"You wait. That Matilda might just follow in her mother's footsteps and become a lawyer." "Maybe. But Ester? It's going to take a village to raise that one. She is so damn smart and knows it."

"Thanks, man."

"Yea. Stay in touch."

James drove Marcus out to the new house and the couples

were completing their walk-through. "How do they look, folks?"

"Perfect. And you finished them on time!"

"Well, let's get to the office and have you sign the papers with Denise. My attorney has already had me sign." He gave the thumps-up to Roger, the supervisor. "Go pick out a bike, my friend. Good work." James got him back to the office just as John Marcus was pulling up with Phillipe in a new Jeep.

"I see you upgraded."

"Yes, your dad insisted."

"Well, let's go inside and talk. Christi, send coffee and water to my office with a roast beef sandwich. Anyone want a sandwich?" Marcus asked.

"We had lunch and then went by the hospital. Francesca is doing well. They got all the cancer and with six months of recuperating, she will be good. The doctors will check every six months, and then every year," John Marcus replied.

"So, Phillipe wants to stay with his mom until she is well enough for him to leave for Europe. I arranged for him to go to a cooking school there and get his degree in culinary and restaurant management. He'd like to have his own restaurant, and you know how I am about education," John Marcus finished.

"Yes, dad," Marcus replied. Phillipe said, "I do not want to be an embarrassment to the family."

"Phillipe, my dad is an honorable man. He is also responsible for his actions. So, you're my big brother and I'd like to get to know you and for you to know my family. You have four nieces and nephews. My wife is an attorney, but she just gave birth to our twin boys. They are about three weeks old."

"So, you're a papa. So good."

"Thank you. Dad said he'd like to upgrade your mother's house, and you know, as an acknowledged Matthew, you will travel with security. I will be setting you and your mom up with a trust, and all your bills will be paid from that. One thing I'm sure my dad made clear is that I run the company. I set the rules and take care of the Matthew families. I'm sure dad will get everyone together to meet you."

"Yes," he said. "Soon."

"As far as press goes, my office will handle all statements and you will have to sign a confidentiality agreement. We all do. If you get married, your wife will sign a prenuptial and any children you have will have a trust set up for them." Christi brought in the sandwiches, coffee, and water. "Dad, I am starved."

"Go ahead, son. Eat while we talk." John Marcus continued, "There is a moral contract you have to sign. Robert, the family attorney, will go over everything with you. We have a lot of money, but with that comes responsibility. Now one thing did come up, you have two DUIs?"

"Yes, I do."

"So, an inpatient rehab. Just to sort yourself out, might be a good thing. It had to be hard growing up without a father; learning who he is and understanding why your mother and him were not together, or why your mother waited so long to tell you."

"Just know you are a Matthew, and my father's son, and you will be treated with the same respect that I am. And did dad tell you that you have two twin sisters?"

"Yes, I met them. They are lively."

"Yes, that's dad issue. Keeping those two under control. I have two daughters of my own and man, they work you." The men all laughed. "Marcus, we are going to leave you to eat. I want to show him around the office and introduce him. And I was hoping you would show him some of the projects we have here later?"

"Sure, dad. Just not on Friday. I'm taking my wife out. We have established date night."

"Good, son. Your wife comes first, or she can make your life hell." I gave dad a smile, "And cost you a pretty penny, eh dad?" With that John Marcus left the office with Phillipe.

Friday morning came, and Marcus left the penthouse before anyone was up. He met James and Mike outside and said, "You guys are going to help me impress my wife. This is the first evening we have been out together for fun since the twins were born and we adopted the girls."

"So why six in the morning?"

"I have a lot to get accomplished before six this afternoon when, Mike, you show up in the company's limo. I plan to take us to the airport where the company's helicopter is. I want to show my wife New York in the evening, and then have Denise make us reservations at Beautique. Mike, go by Tiffany's and pick up a rose-colored diamond necklace and bracelet, with matching earrings. They will have it ready for you to pick up. Have Denise deliver it to the penthouse, along with the dress I picked out from Rosie's. She will have the shoes and handbag with it." James said, "So where do I come in?"

"Well, your job is to make sure all goes well here at the penthouse. The nannies will be here, Hilda will have dinner, and the nurse is here, also. I just want you on duty as I plan to make a night out of it. I also plan to have a long morning, then I am taking her on a mountain motorcycle ride, along with a picnic. Hilda will have that covered," Marcus said.

"It'll be hard to get her to relax away from the children. But I want this to be the beginning of our every other weekend thing. I want a special weekend that will be memorable. Then Sunday, after church, we are all going to the Central Park Zoo. I plan to show them all the park has to offer. So, our Saturday will be short, as I know she will be tired. We will eat at the Dancing Crane. We are going to need at least three or four security people for all weekend. So that's the plan. We are going to take the boys with us, both nannies will go, and maybe a woman security guard. Mike, if you cannot do all three days, I understand, just give me your best team. James, you have Friday and Saturday here with the kids."

"Hey, I will volunteer for the Zoo also," James said.

"Yea, I think you can count on both of us for Sunday. Sounds like too much fun," Mike added.

"You're going to need help carrying those kids," James said.

"Yea, I think we will use carriages for the boys and maybe strollers for the girls. I know it will be a long day, but I kind of want this to be special."

"Alright, so I take it you are headed to the development early to check on things? Even though you have competent help?" Mike asked.

"Yea, I've got seven houses to get finished, and my own, so I want to sign checks and get everything over by three p.m. today. Mike, have everything delivered to Sam by three. You call and tell the pilot to get the helicopter ready." Mike asked, "So you're going to pilot it?"

"Yes, I've never taken my wife

up." "Which motorcycle?"

"The Harley. Have it ready by two p.m. and we will be finished by seven that night. And I want the limo with driver ready at 7:30. So, guys, that's the plan."

"Okay, we are on it."

"So, secrecy and all that."

"Yep," Mike replied.

"Marcus, leave it to you to set the bar so high. The children and Sam will love it."

"It's all on you to set up. It's just I want this to be a celebration of us as a family," said Marcus. Mike replied, "Well, I think it is going to be a blast."

At exactly four, Mike delivered clothing and jewelry with instructions for me to be ready at six.

"Yes, sir," I said as I went upstairs to look at the dress. It was beautiful, but I'm not sure it will fit. My curves were bigger now, my breasts had increased, and my butt was rounder. Exercising helped, but my figure had changed. I took a shower, shaved, and moisturized my body. I had recently had a Brazilian and gotten a manicure and pedicure. A quick nap would be a good idea. I set the alarm for five. An hour should give me plenty of time to dress, do my makeup, and style my hair. At five, the alarm went off. Peter sent up a glass of wine and a cheese and fruit plate.

"Something to nibble on," he said, setting the tray down. The dress fit beautifully; my new curves were perfect for this style of dress. With my makeup complete, I started doing my hair. It was its usual curly mess. At exactly at six, the doorbell rang. Peter called up on the intercom, "Mrs. Matthew, your date is here." The girls were in the foyer waiting for me to come down. Marcus was in a silk-lined black suit and a white silk shirt. He looked gorgeous, as usual. I came down the stairs and Ester said, "Mom, you look like a princess!"

"No," said Matilda, "You look like a queen!" The jewels were sparkling. Marcus stepped forward and said, "Sam, you look like a vision. Ready to go?"

"Mom," said Matilda, "Can we get a picture of you and dad?"

"Sure." Marcus put his arms around me. Matilda took the

picture and Ester kissed her daddy. Matilda took another picture. "Bed on time, girls," Kelly said. "You two have fun."

"The girls and boys will be fine. Let's go, darling. The car is downstairs." We went down in the elevator and the door attendant got the door to outside. The driver got the limo door. Inside, Marcus kissed me and said, "You look so beautiful."

"Marcus, you went overboard...the clothes, the jewelry."

"Sweetheart, I want you to have a taste of what our family life will be like."

"So, where did you get dressed?"

"At Mike's. And he is the security on duty tonight." The driver took us to the airport to the Matthew's hangar where I saw the company's helicopter. "Well, sweetheart. You had never seen the second-best place to see the sunset."

"I am guessing from the air?"

"Yes. I am an excellent pilot. With helicopter *and* planes. I've been trained on all." The pilot was standing by the helicopter, "She's ready to go."

"Thanks, Frank." Marcus helped me up into my side of the cockpit and then he went around to the other side.

"Sam, I have a check list to go over and then we can take off." It reminded me of Joseph and his carefulness in adjusting my harness when we were rappelling and when we flew. *No. No more thoughts of Joseph. Tonight is about my husband. No other man should be on my mind.* He put the headset on my ears and then his own. "It will help us to talk."

He started the engine and the propellors started to turn. I began to get butterflies in my stomach. I squeezed his hand that was on the stick. He smiled and said, "I love you so much. I promised you an exciting life, and I am going to make it always happen. And if I do not, then kick me, darling, in the head. Nothing is more important than you."

The sites over Manhattan were breathtaking. We flew over the Statue of Liberty and then the sun started to set. It was incredible. "Marcus," I said, "Yes, I will marry you." He laughed. We then began to descend. Our car was there waiting, and Mike was in the van behind it. "The next stop is dinner, dancing, and the chance to show off your new curves. The boys are fourteen weeks old, and you look amazing," Marcus said in awe. The car pulled up in front of the nightclub, Beautique. "I'm impressed, darling. This place is extremely hard to get reservations."

"Well, it helps to know the owner." We went inside and were seated so we could see the dance floor. We could see several celebrities there; several came by the table to say hello. We ordered wine, caviar, and a seafood dish, with chocolate mousse for dessert. Then there was an announcement that a song was being played for the Matthews. It was the song Elton sang when we saw our first sunset together, "Your Song." It was after three when we left the club. Surprisingly, I had a lot of energy. "Would you like a nightcap or go home, Samantha?"

"I've wanted to rip that suit off your body. I want to have kinky sex and make love to you the rest of the night."

"Well, I will not argue with that. Home, please." Marcus called Mike, "We are headed home my friend."

"I do not blame you. With a woman looking like Samantha does, I'd skipped dinner." Marcus said, "Stop flirting with my wife. See you tomorrow."

"I will be ready," Mike laughed.

"So, what's tomorrow?"

"After we sleep in, you will see. Remember, we get this Saturday. Kids get Sunday after Church." Mike rode the elevator up with Marcus and I. It was obvious to both men that I was tipsy. The elevator stopped at Mike's floor. "Can you handle your wife?" Marcus gave Mike a smart look, "Yes, I think I can handle my wife."

"Well, I mean, she's kind of drunk." Marcus said, "She really enjoyed herself and really needed this." Mike got off the elevator at his floor and we went to the penthouse. Night security was outside the door. "Good morning, Mr. Matthew and Mrs. Matthew. How was your evening?"

"Fantastic, thanks." He opened the door to the penthouse, and we went in. All was quiet. Everyone at this hour was asleep. I was leaning on Marcus for support and said, "Let's take the elevator up to our suite."

"Good idea."

"Wait. Let me take off my shoes. I'm not too steady on my feet, thanks to you."

"Good idea. Better yet," Marcus picked me up, pushed the suite button, and the doors opened. He sat me on the chaise lounge in our room and removed my shoes. He rubbed my feet and I laid back on the lounge and said, "Oh, that feels so good." Marcus took off his jacket, shirt, belt, shoes, and socks. "Sweetie, let's get you out of this dress." I was not sloppy drunk, just tipsy enough not to have inhibition. I leaned forward and said, "Will you unzip me please?"

"Of course." Marcus leaned forward and slowly started unzipping my dress. As he unzipped my dress, he began to plant kisses down my back. He pulled me to my feet and pulled my dress down to the floor. I kicked the dress to the side.

Standing before him was a vision of sexual energy. Sam had straps holding up her stockings, with only a bra and panties on. She was all curves and was aggressively pulling at the straps of her stocking. "Here let me do it, sit down." He said as he unhooked her hosiery and slowly rolled them down her legs until he reached the end of each foot. Her panties were G-string, and he ran his hand up in between her legs and began to massage her clit. She began to moan. "Marcus," she said, "Husband, I have to rely on you to control yourself, because right now, I want your hard cock inside of me."

"Sweetheart, I know the rules." He pulled her back to her feet and took her panties down, kissing between her legs as he pulled them down. She leaned into him, and he engulfed her with his mouth, searching her with his tongue. This was the raw side of her sexual prowess. When her passion takes over her, she's out of control. She tried to remove her bra but was having a problem with the hooks. He reached around behind her and flicked the clasp open. Her breasts fell out of their constraints and into his hands. He kissed each breast. She was wet between her legs; her hair was falling all around her shoulders. All he could think was, *This was not a wife, but a sexual vixen.* She went to take off her diamond necklace, "No sweetheart. I want you naked, jeweled, and in my bed."

He picked her up and placed her in the middle of the bed. He quickly removed his pants and underwear. He was so hard and ready. "I'm going to have to slow myself down, otherwise, I am going to ravage my wife." She pulled him on top of her and began to passionately kiss him. She was saying, "Fuck me hard, Marcus."

"Darling, how about we slow down and enjoy ourselves?"

"No, I want you now."

She moved on top of him, her hair falling in his face. She began to kiss down his stomach until she reached his cock. She wrapped her tongue around him and began to suck and pull. He knew if he did not stop her, he was going to come. "I wanted us to cum together," he panted. He flipped Sam over and got on top of her. With one hand, he held her hands above her head and with the other hand, reached under the pillow for a condom. He used his mouth to open it. She was wiggling in desire, "No Marcus, no raincoat. Let's just go for it, like before the twins."

"Sweetheart, the twins are three weeks old. No way am I taking the responsibility for you getting pregnant tonight. That's a risk we must agree on when your mind is clear." He put the condom on with one hand and slid her towards him. He moved her legs apart and thrust forward into her wet core. She arched forward and sat up in the bed, with him inside her. She groaned and said, "Fuck me. Now."

He began to move up and down, bringing her right to the crest, and then letting her back down. He knew he was trying to make the orgasm last longer for them both, but with no luck. He felt her clamp around his shaft. She was meeting thrust for thrust, then she began to quiver. "Fuck me."

"Oh, shit. Marcus, I love you." He buried his face in her hair and shuddered. His climax felt bone-shattering. He held himself on his elbow and moved her hair back. "God, darling, what have I created?"

"Tonight, I am a woman who is showing you that I need sex as much as any man. I need you to love me to death." He reached down, removed the used condom, and tore open another one. He began to slow the pace down. "Let me make love to you now, please." He began to kiss her passionately and she met him kiss for kiss. Then she rolled over on her stomach and he pulled her ass up to enter her from behind. So much for making love. She came and he felt spent, but she was not ready to quit. "Darling, you have exhausted me."

"Sorry, sir. I took a nap. Now make love to me." He began to squeeze and kiss her breasts and her neck. She was getting aroused again. He got another condom out and tore it open.

"Darling, one of us is going to be sore tomorrow. My dick feels raw already."

"Are you okay?"

"Yes."

"I told you I want the man I married." So, this time he made love to her, and they climaxed together. This was a record for him, that he could stay hard that long and recover that fast. Finally, he collapsed next to her.

"Thank you, husband, for a wonderful night." By this time, it was five in the morning, and they were planning to get up at one. He took all the used condoms and wrapped them in toilet paper. She had the sheets wrapped around her, but he wanted to get an aspirin in her and a glass of water. He knew she would be dehydrated if she did not. So, after several attempts, he got her to wake long enough to take the aspirin and drink the water.

"Samantha, do you need to pee?"

"No. Well, maybe." She gets up and closed the door. She likes to keep some aspects of their marriage private. He heard her turn on the shower again and went to join her. They took turns washing each other, dried off, and fell into bed exhausted. It was now 5:30 a.m. They were supposed to be ready for Mike at two. She entwined her body with his, and they fell asleep.

I woke up and looked at the bedside clock. It was one o'clock.

Marcus was laying on his stomach. No covers, his nude butt so enticing. I crawled down to the foot of the bed and kissed his butt cheeks. Then I started planting kisses up his spine. He began to move around, "Am I dreaming or is that random woman I brought home last night ready for another go round?" He flipped over and pulled me up between his legs and kissed me deeply. "I'm just trying to repay my gratitude. It's one and we slept most of the day away."

"No, we have an hour to meet Mike in the garage." He grimaced a little and picked his penis up and said, "Samantha Matthew, my dick has the skin burned off of it." I laughed, "Well, I told you, we're playing in the major leagues, and I remember at least four home runs."

"Well, darling, you are going to need to give me a day to recoup. Let's grab a shower. Wear jeans, a t-shirt, and your bike jacket. I'm taking you to another favorite spot I like to ride. Hilda is packing us a picnic." He slapped my behind and jumped off the bed to shower. I would not admit it, but I was feeling sore myself. I got in the shower with him, and we took turns soaping each other up. Last night was washed off, and we were ready for a new day. Marcus had on his jeans and no shirt; I was still in my robe doing my makeup when we heard a knock on the door. "What do you want to bet it's the girls?" Marcus, reached for a t-shirt and said, "Come in." It was the girls. Ester ran and jumped in Marcus' arms and Matilda entered quietly. "Mommy, is it okay if we come in?"

"Of course, my darling. Your dad and I had a late night." "We just wanted to make sure you got home alright." Marcus looked at me with understanding. "Yes, it was late, and everyone was asleep."

"So, what did you two do while we were out?"

"We made popcorn balls and watched a movie."

"We knew you would be back," Ester said.

"Yep, we are back. But it is still mommy and daddy's time, so we are leaving in about thirty minutes."

"Then tomorrow, after church, is family day," said Marcus. Ester squealed, "We are going to the zoo!"

"That's right," said Marcus, "So today, I want reports on what animals they have there and make a map of where you want to start first." Matilda said, "cCn we draw pictures too?"

"Of course, you can, what's a report without visuals?" I added.

"Now scoot along, we want to check on the boys before we meet Uncle Mike." The girls left the room. "Honey, I had not thought that date night would bring back their parents' accident," Marcus said. "Remind me to ask the psychologist about how to reassure them."

"Good idea," I spoke. We took the stairs down to the nursery and Teresa had the boys on the floor doing floor exercises with them. Marcus walked in and picked up Jacob. I picked up Jared. Marcus said, "You didn't miss mommy and daddy at all? Did you?" Jacob gave one of his famous smiles from ear to ear. Jared snuggled up to me. "You may not have missed me, but I missed

I you." I kissed Jared on the head and then we traded babies. "So, Teresa what are you doing with the boys?"

"This exercise helps them strengthen their bodies so they will be stronger to turn over, and then eventually crawl."

"Well, you guys have a wonderful day. And thank you. We are headed out this afternoon for a motorcycle ride. We will be back by seven. Tomorrow is church and family day, so we will need to rest up."

"I have everything packed for the boys. We are all looking forward to the zoo. I've never been there," said Teresa. "It will be great. Come, sweetheart. I'm sure Mike is already in the garage."

Marcus walked to the kitchen and Hilda gave him a picnic basket. "Have fun, Mr. Matthew. We have everything under control here."

"Thank you," I said back to her. We took the elevator to the garage and Mike was already there with Denise. "Glad you could make it, Denise. Mike said he was bringing someone."

"I hope it's alright, Mr. and Mrs. Matthew?"

"Yep, it's good to see this ugly man with a beautiful woman for a change."

Mike threw a water bottle at Marcus. "Which bike, old man?"

"I will take the Harley and you take the BMW." Marcus strapped the basket on the back of his Harley. "Mike, lead the way."

"We're going up toward Bear Mountain, west of the Hudson?

All the way up King Highway?" he asked.

"Yep, you know it. It will be beautiful. A breeze off the water and there are a lot of good places off the road to picnic."

"Okay, Marcus. I'll lead until we get to the highway, then you pass me and stop when you find your place. Then we will ride up a little further to give you guys privacy."

"Actually," I said, "I'd love for you to have lunch with us. My husband has about worn me out." He laughed, gunned the motor, and said, "Ready?"

"Yep." I snapped my helmet and put my arms around his waist. Mike led us out of the garage and past the door attendant, who was opening the door for James, the girls, and Buddy. Mike blew his horn. All three waived. Mike spoke through his helmet to Marcus, "I guess I have to make this up to him?" Marcus laughed, "He works for you. You give out the assignments."

"True," Mike said.

Mike led the way along the west side of the Hudson. The breeze coming off the water felt divine. Marcus reached and pulled my arms tighter around his waist and said through his helmet, "Hang on, darling. I can't lose you now." These two men were so competitive, it became a race to get up to Bear Mountain. Then Marcus signaled Mike that he was coming around. Mike gave him the thumbs up. In about thirty minutes, Marcus pulled off in a secluded area close to the river. It was like a little private cove. Mike pulled up next to Marcus, "I thought you were going here."

"Samantha, we used to come here as boys and often skinny-dipped here in the water."

"Spare me the details. I'm sure you were not alone." Marcus laughed, "It was the only place we could escape dad's security."

"Oh, that's how it was?" Denise said. "Yep. We were inseparable and always giving his dad the slip. We would have never gone anywhere as teenagers. Marcus' dad kept us under his thumb." Marcus took the blanket out of his saddlebag and unstrapped the picnic basket. "Girls, we got you here, now you can fix our plates."

"No problem. I feel extra pleasing today, my love." I opened the basket. Hilda had packed plates for sandwiches, tuna and chicken salad, pickles, deviled eggs, cheese, and crackers. There was also fruit, bananas, oranges, and chocolate chip cookies. There were bottles of apple juice and sparkling water. Denise said, "No wine?"

Mike said, "No. The boss does not like the drivers to drink, nor the passengers on motorcycles. He's afraid somebody might fall off."

"Makes sense," said Denise as she handed Mike a plate. "Darling, apple juice or water?"

"Water. I need to rehydrate after last night," Mike laughed. "Rough night?" Marcus winked at me, "Yea the worst." After we ate, I stripped off my jeans and went into the water in my t-shirt, bra, and panties. Marcus peeled down to his boxers and joined me. Mike did the same and said to Denise, "Come on in. The water's great."

"No, I am good. You three enjoy yourself." After a while of horse play, we came back to the shore. Marcus pulled towels out of his other saddlebag and began to help me dry off. I turned and dried him off. We slid our jeans back on. Mike dried off but did not put his jeans on quite yet. "Hey, let's skip stones?"

"Okay," said Marcus. "You first, then the girls. I go last." Denise said, "I grew up in Brooklyn. I never skipped a stone."

"It's pretty easy," I said and sailed one into the water that skipped three times. "Nice, wife."

"Okay, Mike. You go." His made four skips. He picked up a stone for Denise and put it in her hand, then took her wrist and showed her how to bend her it to sling the stone. The first one dropped and the second skipped once. Denise said, "I did it."

"Yep," said Mike, "Nice one."

"Okay, Marcus. Your turn." Marcus looked around for the right stone and threw it. It skipped six times. Mike said, "Marcus has always been unbeatable."

"Yep, I hold the record." We sat on the bank of the river and ate some more food and all the cookies. "It's six o'clock, guys," said Marcus. "We need to head back." He reloaded his motorcycle and said, "I'll head back to the garage. You take Denise home. See you in the morning."

"Family day, would not miss it." Before I put my helmet on, I kissed Marcus on the lips. "What a great weekend and what an enjoyable day. And what is this with Mike and Denise?"

"He likes her. He's laid back and she's super organized. Maybe it's a casual thing."

"Or," I said. "She wants to get laid by a good-looking man. Who made sure she saw his goods?" Marcus laughed, "And my wife, did you like what you saw?"

"You'll see when you get me back home, darling. However, we do need to eat dinner with the kids, and tuck them in. Or did you forget you have children?"

"Nope, first thing on my list after a quick shower. See them at dinner and look at their reports."

"And I want to help feed the boys. They are growing so fast. Already trying to crawl. I am looking forward to our honeymoon."

"Will you marry me,

sweetheart?" "Yes. Yes, I will."

It had been a fun and passionate two days. Even though we had enjoyed each other and reconnected our intimacy, we were ready to go home and see our kids. Marcus started the Harley. "Leaving now will give us enough time to grab a shower and eat dinner with the children. Is that what you want to do?"

"Yes, darling. I loved our weekend, but I am ready to get back and start family day." Marcus said, "That's the woman I married. Recharged her batteries and she is ready to tackle family life again." We got back just in time to grab a shower, throw on shorts, and let Hilda know we would be joining the kids for dinner in the dining room. She said she had the maids already set our plates. She knew we would be back early. She had prepared beef stroganoff, a salad, and a fruit plate. She and the girls had made a pineapple upside-down cake. When we entered the dining room, at Marcus' seat were the reports and the map, and pictures of zoo animals. There were even pictures for the boys. There was a map showing that they wanted to start with the Bear and Duck Statue. Their great-grandmother said it was their dad's favorite. The girls rushed first to me, and then to Marcus, and gave us big hugs. Marcus tickled the girls, hugged them, and said, "Let's eat. I am hungry."

The maids and Hilda served the stroganoff with noodles. It was fun showing them how to eat something new. Matilda was no longer a vegetarian, as salad and fruit did not look as appetizing as the stroganoff. Hilda stood and watched. "Join us," I said. "No, Mrs. Matthew. This is family time."

"Now Hilda, you had been with me long enough to know that you're a part of this family. Thank you for the picnic lunch," said Marcus.

"It was spot on," I chimed in. Hilda did not have any grandchildren, nor had she every been married. She was loving the kids like she would her own grandchildren. Peter stuck his head in and said, "Welcome back. Your father and mother are here and have asked you to set another plate." Saul and Margaret entered the dining room and sat down. The maids brought them a place setting. "Hi, dad. Are you here to see your daughter or your grandchildren?"

"Do not be offended, but our grandchildren. We thought you'd still be on your date, but I see you were missing your brood." Margaret smiled, "Look at the gleam in these eyes around the table. Absence makes the heart grow fonder." The boys were just watching from their seats. You could tell they were beginning to recognize faces. Margaret picked up Jared and he made gurgling sounds as if he wanted to talk to Margaret. "For sixteen days old, they are really alert and responsive." Saul said, "So tell us, girls, about your plans for the zoo."

There was constant chatter about the animals they wanted to see. Matilda said she wanted to go to the museum and see the art and exhibits. She had drawn a picture of the building. It was already apparent that she was talented in sketching. "Darling, our girl needs to take some art classes. Let's set her up an easel on the terrace so that she has her own private place to draw." Marcus said, "I think I can make that happen." Matilda smiled and said, "Can I have real paints?"

"Yes, of course." Her dad said, "And when you're ready to show your work, we will have the rest of the family over for your first exposition of your work." She was excited and said, "And maybe I can sell some of them?"

"Maybe," Marcus said. Saul, or Grandpa, as he had accepted his role, said, "I will be your first client." Hilda brought out the upside-down cake that she and the girls made. She had cut all of us a small piece, "This is delicious!" Marcus said, "I hope you two do more cooking. Grandmother Isabella kept me in the kitchen and taught me to cook. I enjoyed our time together, plus I am a rather good chef. Even if I say so."

"I can vouch for that. Your daddy's first meal for me was so good," Grandma Margaret said. "It's getting late. I bet you need to get to bed early tonight."

"Grandma?" Ester said, "Will you read us our book?" "If your parents say it's okay?"

"Sure, the girls will enjoy that, and we can spend time with the boys," I spoke. They scurried from the table, "We are ready to take our showers and get ready for our story!" Margaret's three children had not given her any grandchildren, so she enjoyed her role with our children.

"Dad, you want to join us for some brandy in the library?" I asked.

"I'll join Marcus for the brandy after I hear the story grandma reads," he spoke. So, we picked up the boys and went to the nursery. Marcus gave Jacob his bath, while I got Jared undressed. He loved his bath time. Next came the bottles. The boys snuggled up close to the warmth of our bodies. Being close to the person who made you feel loved was all that mattered. Jacob was finished being dressed by Marcus, so we swapped boys. Jacob loved to drink his bottle. He greedily grabbed it with both hands and shoved it in his mouth. "That boy's definitely a builder. He's just strong." I gave Marcus a sarcastic look. "Just saying, honey." After a while, they both were getting sleepy. "Ready to go to bed?" Marcus kissed Jacob and put him in his bed after he burped him. Jared had fallen asleep while I was rocking him and telling him about my day. We left the room as the night nurse was coming in. Teresa had left right after dinner to get ready for tomorrow. She had the boys packed, except for bottles, and had church clothes laid out and casual clothes for the zoo. We peeked in on the girls. Margaret was reading Charlotte's Web and had gotten to the part where Wilbur and Charlotte were talking about her making a web. "Time for bed, girls. Kisses for everyone, then lights out and white noise on." I had white noise played in both the girls' room and the boys' room. I also had it in our room. I had read it was proven for a restful sleep. Saul said to Marcus, "How about that brandy?" Marcus said, "I'll lead you to the library. Ladies, would you like to join us?"

"I'd rather have tea, darling. So, I'll fix me and Margaret tea in the kitchen."

"You two catch up," Marcus said.

Saul and Margaret left at nine-thirty. Dad kissed me on the cheek and said, "I knew Marcus was the better man for you."

"And how's that dad?"

"I just knew."

"I love you, dad. Have a goodnight." I kissed Margaret's cheek. "Thank you for making my dad so happy." They left and we went upstairs to get ready for bed.

"It'll be an early morning with church at nine. Come close, my darling." Marcus kissed me passionately and held me. We both fell asleep cuddled together. Next morning was church, so everyone was up by seven and had breakfast. We were ready to leave by eighty-thirty. The driver was downstairs waiting. "Thank goodness we had the nannies to help get the children ready," Marcus said. "This is a lot of work to get them all dressed, fed, and out the door." He had put on some gray dress pants and a white shirt. I wore a simple summer mid-length dress with a matching hat. The girls were dressed in simple summer dresses. Ester had chosen a long one. Matilda stuck with a simple, pink frock. They both had on their lacy socks and saddle shoes. The boys had on simple one-pieces with bare feet. Both nannies had organized snacks, bottles, diapers, and everyone had a casual change of clothes. The idea was, after service, we would all do a quick change in the church bathroom.

We got there on time, and already in the Matthew's pew were Marcus' parents and his new half-brother. We created a stir when we entered the church; it was the first time we had all the children in public. Ester and Matilda wanted to sit by Grandmother Isabella, which delighted her. Teresa had taken the boys from their stroller. I had one in a baby sling that went over my shoulder, and she had the other one. The priest began by congratulating us on the arrival of the four children, then the hymns began. Isabella was directing the girls. Both boys were asleep. Then the priest called for the children to come up front for a story before he would dismiss them to Sunday school. The girls were reluctant to go, so Marcus took their hands and walked them up. They seemed comfortable after that, and when the priest began to tell his story and ask questions, suddenly Ester took over the conversation. She was going to be our live wire. The priest dismissed them, and they went with their Sunday school teacher while the adults finished the service. So far, so good on the boys. Jacob had woken up, but a quick bottle, and he was back to sleep.

Once service was over, everyone paid their respects to us. Marcus showed everyone where they could change clothes and get the boys a fresh diaper. People may have thoughts about the paternity of the boys because of some of their features, but no one would question it, as the Matthews were big supporters of the church. By the time we got dressed, all the church members had left. Marcus was talking to Phillipe about his mother and whether they had found a house yet. He said they had selected one and were scheduled to move in two weeks. His mother was doing well. Marcus' dad and mom had been spending time with them. His dad was trying to get to know his thirty-four-year-old son. The family had been incredibly supportive of his dad's past relationship.

It was time to go to the park. Mike and James were riding in a separate van for security. Our driver helped load the boys in their seats and strap in the girls. The nannies were between the children, and Marcus and I sat across from them. I could not imagine what it would be like when there were more children. Marcus wanted at least two biological children of his own. I understood his desire and supported his need, but I just wanted to get some age on the boys. I was ready to go back to work once we went on our honeymoon, and I could not wait until the new house was finished. His crew had completed four more homes in the development, so now the crew was focusing on our house.

We finally were on our way to the zoo, our first real family outing. Mike and James had put an extra security woman on our trip. She would meet us at the Bear and Duck statue, where the girls wanted to start first. When we arrived, James helped Teresa get the boys' carriages out, and put them in them, covering them with blankets so that they were not visible to the crowds of people who would be curious to see the blended family. The boys had not been photographed by any photographer for any gossip magazine and we were trying to control the press until we had to broach the subject of paternity. They were dark-skinned like Marcus but looked like Joseph. There were several-racial marriages in Joseph's family, that had made him light-skinned, and now with me as their mother, they were more olive-skinned toned. This made them seem more of Spanish descent, like Isabella. No one in the family asked, and only Margaret and Saul knew the truth, but no one cared. Marcus was happy and that is all his family cared about.

"Wait, girls," I said, "Until everyone is unloaded, and the backpacks are unloaded for each of you, please. If you're going to the duck pool first, you will need to change into flip flops." Marcus had rented a pushcart for the girls to ride in. It was shaped like an elephant. Mike was pushing the girls and James was walking behind the family. Teresa and Kelly were walking along side each of the children's cart and carriage. Marcus had taken control of the carriage. For a normal family, safety in a public park was important, but when you were a child of a multi-billionaire, security had to be top priority. Too many children of the rich and famous had been kidnapped or accosted in public.

We reached the ducks and water and the girls started climbing out of their cart. "Slow down, girls," Mike said. He unbuckled their straps and said, "Stay where we can see you. You see the woman who is standing next to the bear?"

"Yes, Uncle Mike."

"That is Shelly. She is here to help watch out for you. You two remember what we talked about with safety and what's the most important thing you can do if someone bothers you?" Ester, in a high-pitched voice said, "Yell!" And that is what she did, bringing attention to our little group. "Ester," Marcus said, "Remember to remind me of the story of the boy who cried wolf. Now put your flip flops on and take off to the water." I had the video camera going and alternated with taking pictures. It was a nice, breezy day; perfect for an outing. After the duck pond, the girls wanted a snow cone to eat as we went to visit the monkeys. Then we moved on to the bears and then the giraffes. One giraffe tried to take a lick of Matilda's snow cone. This brought giggles to the girls. There were kangaroos, birds, rat-like animals, hippos, and porcupines. All kinds of exotic animals. We went into the bird sanctuary and the keeper put birds on the girls' shoulders. Everyone was having fun, but it was getting time to feed the boys and change their diapers. We went to the baby changing building and freshened the boys up. So far, they had slept in the warm breeze.

"Who's hungry?" I asked. Both girls yelled, "Me!" So, we went to the outdoor restaurant and got seated and the men went to order. There were hot dogs, pizza, corn dogs, and fries, with lemonade to drink. There was a lot of ketchup to be wiped off faces and hands. The nannies had packed wipes and hand sanitizer to clean the girls up. Then, they had to go to the bathroom, so another line, but they waited patiently.

"Okay, we have snakes, butterflies, bugs, and the fish to see before we go to the art museum."

"Snakes! Snakes!" they said. "Dad, that's what we wanted the boys to see!"

"Okay, snakes it is." A zookeeper there put a snake around Mike's neck, then he asked the girls and I if we wanted to hold it. We all said no, except Kelly. "I like snakes," she said. "They are very affectionate. Just pet their head." They stroked the snake's head. The boys could care less about any of the pets. The warm air kept them sleepy. "Let's go to the aquarium and have ice cream while the dolphins perform. Then we will see the butterfly house, and last, the art museum."

It was getting late, but the girls were determined to see it all. "Daddy, can I ride on your shoulders? I'm tired of riding in the elephant." Marcus took Ester and put her up on his shoulders. Kelly pushed Matilda. The butterflies were everyone's favorite. There were hundreds of species and if you stood still, they would land on you. Matilda said the bugs were "icky." They even had a bug cafe, but only Uncle Mike would try the chocolate-covered ants. James tried the cookies with ground beetles in them. He said they were good. Last was the art museum. Matilda admired a painting. "May I sketch something, mommy?"

"Of course, darling. And if you would like, we can come back."

"I'd like that." Everyone was wanting a frozen lemonade and souvenirs. Marcus said, "One item a piece." The girls picked out ant suckers for Phillipe, Hilda, and their grandparents. Then there was a stuffed monkey for Matilda, and Ester chose the bear. I got butterfly pins for the girls' hair. The boys were starting to get hungry again and undoubtedly needed a diaper change. "Let's take the kids back to the van, clean them off, and take care of the boys."

It was going on five and it was time to call it a day. Mike telephoned Shelly, thanked her, and said she could go now. James caught up to the family and everyone waited as Teresa and I took care of the boys. Marcus wiped Ester's face with a wipe and Matilda did her own. The guys loaded up the children and we got back in time for dinner. Hilda had fixed salads. She said she did not think anyone would be very hungry. They gave the bug cookies and sucker to Hilda and Peter, who said they'd save it for later. Baths, teeth brushed, and within minutes, the girls were asleep. Both had their new stuffed animals next to them. Both nannies went home, along with Mike and James. "Honey, it was a wonderful day," I said to Marcus. He kissed me and said, "I really enjoyed the children, but I am bushed. Let's go to bed."

The days went by fast. It was already time to celebrate the girls' birthdays. We decided to celebrate the girls' birthdays with a party with the family at Central Park.

They wanted bounce houses, water slides, and games. The grandparents came baring gifts. Isabella had bought each of them a box of new school clothes, uniforms, dresses, jeans, t-shirts, shoes, and socks. Grandfather John Marcus had brought a miniature doll house with furniture and a little family that occupied the house. Paige and Penelope had games and an Apple watch. Uncle Rick and Scott had bought birthstone rings for each girl, as well as a tiara for them. As they said, "All princesses needed a tiara." The girls loved their uncles and often hung out at the house with Rick or went over to Scott's house and helped him garden. Uncle Phillipe had bought cookbooks for children. Saul and Margaret, not to be outdone with gifts, bought a pony, which they promised to keep at the estate until our house was finished. Uncle Mike, who was there with Denise, brought each girl a bike with the promise to teach them how to ride. Ester's bike was pink and Matilda's was blue. Both were all decked out with baskets and tassels on the wheels. I hired a photographer, who took all the pictures. Matilda and Ester were so overwhelmed with the family turnout that much of the time they were in tears or throwing their arms around the guests. The children who were in the park that day had been invited by the girls to participate. I was proud of how generous they had become. The boys, who adore their sisters, gave them books to read. A first edition of *Little House on the Prairie* by Laura Ingles Wilder. Marcus and I gave them money and asked them to donate it to a charity of their choice. They decided on the ASPCA. They had been thinking of all the animals they knew needed homes and had both said they'd like to start volunteering there.

There were cupcakes in a tower instead of a cake. Margaret had brought homemade strawberry ice cream. There were balloons tied all around the park. Everything was done in pink and white. There was a magician who came to perform magic. Ester fell in love with his rabbit, so John Marcus bought his white rabbit and swore they could keep it at his mansion until our house was finished. The nannies came and had bought art supplies for Matilda and a child's sewing machine for Ester and had promised to teach her to sew. At the end of the party, the girls were tired and happy. They recognized that they were surrounded by love. Their father's grandmother came, with the assistance of her nurse we had hired to care for her. She brought a picture album of their biological parents and told stories of her grandson, who she missed. The boys were begging, trying to get the girl's attention by holding out their arms to be picked up. Matilda and Ester cleared everyone out of the bounce house, and with the aid of the nannies, put the boys in and ever so gently bounced the boys. They all four laughed and laughed. The children had bonded.

In a month, school would start, and things would be changing again. Marcus was determined to get our house finished by spring. The girls would go to the same Catholic school their dad had, so one of us would have to drive them, or the nanny would. Kelly would be going back to school, also. Teresa was still undecided if she wanted to take graduate classes. She was content now, helping raise the boys. Marcus had not wanted the boys hair cut yet, so soft brown curls fell around their head. They had begun to look more like me. It had been a super fun day, and everyone was tired. Thank goodness for the help cleaning up. The girls were each in a grandfather's lap. Ester was in John Marcus's lap and Matilda in Saul's. This was the first extended family they had had. Their biological mother, Lisa, had been raised partly by her mother, and then in and out of the system, which meant foster care. She had a mother out there, but she did not want anything to do with the girls. She had been young when she got pregnant with Lisa and had put her in the system. She had been in and out of Lisa's life. Marcus had made sure she had a home and help. But she had always had a drug problem, so right now she was in a halfway house. Marcus was opposed to her having any influences on the girls, and it seemed if the money and care was there, she was content with not seeing them. She had easily signed over her rights to us and their adoption had been sealed a month after the girls came to live with us. All seemed well in the Matthew family.

The boys were now three months old and had started rolling over and recognizing faces. They were smart. School was starting soon for the girls. Marcus was trying to get our house done sooner, but one thing after another was causing its delay. Marcus started talking about our honeymoon and where he was going to surprise me. We had sex every night and sometimes during the day if we could slip it in. Our family life was going well. Joseph had called and said he would come for a week while we were on our honeymoon. He said he would be bringing Sophia. He was bringing a nanny with him. Emily wanted some alone time, he said.

The days went fast. Soon the boys were three and a half months old and trying to sit up without assistance. They had begun to roll everywhere, especially if they saw something they wanted. We took them to work with us. Sometimes Jacob was with Marcus and Jared with me, or I took them both to my office that was equipped with a nursery. Rick had the office totally under control, and even though I could take another month of maternity leave, I wanted to get back to work. I liked being a parent, but I liked working, so I was going to juggle both. Of course, I had plenty of help juggling. Anytime I brought the boys into the office, Teresa came with me.

Rick had construction started on the firm's new daycare that was already going to be needed. Two of my attorneys were pregnant and expecting soon. We had children, whose parents worked in the building, that wanted to reserve spots for their children. Rick had hired two teachers and some interns from the local college. All qualified to take on managing the daycare. It had not taken him much effort to get a license to open the daycare, but our capacity was twenty-five. So, it was filling fast. I had asked for the Montessori method to be taught. It was important for children to learn from each other. Both teachers had been trained in that method and Mrs. Sherry would manage, as well as teach. She had the kids three-year-old and older. We stopped at five years and Mrs. Shelia had the three months old until two years old. There was an intern in each classroom studying child development, so they got intern credit by working for the daycare.

My boys were over 3 months old, but I was not ready to trust them to daycare. Rick had developed a parental leave policy. Each parent received three months of leave that was covered by the firm under our insurance coverage. It gave them time to adjust to their new baby. It was an experiment that eventually would benefit the firm. If their children were well cared for and they could see them, studies showed that their productivity was better. Fewer days were missed from work. Everyone thought it was great idea.

Matilda and Ester were starting school Monday, so they were going to bed early the night before. They had their uniforms ready. Both girls were excited, but a little apprehensive about being taught by the nuns, so Marcus and I would go on the first day with them. Matilda was ready for kindergarten. The girls may be in different classes, but they would still see each other throughout the day. That made the girls seem more at ease, but we knew eventually they would find their own way and their own group of friends. There were two nuns in each room. Their day would be filled with music and art, as well as the core subjects. There would be church and the learning of the Catholic faith. Marcus had insisted they play soccer. Through classes, they were taught the fundamentals of the game. They were also taught French and Spanish. They got home at four and Hilda always had snacks for them. Then it was homework, music, and soccer practice. Free time came before dinner, and usually, Matilda would be on the terrace painting with her art teacher. Ester was usually on the computer. She loved learning. Buddy still was a part of their schedule. Twice a week, Saul picked them up and attended a Hebrew class with them. Of course, that's when they visited their pony and rode her. They had named her Rose.

John Marcus and Isabella would take them for a sleepover every other weekend, and that's when they played with their rabbit. At dinner, Marcus wanted to hear about their day and would give them a new word to learn or a report to write that might affect their life. He assigned them math problems that he expected them to solve the next day. He kept them busy. The boys had reached four months and had begun to crawl. Jacob was the first, but instead of crawling on his knees, he stood on his feet with his hands on the floor. His little butt was always stuck up in the air. Jared was a roller, he simply rolled everywhere. That was fun to watch. Both boys were on bottles that contained breast milk from donors. They had been introduced to watered-down apple juice, and the pediatrician thought, in another month, we could introduce some rice cereal to their diet.

Marcus began to push for dates for our honeymoon. He had special plans for us and wanted us to get away for three weeks.

I was on board, but then I had a feeling that I'd miss so much. He said, "Sweetheart, I need this. So much time is given to the children and to work. I miss us."

"You're right. Let's plan for the first of September. The boys will be five months and the girls will be busy in school. Margaret can come over with Saul, as well as your parents. Mike and Rick will be here with Joseph."

"My sisters will be here. The kids will be so busy. They will miss us, but not like you think. The boys have no idea about time, so it would be a suitable time to go. And you can Skype every day. I need my wife. We need the intimacy with each other."

"Darling," I said, "Let's go." I went into his arms and kissed him. Marcus needed to feel number one in my life, like we had promised each other. My husband was telling me he needed me alone for a while. He did not want our life to be humdrum. The chase was the most fun part of the relationship. It has nothing to do with love and being a dad. He was a man and wanted me alone with nothing but him on my mind.

"Where are we going? So I know what to pack."

"Remember the ranch I bought for you in Wyoming? Well, there are colts being born. I'd like to see what we own and spend time with you there. So, jeans, western wear, and boots. Well, something for a special evening, but yes, we are going on cattle drives and fly fishing. Riding trails. Our place is close to Yellowstone, and it's set up to breed Arabian horses. You can see bears, antelopes, deer, coyotes, and wolves. It will be an exciting time to be together, doing something we have never done."

"Set it up, Marcus."

"How about us leaving in a week? The girls will be in school. The boys will be good with Teresa and the nurse. The family will keep them busy. Joseph has agreed to come, which will be good for him."

"A week from today, I will be ready." He picked up his phone and said, "Mr. Hill, my wife and I are coming up the first day of next week. I will fly in on the family jet. Will you park a jeep at the airport for us? I am not bringing security, but I am sure we will be alright with your people there. Just give us the biggest cabin, until I decide what I want to do. See you Monday." Marcus had a broad smile on his face. He needed this. I was sitting in a chair in the nursery holding Jared. He kissed me on the head, then Jared.

"I am going out to the house to see if I can speed up the building process. I also need to go over some things with Denise."

"Marcus, I'll call Rick and tell him I will be gone from the office so he will have to take charge of things."

"Talk to your parents and I will talk to mine."

"Yes, I will," I responded. He was visibly excited. I wanted that look in his eyes all the time.

We were all packed and ready to go. We had told the girls and they were curious about the ranch. Marcus said, "Maybe on your Christmas break, me and mommy can take the whole family."

"We understand, daddy. You need a date vacation with mommy. We like it when you and mommy are in love."

The jet was ready to take off at ten. We'd get there by seven in the evening, then we would drive the thirty minutes to the ranch. After we got to the ranch, we met the Hill family. They had been running the ranch for years and Marcus had asked them to stay on. They had several different sources of income and did not need to sell. Marcus just offered a price that they could not turn down.

It was a rugged drive to the ranch, and I was tired. When we got there, they had dinner of roasted lamb ready for us. I especially enjoyed a glass of wine. They showed us our cabin and Marcus said, "Darling, be ready at seven so we can tour the ranch. I can already tell that I want to build us a large cabin for our family and the rest of the Matthew family." I went to bed and Marcus hugged me and kissed me passionately. "I am ready for this adventure, my darling."

"What time is it?" I asked Marcus.

"It's time for you make love to your husband. We used to never skip a day. I want that back, Sam. No matter how many children we have, I always want us to be available for us." He began to nuzzle my ear. Then he reached between my legs and began to massage my clit while holding my hands above my head. I began to wiggle and moan. Neither of us were that tired; it must be the mountain air. Somehow, I got loose of his grip and rolled on top of him and sat on his hard dick. Just the insertion of his dick made me quiver. He was pushing up into me, but I wanted control of this, so I reached in my bag beside the bed. I jangled something familiar in his face.

"Remember these?" He smiled, "So it's going to be like that?"

"Yes. You are going to be chained to this bed and I going to have my way with you." Marcus responded, "Please, do." I cuffed both his hands to the bed and got out a bottle of cinnamon edible rub and began to pour it on his body. I started with his chest and began to lick off the tasty candy rub. I started moving down toward his pelvic area and he began to twist and try to get out of the handcuffs. He knew what was coming; I poured the hot liquid on his dick, and it began to burn. "Jesus, Sam," he spoke. Then I began to quickly lap up the liquid using my tongue like a whip. I began to nibble his dick. By this time he was pushing his body to my mouth. I took him all in at once and made a loud sucking noise as I put my lips around his dick. "Sam, I am going to explode," he said. I then mounted him until we both climaxed. I unlocked the handcuffs. Before I could catch my breath, he turned me over on my stomach and pulled my ass up so he could enter me from behind. He rode me until we both came and collapsed from exhaustion. He kissed me, licked his lips, and said, "Cinnamon, I have to remember that. Sam, still up to your tricks. I like that." He smacked my bare bottom, "Better get some sleep. Breakfast is at seven, then we are going to tour the ranch on horseback and just see what we own here in Wyoming. Samantha Matthew, will you marry me?"

"Yes, darling. Always."

"Marcus, you know we did not use extra protection during sex."

"If you get pregnant with my baby, Sam, I would love it. It would be yours and mine. Do you understand how I would feel?"

"Yes, darling. I know you love the brood you have at home, but one that is ours biologically together, I understand that is part of the male psyche."

The next morning Marcus got up and went to the shower. I showered after him and put on my jeans and shirt. As I was putting on my boots, I noticed he was already dressed. It was obvious how happy he was to be here at this ranch—our ranch. We left the cabin for the main cabin where breakfast was being served.

"Mr. Matthew, we feel like you should be in the big house. After all, you own the ranch."

"Mrs. Hill do not worry about our accommodations. I will probably build my family a home here eventually." She handed him a mug of hot coffee and said, "Well, we are glad to meet your wife. We have breakfast ready for you, then we have horses and a guide to show you around."

"That sounds great." He sat down and reached for one of the homemade biscuits and slathered it with butter and strawberry jam. He said, "Sam, have a biscuit. They are delicious." I took a biscuit and some scrambled eggs. He reached over and tossed my hair back, "You are going to enjoy today, my sweet. You will have a horse between your legs all day. Do you think you are up to it?" I knew he was making a reference to last night. I smiled at him, "I am pretty sure I can keep up." The biscuit was good, and the eggs were from the hens they raised on the ranch. Because they lived so isolated from the city, they grew almost everything they ate.

Outside was a ranch hand holding the lead on two horses. The one I wanted had a painted face. It was beautiful. "Ma'am, he is gentle and easy to ride."

"Mr. Matthew, this Arabian has a little fire in him. I hope you can handle him. He bucks a little at first, just to show you who is boss. Then he will settle down and ride just well." Marcus took my reigns and said, "Sam, let me help you up." I put my foot in the stirrups and pulled myself on to the horse. I reached over and patted her pretty face. She would not give me any trouble. Marcus put his foot in the stirrup and when he began to pull himself up, the Arabian began to move around. Marcus pulled tight on the reign and started talking to the horse, which began to settle down. Then he mounted the horse and was ready for our guide to show us around. We rode east of the wind river; the rocks and cliffs were breathtaking. The guide explained to us that this was considered a working ranch. They had sheep, cattle, goats, and grew most of their food. They also raised the Arabians to sell or to stud out.

"How about the trainer I sent here? How is he working out?" Marcus asked.

"Well, old Frank, as we like to call him, said to tell you after lunch he had a surprise for you." It was getting to be lunch time and James, our guide, walked his horse up to a clearing where a wagon had been set up for food. The cook was roasting a goat.

"Honey," Marcus said, "I know how you love animals, is this

going to bother you? If so, we can ride back to the house."

I said, "And miss this opportunity to be a real cowgirl? No way. I am loving it." I got off my horse and went over to the wagon where they were serving beans, fried apples, bar-b-que goat, and cornbread.

"Marcus, I cannot wait to bring the kids here."

"We will have to wait until they get a little older. The girls need to keep up with their riding lessons for now." He got a plate, and I could tell from the expression on his face he was enjoying the food, the ride, and the experience. After lunch, we went to the barn and found Frank tending to a pregnant female Spanish Arabian. He was feeling her stomach and was looking to see if she had dilated yet. The horse began to move around, and Frank was careful to direct her to the fresh hay area.

"Hi, Frank." Marcus shook his hand. Frank reached for Marcus' hand. "Well, we should have our first colt that has been bred for racing. She was bred with a Kentucky racehorse called Nadal." I went over to this beautiful Arabian mare. You could tell she was in labor and began to pant. Frank led her to the fresh straw in her stall. I patted her head as she laid there trying to push out her baby horse. I knew what she was going through; the body's instinct to push the baby out and the pain of every contraction. I talked to her quietly as the process took place. Frank said, "I see the legs." He kept rubbing her stomach, it seemed she was too tired to finish, which happens sometimes.

"Marcus, we are going to have to pull the baby out or we will lose the colt. Put those gloves on and grab a leg." Marcus did as he was told. "Now be careful so as not to break a leg. Pull at the same time as I do." They both had their hands inside the horse. I stayed by her head and laid my head on hers and just kept talking to her. "Okay, Marcus. Pull with me." A strong pull and the colt came out. Frank quickly rubbed the sack of the new colt and, just as quickly, the afterbirth came out. The colt was beautiful, black, and very tall. Frank said in about thirty-nine minutes the colt will try and stand up to nurse. The mother horse had already stood up and was nudging her baby to stand up. It was a boy colt and seemed strong. He got up awkwardly with its legs spread far apart. Finally, he stood and was able to walk to its mother. He reached under her stomach and latched on to a tit. The colt was so tall that he had to bend down to reach under his mother's stomach. The birth process seemed the same for humans and horses. It made me angry that men simply had no clue what women, and this horse, went through to have a baby. Women may have advanced, but if we bear children, we were dependent. Yet, I had been so eager to have Joseph's boys and now Marcus wanted his own. I was beginning to think about Kenneth, who simply treated me like a piece of meat. A tear ran down my face—that baby I aborted would be forever on my mind.

"Sam, darling, are those tears of happiness?" Marcus asked. I brushed the tears away and said, "They are tears of mixed feelings." He came across the stall and put his arms around me, "I got you. I will always be there for you, no matter what. I love you, darling. Isn't he beautiful? This was my surprise for you. He will be our first racehorse. His dad is an old Kentucky derby winner, retired."

"I know you were trying to show me something beautiful. I

am just so emotional, Marcus."

"Let's take a walk. There is a trail that leads to a path along a riverbank," he spoke. "Let's see if you learned anything about skipping stones."

He picked up one and threw it and it skipped five times. I said, "You know no one can beat you, but here goes." Mine skipped five times, he swung me around. "See? Partners. That's what that means. You and I are just made to go together. I hear this river is full of trout, how about some fishing?"

"I'd really like that, Marcus, but you will have to teach me how." He called the ranch hand and asked him to bring out supplies to trout fish and have a picnic supper. We were going to stay out awhile. The ranch hand drove up in a jeep with a horse tied behind. "Mr. Matthew, if you are going to be out late, you'll need transpiration to get back. Also, you might want to take this gun just in case you run into a wild animal like a coyote, bear, or fox." Marcus took the gun and the basket of food and said, "Thanks." The ranch hand, Pete, got on the back of the horse and rode off. Marcus found a perfect place under the trees. You could see the trout jumping. We cast our lines and it was as easy as picking them up. Marcus pulled the line out and showed me how to cast. After we caught twenty trout, we put them in the cooler with ice and opened the picnic basket. It had baked chicken, potato salad, fruit, cheese, and a loaf of homemade bread. There was macaroni salad and fruit pies for dessert. There was a couple bottles of wine, cups, plates, and silverware. It was a feast. I laid back in his arms after dinner to rest. I was almost asleep when he whispered, "Sam, do not move."

I opened my eyes and standing by the riverbank was a bear, catching trout in its paws. "Stay still. Let's watch and see what he does." Marcus moved the gun closer to him. We laid in silence and watched him catch fish and sling them on the bank. After a while he sat down and started eating the fish. He paid no attention to us. Marcus started to move slowly. He picked up the basket, blanket, and gun, then said, "Get in the jeep, Sam." I moved to get in the jeep and as we drove away, I took a picture. The bear never moved from eating the fish. Marcus laughed, "What a treat! A new horse, a bear, trout—what more could we want?" "Well, I'd like to talk to the kids tonight, please."

"No problem. It's been two days, let's see if they even know we are gone."

We called at 7:30 p.m., which was right before bedtime. Marcus emailed Kelly the video link and she hooked it up for the girls. "Hi, mommy and daddy!" the girls said. They were in their pajamas and were excited, "Uncle Mike and Denise are here to have a sleep over. Paige and Penelope are here, too." It was Friday night; we had been gone two days. Mike stuck his face in the camera, "Hey guys, hope it is okay. We had dinner and ice cream sundaes. We are camping out in the living room. Denise and I picked them up after school and we went to picked out their sleeping bags. So here are the girls."

"Thanks, man. Sounds like they are having fun."

"Denise's idea. Your sisters are in with the boys," Mike said. Ester got back in front of the camera and said, "Daddy, how late can we stay up?"

"Well, I think you should see what happens. Have your aunts and Mike read to you and do whatever you plan and see how it goes."

"Hi, mom," said Matilda, "How was your day?"

"I have to tell you girls, it is beautiful here. I want you to see the ranch. We saw a baby horse born today. Your dad helped the mother have the colt. We have ridden horses and we went trout fishing and we saw a bear eating trout."

"Oh, Mommy, I'd like to see that." There was a voice calling the girls; it was Hilda. "Popcorn is ready!" So, they left the screen and ran out of the room. "Hey," Marcus said, "Can we have a hug goodnight?" They both put their arms around themselves and hugged their own bodies and blew kisses.

"Girls," Marcus said, "I want, you to look up our ranch and write me a report about it. And one on trout fishing, ready for Sunday when we call."

"Okay, daddy."

"We love you," I said. "Kisses." And off they went to get popcorn. Kelly got back on the video conference. "They are so happy and excited."

"So, no missing mommy and daddy?" Marcus asked.

"To be honest, sir, not yet. Too much going on."

"That's what I want to hear. You think you will be able to get them down at reasonable hour?"

"Yes. Mike has promised they will be asleep by ten. He took

them to get sleeping bags, but he also took them and Buddy, to the park and they jogged before dinner. I have already seen some yawns. We are going to have reading time at about nine. And your sisters are going to play music after that, so I am fairly sure they will fall asleep."

"Take lots of pictures please," I spoke. Kelly

said, "Would you like to see the den?"

"Sure," Marcus said. Kelly took the laptop to the living room and showed us the den. There were pink and yellow sleeping bags and pillows everywhere.

"Honey, I got to get our new house finished. Look at the den. A few months ago, it was an orderly bachelor pad."

"Sorry, you asked for this."

"And I love it, mommy," Marcus said. The adults had gotten out our camping sleeping bags.

"Hi Denise," I said, "Thanks for your help."

"This is fun. But Mike and I both said we do not know how you do this, every night and every day. Balancing work, having time for each other, and time for yourself. It's like a twenty-four-hour job. I know I could not and would not want to do it, with the boys in addition to the girls."

"Thank goodness for Teresa, Hilda and Peter." Buddy ran by and got on a sleeping bag. Peter came through, "Sorry sir. I am taking Buddy out for his last walk. The girls asked if I would mind tonight, I said yes, as long as I am not expected to sleep in one of these sleeping bags.'"

"So," Marcus said, "They used negotiation and charm?"

"Yes, sir. I have to say, the girls have been very cooperative."

"Kelly, will you take the laptop to the nursery?" I asked. Paige and Penelope were holding the boys. "Goodnight," Kelly said, "We are doing great. Have a fun time." Teresa took the laptop and held it up to Jared first, who was having a bottle given by Paige. She pointed to the screen. "Hi darling," I spoke.

"Hey, little man," Marcus said. He looked at the screen, recognizing our voice and then went back to his bottle. Paige had him in his pajamas. "They are so sweet and cute. They were crawling around this afternoon, and we played games like peek-a-boo. I am reading to them now; I think Jared will be asleep soon. Marcus do not cut his hair. These curls are beautiful," she spoke. "I hope you will let it grow."

I chimed in agreement, "I'm hoping to let it grow for a while. Where is Jacob?" Penelope had him and was rocking him on the rocking horse. "Hey, big man."

"Dada," said Jacob. His first word. "Yep, he calls everything dada. We worked on it today. But at least it's a word. We have recorded the boys and taken plenty of pictures. I hope you two have a fun time. Don't worry about the kids. They're getting plenty of attention and as you know, that's all they want."

"Thanks, sis. I'm glad you two pitched in."

"Hey, we want to be good supportive aunts. Dad and mom

plan to take them to church Sunday and have plans for them to spend the afternoon at the house. We got this."

"Give them kisses," I spoke. We turned the video off. "See, honey? They are so young that this is the best time for us to be away. And keeping them busy is the key. They do not understand time. So, it's a perfect time for you and me to get away."

"You're right. But Jacob said dada. That's just not

fair." Marcus said, "What can I say? He loves his dad."

"Yea, we know that 'd' words are easier to say first. If you read the baby book on development, he is right on target to start saying words that start with 'd'," I replied.

"Come here, sir, and let me show you who loves you best." I pulled him to me by his t-shirt and started kissing him passionately. I ran my hands underneath his shirt and rubbed his chest. He took his shirt off, then I tugged his jeans and unbuttoned them, sliding my hands deep into the front of his pants, down to his groin area. He was already hard. I pushed him back on the bed and straddled him. I kissed him on the lips and searched his mouth with my tongue. I started nibbling down his chest and bit his nipples. He began to moan with pleasure. I sat up, pulled my t-shirt off, and shook out my long curly hair. I unhooked my bra and let my breasts fall forward. Marcus reached up and moved the right one into his mouth.

"Darling," he said, "I love how your body is so voluptuous after the boys."

"Yes, it seems no matter how much I work out, that some

areas of my body are going to remain unchanged."

"Yea, all the good areas." He flipped me over on my back and tugged at my jeans until he had them off. Then he pulled my panties off and without taking his jeans off, he pulled his cock out and rubbed it along the lips of my vagina, until it was wet and ready. All the time he was kissing me passionately.

"I am ready to have you, Samantha, and I staying in the raw. No raincoat."

"Fuck me, darling." And with that, he rubbed his dick along the lips of my vagina and plunged in deep, rubbing against my clitoris. He began to move up and down and I met him thrust to thrust. I felt my climax coming to the peak, just as I got there, Marcus, too, was peaking. I could feel his warm release come into my body. He momentarily rested on his elbow, "Darling, let's get a shower and get some sleep. We are supposed to help with a cattle drive tomorrow morning. I want you to be up for this. We are moving them to another pasture so they can fatten up to be sold." We both got into the shower, dried off, and went to bed naked. It was 11:30 at night and we had to be ready by five a.m. We would have a cup of coffee, a sausage and biscuit, and start moving the herd on horseback.

Next morning, after the quick breakfast, we each mounted our horses and put on a riding helmet. Our job was to move the herd from their summer grazing area, which was adjacent to the national forest, and gather the rest of the herd, which was scattered in a fifty square mile area of forests and small clearings. Pete was our wrangler that was paired with us. The cook had fixed a picnic lunch, as we would be out for about seven hours.

Marcus loved this work and was in better shape to do this strenuous task than I was, but I was determined to keep up. You could tell that he was getting great satisfaction finding the cattle and loading them into the trailers that would take them to the lower ranch for the winter. The ranch had over 120 horses, Arabian and Quarter. Marcus was riding an Arabian and I was riding the same Quarter horse that I had when I first got here. I loved her brown and white face. We had bonded, and Marcus said we would designate her as my horse.

We were riding western style, so the horses were taught to respond to the reign. Marcus had insisted that our girls train in western riding. It made sense, as his plan was to bring the girls here to ride. I would be ready to do some yoga when I got back to relieve, what I knew, would be some sore muscles. We crossed the Wind River Valley. The scenery was beautiful. There were no people in the area where we were driving the cattle. The closest ranch was thirty miles away. The ranch was self-sufficient. The garden grew plants like rhubarb, strawberries, spinach, carrots, potatoes, peas, lettuce, beets, and Swiss chard. With the beef and lamb from the ranch, and with its great chef, I could not wait to see what he had planned for dinner after this ride. And a glass of wine. Marcus rode over to me, "Sweetheart, if you want to cut our ride short, I can have a jeep come and get you to take you back."

"No, sir. I am fine. I am working up quite an appetite. I was just thinking about what dinner would be tonight." Marcus laughed, "So your mind is on food? Honey, we will be stopping for lunch in about an hour. Samantha, I really needed this. How about you?"

"You're right. It is a real stress reliever. We should make this a retreat for the people in both our companies. I'd like to see Rick on a horse. I bet that'd be a sight." We stopped and the ranch hands put out the picnic lunches. There was roast beef sandwiches, chips, apples, cheese, pickles, and apple turnovers. They had water for us to drink. We broke for an hour, then it was back into the saddles. About another three hours and we would be back at the ranch.

When we got back to the main ranch, Marcus and I went to our cabin and showered. We were both tired, but it was a relaxed tired. I put on a comfortable sweatsuit, as I planned to get in twenty minutes of yoga before dinner. I left Marcus laying on the bed.

"You better not get too comfortable. You will miss dinner."

"I'll be there. My stomach is not going to let me go to sleep. I am hungry." I threw him a kiss and went to join the others for yoga. The stretching was good and afterward, I met Marcus for dinner. We were having steak, potatoes, peas and carrots, a Swiss chard salad, fresh-baked bread, and strawberry-rhubarb pie. Wine was plentiful. Marcus and I, after we ate, decided we go for a short walk, then go back to the cabin. He kissed me and said, "I never thought I'd say this, but I just want to sleep."

"Me too, darling." So, we got into bed, spooned together, and slept until noon the next day. We decided, after getting up and dressed, to drive into the nearest town called Dubois. First, we decided to explore the Dubois Museum, then eat at the Cowboy Cafe. It was a bar and restaurant. It had a dance floor, and a lot of ranch hands were there hanging out to see if they could score tonight. Some of the women were local ranchers, ranch hands, and just bored homemakers having a night out while their husbands were out of town or on a cattle drive. The excitement in this town was horses, cattle, and not much else.

Life was relaxed and easy. Sometimes there was a rodeo in town, and sometimes a small fair might come through. Tonight, it was dinner and a little dancing for us. Marcus said, "Let's order some of their well-known bourbon and a couple of rib-eyes, salad, and a baked potato." Marcus was really enjoying the ranch hand life. I could see this handsome man hanging out, and every available, or unavailable, woman making a play for him. Tonight, no one knew who we were, no security. Tonight, we were a couple looking for a little fun. The food came and, as usual, it was cooked to perfection. Marcus downed his drink and ordered two more. I had only sipped my drink and could already feel the effects of the liquor. Smooth, but with a touch of heat going down. Halfway through our meal, another drink came Marcus' way. It seemed that one of the ladies, even though we were plainly together, was taking the chance to introduce herself by sending him a drink. He looked at me and laughed. "Seems the women are forward here." He told the bartender to send it back with his thanks. But unless there were two drinks, he was not interested. "Kiss me, sweetheart. Like you mean to tear my clothes off right here. Brand me like a cow, so these women know who I belong to." I leaned forward and kissed him, pushing his mouth open with my tongue. I explored his mouth that tasted like bourbon, and he reacted as I knew he would; the bulge in his pants told everyone in the room that he was turned on with the woman he was with. We parted and started to finish our meal when the bartender brought us over a bottle of bourbon. He said, "That was Ms. Rosie Burns. She owns the ranch about twenty miles down the road, called the Diamond Circle Ranch. She said to tell you she meant no harm, but just wanted to introduce herself."

Marcus said, "Thank you," to the bartender and went over to Rosie's table. "I want to thank you ma'am, for the liquor. But I'd like it if you come over and have a drink with me and my wife. We are here visiting a ranch down the road and enjoying our honeymoon." Ms. Rosie was about 64, but a beautiful woman. She was dressed in a leather skirt and denim shirt. She had kept the gray out of her hair. She had money; it was apparent by the jewelry she had on.

"Have a seat," said Marcus as he moved another chair to our table.

"Hi," she said to me. "Excuse me if you thought I was a little forward, but your man is the most handsome man in the room. And obviously, not from here."

"Oh, I know I am a lucky woman to be here with him. Sometimes it's hard to get away from our four children and relax," I replied.

"Your husband said you are on your honeymoon? But you have four children?" Marcus said, "Yes, ma'am. Twin boys and two little girls."

He pulled out his phone and showed Rosie our children. "Well, you two deserve this bottle of bourbon and a night on the town. Dinner is on me." We talked to Rosie for about an hour on cattle and the drought. Then the music started up and a ranch hand came over and asked her to dance. "Excuse me, but I do love to dance." Rosie, being a widow for some time, was about to add a little excitement to her night.

"Sam," Marcus said, "Let's dance." And he stood up and offered me his hand. I knew I was tipsy, but he was so inviting.

"Darling, you may have to hold me up." He laughed, "Yes, I can tell. So, come close, and let's let the heat between us move us to the rhythm of the music." I was in his arms, and I could feel the hardness in his pants and the fever beginning to rise between my thighs. I also knew that I had drank enough to lose all my inhibitions, so tonight, it was a good thing that we had decided to stay in town.

The first week of the honeymoon had passed fast. We called the kids every other night and so far, they were just too busy to talk very long. The babies were getting more mobile, and Jared was now saying 'dada' also, but he also had started saying 'dog.' He loved Buddy to be around in the nursery. The girls had a shopping spree with Isabella. She had also bought them each a charm bracelet. Dad had taken them riding. Saul and Margaret were there for dinner and Saul was looking over their homework. This week, Joseph was coming with Sophia. He would be staying in the guest room and Sophia would be staying in the nursery with the boys. He had brought his nanny to take care of Sophia. We called to make sure all was going well with his visit. The boys looked a lot like Sophia, but nothing was ever mentioned. Only Saul and Margaret knew the real story. The girls accepted Joseph as the boys' godfather, like Mike, Rick, and Scott, were their godfathers. Rick and Scott had been over to meet with the kids and Joseph.

The office was running well. Denise had Marcus' office under control. She had reported that the house was moving ahead faster than planned and would be finished after Christmas. We had decided to spend one week at Yellowstone. But tonight, we were not thinking about kids, work, or anyone else.

Marcus was a smooth dancer. He twirled me around and I kept up with his waltz, even though I had never danced in cowboy boots. The music ended and Marcus said, "Darling, are you ready to go?" I knew I was out of my head, but I knew I wanted this man very much. He picked up the bottle of bourbon given to us by Rosie and left a tip. We waved to Rosie who had her arms around the same ranch hand. She winked and said, "Have a goodnight."

The hotel was within walking distance, so Marcus and I decided to leave the jeep and walk over to the hotel where we had reservations. He told the man behind the desk to have someone bring his jeep over. He gave the man fifty dollars, and we took the keys then went up in the elevator to the eighth floor. Marcus had booked the only suite in the hotel. It was decorated tastefully, but had the ranch feel. There was an electric fireplace lit and a plate of cheese and fruit. There were bottles of water. I started removing my boots and fell back on the bed. Marcus reached down and pulled off my boots and socks. Then he unbuttoned my jeans and pulled them from my body. I reached down and began to unbutton my shirt. He pushed my hands away, then took each side of my shirt and tore it open. Buttons popped off.

"Now, my darling, I remember a night when you got me drunk and seduced me. So, sweet girl, it's payback time." He pulled my body to him and tore my panties off. He unzipped his pants and without removing them, pulled his cock out. He pinned my arms back and kissed me hard on the lips. He parted my legs, and without any more foreplay, he rammed his cock into me. I was wet and came as soon as he entered me. His aim at my clitoris and g-spot had been right on. He began to move back and forth, and I felt his length getting longer.

"Marcus, I love you darling, but you are taking a big risk tonight. I am fairly sure your Catholic birth control efforts, and the fact that it has not been 30 full days, is going to cost you." He laughed, "Sweetheart, I'm going to fuck you most of the night." He finished coming. I could feel his release sticky between my legs. He took off his clothes and removed my bra. He had something shiny in his hands. "They say payback is a bitch." He had silver balls in his hand and pulled me toward him once again. He spread my legs and put the balls in his mouth to get them wet and pushed both into my vagina. Then he turned me over on my stomach and began to run his cock into my vagina from the back. The fullness of the balls and his cock made my clitoris explode.

"Marcus, darling, give me a chance to catch my breath." He finished coming and pulled the balls out.

"It seems like I remember handcuffs and not having a choice."

"Well, okay." My head was spinning.

"Here, sweetheart. Drink some water and take this aspirin.

You look like you might be sick." Last thing I remember was falling asleep or passing out. He was wiping my body off with a warm rag and covering me up with a blanket. Marcus took a quick shower, ate some cheese and fruit, and drank some water. Then he joined me in bed. "I love you, Samantha. I will always love you." I was out of it and said, "Make love to me." Marcus began to kiss me passionately and waited for me to respond. I kissed him back and began to move down his chest with kisses until I finally got to his groin area. I spit on my hand and began to rub his dick until he started to groan. He reached down and pulled me on top of him. He propped himself on his elbow and kissed me. He moved on top of me and began to push his cock into my core. We moved together in unison until we both rose to the peak of our orgasm. I rolled over and snuggled down into the blankets. "Rest, my darling." He was still nude but seemed restless. He got up, turned the television on, and turned the volume down low. He finished the cheese tray and the fruit, then drank another bottle of water. I was sleeping soundly until I started dreaming. I was locked in a room, and I felt fear in my dream. The man was coming toward me. In the dream, I started yelling for help, but the words would not come out very loudly. Finally, I remember screaming, "Please help me!" Marcus came to the bed and took me in his arms and said, "Sam, you are safe. I am here with you." He curled up beside me and wrapped me in his arms. He knew that I was having a night terror and had been advised to ask me to stay in counseling. The things that had happened to me as a teenager would never go away. The trauma of so many men who had abused me would never go away. I knew how Marcus felt about my past. He wished that he knew all the men who had abused me, he'd take care of all of them. He had taken care of

Kenneth. He had bankrupted him, and he had moved to Florida. Saul had taken care of my father and stepmother. They never discussed the details, but Marcus and I knew it was not a good thing for them.

The next morning, I rose early and showered, then was on the phone making arrangements to take her out up to Yellowstone National Park. He wanted first to fly over it by helicopter, and then find a cabin so they could do some hiking. Sam was worn out from the night before; she was sleeping soundly. She began to move around about noon. She got up and her blanket fell from her naked body. She ran into the bathroom, lifted the toilet lid, and began to throw up. I came in and held her hair back and grabbed a wet washcloth. "Marcus, I drank too much. I feel weak." I helped her up and turned on the shower. She stood under the warm water. "Gosh, a shower feels good." She rubbed the washcloth with soap and said, "I have bruises on my legs close to my vagina. And I feel like I was rode up hard and put up wet, as they say."

"Honey, I am so sorry. You were so willing to please me and let me do anything to you. You enjoyed it."

"Oh, I did. I just wished I could remember more of the night." She had a towel wrapped around her naked body.

"Here, darling. Take an aspirin and drink a bottle of water."

"I am a lightweight when it comes to the hard stuff. Take

that bottle Rosie gave us and give it to Saul." It was moving toward two o'clock and she had fallen back to sleep. He got on the phone and postponed his plans until tomorrow. He called downstairs and told the owner that they will be staying another night, and in an hour, to send up a petite steak, some scrambled eggs, toast, and some hot, decaffeinated tea. Then he called Joseph and asked how it was going. Joseph turned on the video camera and said, "See for yourself." They were all in the nursery, the boys were sitting under a tent that the girls had insisted Joseph make. Sophia was laying between the girls with flashlights. Everyone was dressed for bed. The boys and Sophia had bottles and Joseph was reading Charlotte's Web.

"Man, I do not know how you and Samantha do it. I am as tired as they are."

"So," Marcus said, "Are you camping out tonight?"

"Looks like it. The nannies are changing diapers, giving baths, and leaving the entertainment of three crawlers to me. Sophia had been learning from the boys." Buddy suddenly appeared in the camera. "And of course, we have to have the dog with us." Joseph was enjoying them. The boys were five months old, Sophia was six months old, and the girls were three and five. Joseph held the camera where the boys could see him. Jared took his bottle out of his mouth and said, "Dada." Jacob just kept drinking his bottle as usual. Food came first for Jacob.

"Hi, Daddy," said Ester. "Are you and mommy having fun on your honeymoon?"

"We sure are. We had so much fun last night that mommy is

still asleep. Otherwise, she'd want to talk to you."

"That's okay, we are having fun with Uncle Joseph. He said he used to take mommy camping so he made us a tent. It's so cool and we have been making shadow animals in the tent with the flashlights."

"Matilda, how are you?" Marcus asked. "I am good, daddy. But Ester is hogging all the time with Uncle Joseph. Daddy, can you tell her not to be so bossy?"

"How about you two look up the word compromise? And tomorrow, you tell me what it means and your plan to work it out. And Uncle Joseph is in charge."

"Uncle Joseph, a lot of times I have the girls research and do reports to settle their disputes on their own. And girls, allowance time will be coming up when we get back. I hope I get good reports from everyone. I love you guys." Jared was asleep, Sophia was laying on Buddy, and Jacob was still drinking his bottle.

"Well, Joseph, enjoy. You are leaving on Friday?"

"Yes, Emily misses Sophia and will be back from her mother's house on Friday."

"Well, Sam will want to call tomorrow. We will be heading to Yellowstone. I rented a helicopter. That will be a fantastic way to see it."

"You have fun and be careful." The camera disconnected. There was a knock at the door and the server set the food up in the living room. "Is there anything else, Mr. Matthew?"

"No," Marcus said handing him a hundred dollars.

"Sam? Darling, wake up. You need to eat something, and I thought we could watch a movie." She started to wake up and reached for her robe.

"The food smells delicious and I am very hungry." Marcus removed the covers on the food and Samantha poured herself some tea.

"Well, this is a start on getting my good graces after last night. But I have to say, I enjoyed what I can remember."

"Ms. Rosie sent you over some bourbon and invited us to her ranch. I talked to the kids and Joseph, and they are about to exhaust him. He is getting a good taste of what it's like raising little girls. I said you'd call them in the morning. Do you still want to see Yellowstone tomorrow? On our way back, I'd like to stop by and see Ms. Rosie. We only have 20 more days left of our trip. I also want to go shopping for the children. I want to get them some western wear, and maybe some stuffed horses for the boys and toy horses for the girls."

"Well, let's touch base with Ms. Rosie when we get back from Yellowstone and see what she is talking about. Now, let's eat."

"I'm hungry."

"Me too," said Samantha.

***

The steaks were good as always and the tea was just what I needed to settle my stomach. "Darling, I love you and I appreciate you giving me a night of excitement. But tonight, may I fall asleep in your arms?"

"Sam, I just want you to know, I love you now and always. Let me take care of you and our family. I love your fierce independence to fight. But you can lay down your sword when it comes to this man. I will never hurt you."

"Marcus, I feel safe with you. And yes, I feel you will protect your family and provide for us. I see that you are putting me first. I've never had that. Thank you, my love." We got ready for bed. I put on a sexy night gown and Marcus pulled on his sleep pants. I laid in his arms until I drifted to sleep.

The next morning, the alarm went off at 7 a.m. "How did you sleep, darling?"

"Truly like I was drifting on a cloud."

"Good." He leaned over and kissed me. "Ready to start our day?"

"Not until you make love to me. I have an itch and it needs scratching."

"I'd like to think I can take care of that." He began by kissing me passionately, exploring my mouth with his tongue. He nipped at my ears and placed kisses down my neck. I knew from the hardness that he was pressing up against me that he was already turned on. He pulled my gown over my head, and I held my arms up exposing my breasts. He took one breast in his hand and squeezed it, then nipped my nipple and sucked hard. My breasts had gotten fuller since the twins. I had a few curves now that I did not have before, but I had gotten my stomach flat and was still working with a trainer. He moved down to my stomach and placed a finger deep inside me. My brain was already signaling for more.

"Please, fuck me darling." He smothered my mouth with a kiss.

"I thought the phrase was 'make love,'" he whispered.

"I'm begging you, sir, to relieve the tension I feel between my thighs."

"My pleasure." And with that, he spread the lips of my vagina and thrust deep. I was already so wet and about to peak. I immediately came. He plunged twice more, and I could hear his breathlessness, then he rolled to one side and propped up on his elbow, so he did not fall on me with his full weight.

"Wow, what a terrific way to start the day. How about a quick shower and breakfast downstairs then you can call the kids? Our helicopter will be here by 8:30 to pick us up." I got up and laid out jeans and a t-shirt and Marcus did the same. I switched to my trail boots since we might be doing some hiking. Marcus was first out of the shower and he was checking on office stuff. I heard him say, "Have Mike put extra security on the project and the family. Do they know who the man is?"

"No, when the security people caught him, he said he as

working for someone that the Matthews had done wrong."

"Did he do any damage to the house?"

"No, Denise said he had a gas can and apparently was trying to set fire to your house. We got people all over this and you know how Mike is, he will get to the bottom of this pretty quick."

"Keep me updated, please. We got this, have fun."

I was drying my hair when he entered the bathroom. "Is there something wrong?"

"No, just some nut case. But Mike has it. Are you about ready to eat? I am starved. A man cannot live on sex alone."

"Okay." I pushed him toward the door and picked up my laptop to call the kids. Rick called and said, "Just checking in. Mr. Smith called, and he has another project he wants to discuss with you. I told him you were on your honeymoon, and he said it could wait to you get back. He is sending you a bottle of champagne. I gave him the name of the lodge outside of Yellowstone. Baby girl, you better make these next two weeks good. I've been holding off the lions, but some of them only want to deal with you."

"Rick, you're doing an excellent job." I

spoke. "So western boots, size 11?" he asked.

"Pointed toes or square cut?" I replied.

"Leather, of course," he responded. "You got

it."

"Square toes and mix a little blue in that leather. Thanks. See you soon."

We sat down to breakfast—a vegetable omelet and toast. It was nice not to have steak. "I think I've eaten enough red meat to last me a lifetime." Marcus was stirring cream in his coffee. "Yes, but you can see how hard the ranch life is. When the boys are big enough, I want them to spend some summers working here."

"What about our daughters?" I asked.

"Nope, would not trust testosterone around them." I laughed. "So, you have a double standard when it comes to the girls?"

"Yes, I have two wild sisters. I know what I was like when that testosterone kicks in. No, the girls are going to be kept in nunnery school until they are married. Ester already is too flirtatious, and she is only three. Matilda is the quiet one, but that does not mean she will be the responsible one. And I do not want their hearts broken because some jackass tells them he loves them to get in their pants."

"Now, Marcus. Don't you think we will teach them better than that?"

"We can try, but the first night I met you, all I wanted to do was get you in bed." I laughed, "Yes, same here. I have to agree with you, hormones trump good parenting." A man walked into the restaurant and said, "Mr. Matthew, we have landed the helicopter and we are here to drive you to it. Are these your bags?"

"Yes, thank you. We will be right there." Marcus motioned to the server and said, "We'd like to pay our bill." She brought it and leaned over to show him the total. I could tell if Marcus were a single man in this town, the women would be fighting over him. And they did not even know that he was a rich man. He gave her a hundred and said, "Keep the change." She gave him a wink and said, "Hope you and your girlfriend come back soon."

"This is my wife, sugar, the mother of our four children, and the love of my life. But yes, we will be back." Marcus had reserved our suite there for the few days we would be in Yellowstone. Then we would spend the last few days at our ranch. "Darling, let me call the kids. I'm sure they are finished with breakfast."

"Yes, we better before we take off," he responded. I dialed the house number and Peter answered. "Hi, Peter. May I speak to the children?"

"I'm afraid, Mrs. Matthew, they are all out with Mr. Joseph at the New York aquarium. Nannies, security, and all. And I can say with all honesty, that it is nice to have some quiet around the house. Mr. Joseph is like a kid himself. Sorry Mrs. Matthew, but he thinks rules are to be broken." I laughed, "He can be a little on the wild side at times, but remember, he is an attorney and was trained to believe that rules are made to be broken. I'll call his cell, thanks." I dialed Joseph's phone and I could tell he was in one of the underwater exhibits. "I suppose the children are not interested in talking to their parents?"

"Probably not, they are having too much fun. I was an only child and never had a chance to cut loose like these five. Even the babies are different when their sisters are around them, and they bring in the dog–holy hell breaks out. Your staff may quit before you get back. Here's Ester. It's your Mommy."

"Hi, mommy! Uncle Joseph is like Uncle Mike, who is here also. Anyway, I got to go, there is a shark swimming over my head." Then there were squeals of laughter. Joseph said, "Would you like for me to step out of here so you can talk to them?" Marcus took the phone, "Man, try to keep them somewhat in the middle of the road, payback's a bitch. Just remember that when we get Sophia for a visit." Joseph laughed, "Ye,a Mike warned me about your paybacks. But I'm up for it."

"Well, tell them we love them, and their mother said 'kisses.' I'd tell you I miss them, but I'd be lying. This was good for us. You and Emily need to come to our dude ranch. It's a lot of fun, totally a unique way of life."

"I'd like that." Joseph said.

"Let me speak to Mike please."

"Hey, man," Mike said. "Nothing new. He said he was never told who the person was that really hired him. Said he was contacted by a throw away telephone and told if he torched the place, there was a hundred thousand in it. He is cooperating fully, just a druggie that never seen that kind of money. From New Jersey, has an ex-wife, no kids. She barely makes it and has not seen him in three months. But he called her and told her he was going to make a big score. That's all she knew."

"Mike, put her on payroll. Give her $59,000 a year and let's see if she can be of help now. Put her on one of the projects that we got going, that casino we are building. Give her a chance to get some training and let's see what happens. After he dries out, let's see what we can do for him. He turned to crime because he is an addict and has no skills. He is not the one we need to worry about. Have Robert figure out everything with the DA. Anyway, take care of my family. See you in a couple of days. Everyone is handling everything too well."

"Yeah, three weeks. But I'd rather be Uncle Mike a little less. You, Samantha, and Joseph must take care of these wild ones. I like things quieter. Got to go, one of the nannies just informed me that Jacob has shit his diaper. Have to find a place to change him."

"Thanks, man." And he hung up. "Well, the kids seem happy and content. So, let's go and play ourselves." He patted my butt, and I took his hand. "I love you, Marcus. You're a good daddy and husband."

"Sam, you and these kids make me want to be, for better words, a better man. And my mother told me, 'All men are pigs, so just be the best pig I could be.' And my dad was all about the family. Responsibility, working hard. When he married my mom, it was all about making her happy, he fell deeply in love with her, and made sure she had all the attention he could give her. They are good role models, and that's what I want to be for our kids. And Saul and Margaret will keep us all grounded. I'm glad he came into your life."

The helicopter blades began to rotate, and we ducked our heads to get into the cockpit. Marcus was up front, and he handed me headphones and binoculars. "We are flying over first, and then we will land and hike a trail. There will be a guide waiting for us. Hope you're up for it."

"Darling, I am excited," I said back through the headphones. The pilot we had with us pointed out sights of interest and would take us as close in as possible. It was so beautiful. We passed over falls and forest,--so much natural beauty. Then he said, "Mr. Matthew, we will be landing just there, past those rocks. That's where you will meet your guide to take you hiking deep into the forest." He landed the helicopter and we got out. He gave our bags to the guide to be put in the jeep that was waiting for us.

"Mr. Matthew, I am Jake, and I will be your tour guide. It's my job to make sure you do not get lost out here. When we get halfway up this trail, there will be someone there with lunc, then we will hike up to the ridge that overlooks the valley. Then we will hike back down. It's five miles up and back. Do you think you and your wife are up for that?" Marcus said, "I'm fairly sure we can handle it. If not, we can always stop."

"First thing, Mrs. Matthew, I'd like to check your boots and make sure they are tied securely around your ankles. Boots not tied tight enough can lead to broken ankles. Now, I have a first aid kit and a walkie-talkie, but I bet you prefer no broken ankles."

"Jake, check away," I said. "You're right, I would not want my husband to have to carry me back down this ridge." I put my foot forward and he loosened my shoestrings, then pulled the strings and tied them tight. When he was finished with the second one, he handed me and Marcus a backpack, water, granola bars, and some fruit. "We will take breaks along the way. Mr. Matthew, are you good with your boots and gear?"

"Yep, Jake. Lead on." Jake must have been about twenty-seven and in really in good shape. He was very handsome and tanned from being outdoors a lot. His blonde hair was lightened by the sun. He had a charm about him that made you want to giggle like a high school girl. He told us he wasn't married and hadn't found a woman who enjoyed the wilderness, and he was not going to settle. He had too many friends that had done that and ended up divorced or hating life. We told him about how we fell in love and just knew we were meant to have a life together. And that we had four kids. Jake said he liked kids and would like to have a few, but four was a lot. "Tell that to my husband." I said, "he wants more."

"I do," said Marcus. "I promised her that I'd keep her barefoot and pregnant."

"Well, sir. Looks like that has happened so far."

"We have plenty of help," I said, "Or I'd rebel big time."

"Where you from?" he asked. Marcus said, "New York. I bought a small ranch in Wyoming, and we are down here checking it out."

"Yes, that happens a lot. But most city folks get tired of it and then sell it."

"Well, we will see," Marcus said. "I was telling Sam this morning that I'd like our boys to work on ours when they are old enough."

"So, Marcus, what do you do?"

"I own a small construction firm, and my wife is an attorney.

That's how we met. My dad hired her firm, and I was sent in with the check to pay the retainer. And well, it was love at first sight for me, so I chased her until I got her to say yes."

We had reached the midway point. There was a table setup on a flat rock waiting with a picnic basket and a person standing beside it. "Hey Jim," Jake said. "I hope you brought something good to eat."

"Well, you know that." Jim said. "You know Paula makes a great lunch."

"Paula is Jim's wife. We are a small outfit, so we are all like family. These are the Matthews." Marcus reached for Jim's hand, "Call me Marcus. And this is my wife, Samantha."

"Yep," Jake said. "Jim got lucky and found a woman who loves the wilderness, and they are expecting their first child."

"I bet you're excited," I spoke.

"Yes, ma'am. It's a boy, due next month."

"The Matthews have four kids, Jim, and they want more," Marcus said. "I am Catholic, and you know how we are."

I laughed, "And I am Jewish. And to get me to agree to his terms, I have to be treated like a Jewish princess." They laughed and Jim opened the basket to set out baked chicken, a potato casserole, green beans, relish, corn bread, corn casserole, and a green salad. He had tea to drink and apple pie for dessert. We all filled our plates like food was going to be scarce. I was so hungry from the climb, and now I was so sleepy, I was not sure I could make it the rest of the way. Marcus said to Jim, "Give your wife our compliments. The food was delicious."

"Yes," I said. "Now I want to curl up under a tree and nap."

"Well, Mrs. Matthew, we will take a thirty-minute rest, but we want to stay on track with time. About dusk, the bears start coming out and I want us back to the jeep by that time." We laid on a blanket for a rest while Jim cleared everything up. It was his job to make sure there was no food or trash left on the trail. Not only did they not want to attract the bears, but they also wanted to keep the environment free of trash. I was about asleep when Jake said, "Let's get moving." Marcus pulled me to my feet.

"Sweetheart, are you okay to keep

going?" "You know I am," I replied.

"So, let's get moving." About an hour later, we reached the top of the bluff. Jake tied a harness around me and Marcus so that we could get as close to the edge as possible. It was a breathtaking view, one of those places very few people get to see. After he told us all about the history of the ledge, he said it was time to start heading back down the trail. "It goes much faster because the terrain is slanted down. So be careful with your footing, gravity will be pulling you downward. That's when people fall. So, let's check your boots again and make sure they are tied tight, and we will head down. Mrs. Matthew, I'd like you in the middle of us, just in case you fall. Marcus, it's your job to catch your wife if she stumbles. Take it slow. So far, I've never had a customer break anything. Had them fall, scratch some knees, but no broken bones." We did just as we were told and made it to the jeep, just as it was getting to be dusk. Jake loaded all the equipment into the jeep, and drove us to the cabin that Marcus had booked for us for four days. Jake would oversee our sightseeing activities and Paula would be there to provide the food. The cabin was quaint and had all the luxuries one needed. There was an itinerary of activities on the table. All I saw was I had to be ready by seven for breakfast. "Darling, I'm going to take a shower and go to bed. That little hike got me worn out."

"Ah," Marcus said. "No sex? No playing around tonight?"

"Sweet Lord, man, if you are not tired then you can go out and find a bear to play with." He laughed, "Sam, I am tired and will be right behind you."

Next morning, we got up at seven, both of us having slept through our alarms. We heard a knock at the door. It was Paula. Marcus, in his pajama pants, answered the door. "Don't mind me. I've seen worse at this time of morning. At least you have clothes on. Miss Matthew, you must be exhausted, pregnant and all?"

"I'm not pregnant," I replied to Paula who was clearly in her eighth month. "Honey, I've been given a gift. And I can tell right off when a woman's pregnant. I say two weeks maybe a little more. How long have you two been on your honeymoon?" Marcus answered, "About two and a half weeks. We have five days left."

"Well, next time I come by, I'll bring a store-bought pregnancy test. With my string and your wedding ring, and I can tell you the sex of the baby. We do things different here in the wilderness. I'm going to have a home birth with a midwife. We are so far out that by the time I get to the hospital, the baby will be born. Here is your breakfast. I did country ham, a fruit platter, scrambled eggs, and biscuits. There are jellies and honey. Coffee and decaffeinated tea for the misses. I'll tell Jake to go easy on you two this morning, just in case I'm right, which I know I am. See you at lunch. There will be snacks packed for you so you can keep up with your energy needs. Mrs. Matthew, you eat hearty and drink plenty of water. Bye, now."

I was still sitting in the bed, "Marcus," I asked. "Do you think she is right?"

"If so, maybe we need to get back sooner. Pregnant. You know I did not mean for this to happen to us this soon. The boys are five months old, and if you are pregnant, that will put the baby's birth when they are fourteen months old. I'm not worried about handling five children. The house will be finished. We can move all the nannies in, and the nurse, plus Peter and Hilda. My concern is your health."

I was stunned. "Marcus my period was due three weeks ago. I had not given it any thought. I figured it has been late before, and well, I guess, I forgot it. I told you it had not been exactly thirty days for the shot to take affect and I took them at least twice."

"Maybe she is wrong," he spoke.

"If I am, I am. What about you, are you ready for another child?" I asked.

"Yes, Sam, I'd like to have my own biological child. One that is yours and mine. The boys are yours and Joseph's. I love them like my own. They have the Matthew name, but I see Joseph in them every day. And Ester and Matilda are adopted, and have my name, but clearly, they look like their mother. I want one, at least, that looks like me and you. Can you understand that sweetheart? I know it does not matter who their biological parent is; I am their father. But someday, it will be only right to tell the boys the truth, and the girls know they are adopted, and even though we tell them about their biological parents, they are too young to remember much."

"Darling, if I am pregnant with your child, it would make me so happy to do that for you. Let's eat. I am starved." I put my robe on and sat down at the table, then removed the covers to the dishes, "Goodness, if I am pregnant at least I can justify the weight gain. Can you handle me fat again?"

"Sam, I love to see the changes in your body. I do not consider you fat and I know you; you will always get that pretty little figure back. Your vanity means a lot to you."

"Marcus, sit down, sweetheart. It's all speculation until I take the test. And then it might be so early it could show a false answer. When we get back, we will see Dr. McCullough. And you know if I am pregnant, she's going to lecture you."

"I know. I am a greedy pig, as my mother would say."

"Taste the biscuits. They are so good with the raw honey and the homemade butter."

"Oh my God. It tastes like heaven. I have not had country ham in years. Pass me the cantaloupe, please. This is such a good breakfast. Sam, you have eaten everything on your plate?"

"Yes, and that last biscuit is mine. I know, I am just so hungry. Marcus, will you shower first? I am still tired; I'd like to go to back to bed for at least thirty minutes. I am tired, but we did hike five miles yesterday."

"Yes, my love. You nap. I will get ready and go tell Jake we will start the next excursion at nine." I crawled back into bed and was asleep in minutes.

✳ ✳ ✳

Marcus showered and changed into his jeans and t-shirt. He went out the door and found Jake waiting patiently in the jeep.

"Well, Paula told me her suspicions and gave me a strict warning that Mrs. Matthew needs to take it a little less strenuous, so I thought we could drive to the falls and do some trout fishing. Trout is one of Paula's specialties and she thought we could all have dinner together. Paula reads cards and really believes in all that shit. Paula, she lives her life very purely. Wild bee honey, herbs, we have a goat, chicken for fresh eggs. She believes in natural ways. The old ways that are about forgotten. She has written it all down to pass on to her child. I think she'd like to publish it."

Marcus said, "Send me a copy. I have a publishing friend and I know Sam would like a copy of it. If you do not mind. I'd like for her to sleep awhile, pregnant or not. I know she's tired."

"Yeah, let's drive over to my office, and I'll show you the

pictures of the bears we have spotted here and some of the animals we are trying to protect, like the bobcat and the red squirrel. We've been working on a government grant to help preserve these animals and enact some laws that would keep poachers out of our national forest, but under the new president, he has underfunded a lot of the money that funded our natural treasures."

"Well, you are in luck. We have a good friend who is an environmental attorney and a state senator. I'll put you in touch with him."

"That'd be great." We got into the jeep and went to Jake's office, where he showed me what he was working on. Jim was taking out some young environmentalist to find some evidence of an extinct fish, "Good morning, Jim. Your wife's breakfast was right on. I've never seen Sam eat so much."

"Paula's predictions are usually right. So, five kids? Man, you might want to slow down and definitely start that princess treatment before you find yourself in the doghouse. You know it is always our fault, no matter the woman's participation."

Marcus laughed, "Suggestion noted." Marcus went back to the cabin about noon and Samantha was just getting up. "Well, hello sleeping beauty. You certainly took a long nap. Would you like to shower, dress, and have lunch next to a small area where the trout are known to be plentiful? Jake said we could reach it by jeep. Just a short distance from here and Paula will make us a picnic lunch. Their suggestion is we catch dinner, which Jake assured me we would catch enough trout for a good supper, and Paula would cook. Trout is supposed to be one of her special dishes. They would like for all of us—you, me, Jim, Jake, and Paula—to have a family-style dinner. She is picking up a pregnancy test and she wants to read your fortune."

"Sweetie, it's up to you," I replied.

"If this sounds fun to you, then I am for it. But you know I do not place much stock in fortune-telling. You said yourself the test could show a false positive because it's too early to really tell."

"Marcus, this sounds like fun. You know I love games, natural ways, and old wives' tales."

"Yes, please. I'd love this sort of afternoon."

"It'd take me thirty minutes to get ready." He came to the bed where she was sitting, "Sam, if we are pregnant, I really want you to consider cutting back on work. I worry that your health may be affected, and your anxiety levels may increase."

"Marcus, it is what it is. If I am pregnant, I'd love it because it's yours. And of course, I will do what I need to do to be healthy. It's our family and I love all our kids, but I want to have your baby, lots of them." He took her hand, raised her chin up, and kissed her on the lips, nipping them.

"Yes, Mrs. Matthew, I love you and you are the center of my universe."

I got off the bed , pulled my short nightie over my head, and jumped in the shower. "Please God," I whispered to myself, "If I am pregnant, let everything be okay with me and the baby. He is a good man and deserves this. His generosity is so unusual, and I am so blessed to have him as my husband and as the father to our children." I lathered my washrag and washed my stomach; it will be hard to see my stomach stretch out again. I had a few stretch marks from last time, and my boobs and butt were curvier. I am a vain woman; I do not want to be fat and unattractive to Marcus. I am thirty and I am not sure how much older I want to be to have children. Marcus is thirty-four and is as handsome as ever. It's just unfair that the woman goes through all the bodily changes. Isabella is still gorgeous even after having the twins at 45.

She confided in me that she had some cosmetic work done, and wholeheartedly believes in it. Margaret had three children and looks good for her age. She did not worry so much about her body changing. She said Saul had to look beyond just the physical beauty, and what she had was intellectual beauty.

I know I have a mixture of their philosophies, as I had abandonment issues that I am still working on. Marcus keeps reassuring me he loves me for who I am, faults and all. I pulled on jeans and tennis shoes and a t-shirt, grabbed my hat, and went to find the men. They had a small boat hitched behind the jeep. Everything was loaded, including a picnic lunch. They were waiting on me, "Sorry guys. I seemed to be running slow today." Jake said, "That's all right. We are placing bets on who catches the most trout."

"Well, can I get in on that bet?"

"Sure. We are laying three to one odds. What can we put you in for?"

"So, if I bet five dollars that I will catch the most, then you three will owe me fifteen apiece, is that right?"

"Yes, honey," Marcus said, "Is that your bet?"

"Yes, I am feeling lucky." We all got into the jeep. Paula passed us and waved. She was returning from the store. The area we were going to was about a mile away. Jake pulled the jeep up to the dock and Jim and Marcus unloaded the boat. "Come here, Sam, Let me help you with your life preserver. Step over carefully into the boat. There is some sunscreen there you need to put on. It will be hot on the water and with the sun reflecting off the water, you might get a burn." All three men were already dark from the sun and with Marcus' Spanish descent, he was the darkest.

Jim was handling the motor ring and got us to the spot where the trout were jumping, trying to swim upstream. Jake baited all the poles and handed each of us one. I threw my line in and immediately caught some trout. Marcus took the net and helped me get it into the boat. We had a mesh trap to keep the fish fresh by keeping them in the water. Jim caught the next one and Marcus caught the next three. We had five, which was plenty, but Jake said he was not willing to give up that easily. I used the hand sanitizer and opened the picnic basket. There were egg sandwiches and pimento cheese sandwiches. I ate one of each and peeled myself an orange. There was fresh squeezed lemonade.

Then I went back to fishing. The men all had a beer and were eating sandwiches as they fished. Marcus caught two more. Then Jake caught a giant trout. He said, "Well, at least I caught the biggest so far." Jake caught another four and Jim said we reached had our limit for the day. Jake steered the boat back to be loaded on the trailer behind the jeep. He caught the most fish and said he thought the winnings should go to Paula since she is doing all the cooking.

We went back to Jim and Paula's cabin, where she had already begun to prepare our meal. She had coleslaw and was mixing hush puppies. The men cleaned the fish. Paula said, "If you want to freshen up, I put out clean towels. I also have a test kit for you if you want to see if I am right."

"Paula, you know that it's really too early for this to be 100 percent right."

"Yes, I know. But I'm betting on how you look and what I think."

"Okay, I'm going to pee on the stick. I have to go anyway." I went into the exceptionally clean bathroom and washed up. There was the kit on the back of the toilet, so I pulled down my jeans and panties and put the stick under my pee stream. I placed the stick on the side of the sink and washed my hands. In five minutes, the stick turned blue, indicating I was pregnant. Well, it's not too soon. According to the directions, it could detect the pregnancy hormone within three days of conception, which would put the conception date on the night I had gotten tipsy. Marcus had sex with me three or four times, and I had thrown up the next day. I came out of the bathroom. The fish was baking with carrots and onions around them. The smell of the food was heavenly. I was so hungry. Paula smiled at me, "Well, I was right?" I smiled. "It did turn blue?"

"Honey, you are as pregnant as I am. Go tell your man he's going to be a daddy again."

"Marcus, darling, I have something to show you." I held the stick out where he could see it.

✳ ✳ ✳

"This means we are pregnant, Sam."

"Darling, if this is correct and it was able to pick up the pregnancy hormone, then yes, that's what it means." Paula came over to the chair Marcus was sitting in, I was sitting on the arm holding the stick. "She's pregnant, just like I said she was. You're her husband, can you not see the difference in her in the last few days? Tiredness, hunger, and changes in her skin color?"

"She looks like she has a glow about her face."

"That's the hormones changing the pigmentation in her skin. How about her stomach, how have you not seen any changes? The changes are subtle at first. Anyway, after dinner let's see what the tarot cards say. I believe in the spirits that rule the universe. If you are wondering, there are no bad spirits, just the way you interrupt them. Life it what you make of it. Lots of folk could not live in the wilderness, but it suits me. No people passing judgment because of the way I choose to live.

We live our days not by the clock, but by what the sky says and what nature tells us. Nature was our director of life long before Christianity. If you listen and really know your body, it will tell you if you're sick, if you're pregnant. That's why I am confident in having a home birth. I know Jim and the mid-wife will be there if my body needs help delivering our baby boy. Now, I also believe that sometimes we must use doctors. But Jim and Jake have had broken bones, bad cuts, and I stitched them up or set the bone, and they healed perfectly. But, I believe, if say, a bear mangled them? Then yes, I take them to the hospital in a jeep. That would be the fastest form of transportation." Jim came over, "Honey, I'm not sure that we should be telling them everything you believe. These folks are not judgmental, I can tell, and they are deeply in love. So, they understand."

Sam spoke up, "I think all your information is fascinating." Marcus said, "And I'd be glad to help you get your book published. I told them I'd introduced them to Joseph, as they are trying to get an environmental grant to help save some of the animals that are headed for extinction."

"Paula, my body is telling me that that fish smells so good, that it's not going to make it much longer if we do not eat," Jake laughed. "Have some fresh squeezed lemonade. How did you hear about our little business here?"

"I asked around and your name came up. I thought the experience would be one Samantha and I would enjoy. We are different I guess; we are risk takers. I love Sam with my whole being and would love her enough to let her go, if that was what she wanted."

"I guessed that," Paula said. "Fish is ready. I'm going to put it on the table—buffet style—and let you help yourself. And don't be shy, we have plenty of fish. Oh, thanks, Marcus, for the bet money. You are a generous man. That's what I see in you." We all got a plate. The trout, carrots, and baby onions smelled mouthwatering. She had also fixed potato au gratin, one of Jim's favorite foods. Then there was a fresh salad that had dandelions in it, as well as mushrooms and other vegetables from her garden. She had made a garlic dressing to go over it and there was wild blueberry cobbler and homemade ice cream. Jake said, "How about another beer, Marcus?"

"That's great. And Paula, this trout is heavenly. Everything tastes better than anything I have eaten in a long time."

"Well, out here, Marcus, nature keeps your head, heart, and senses clear. Now, Mrs. Matthew, I have a treat for you. I want you to try some goat's milk. It is better for you than cow's milk, and it tastes better. And if you can get your children on it, they'd be healthier. But you must start them while they are young, eating pure, otherwise they won't take to clean eating."

"Call me Samantha, please. I would be interested in advice, on my twins especially. One has always been smaller and the other you cannot fill up. I still have them on breast milk as they are only five months old."

"That's smart," she replied.

"And the girls, they are adopted. Marcus was appointed by their mother as the one to take care of them if something happened to both parents. Unfortunately, both parents were killed in a car wreck. They were two and four when that happened. We've had them six months, and they never talk about their parents. Just occasionally. Marcus knew their mother the best; she worked for him, and she had no other family. The father has an elderly grandmother, who we keep the girls in touch with, and one of them talks a lot about her dad. But they call us mommy and daddy—they have since we first took them in." Paula said, "They are young. It's like a cat will nurse young dogs, and they will grow to accept each other because the basic need to be loved and nourished is inherent in them. People are the same. These little girls needed to have the basic needs of love and security met. Later in life, they may want to know more about their parents, but they will grow up accepting you two as their mom and dad. They feel the strong bond between you two. I say you will have an incredibly happy and trusting heap of children, which is a good thing. This world needs more children who are raised right to become productive contributors to this world of ours. Now, who is ready for wild blueberry cobbler and homemade goat milk ice cream?"

"Me," said Sam, "This milk is delicious. It's thicker than cow's milk and tastes better." Jake said, "Are you breaking out the tarot cards to give us a bedtime reading or something for us to ponder tonight?" Jim said, "Marcus, another beer? We make our own beer, and it will make you sleep like a baby."

"Yes, man. I'm loving every minute of our visit. And I can tell that my wife will stay in touch with you. I will be sorry to have to go tomorrow, but we have five days left of our honeymoon and Sam wants to visit a lady we met in Wyoming, about three hours from here. And then we must get back to our ranch and talk to the people we have running it about some improvements I want to make. I'd like to make some of your suggestions, about creating some other interests for the visitors that come there to stay. I'd also like to include your excursion on the list of things that our guests may want to experience.

"Of course, if that's okay with the three of you?" Jake said, "That'd be great. I like to talk to you about some ideas I have."

"Jake, I'll give you my project manager and you can talk to her. We will make some things happen. Now Paula, break out those cards and some more cobbler please." Jim dished up the cobbler and Jake got Marcus another beer. "Samantha, would you like something else?"

"Just some water, please," she replied. Jim got a glass of ice water. Paula said, "Now first, give me your wedding ring and let's see if you're having a boy or girl. That is, if you want to know, Samantha?" She took off her wedding ring and handed it to Paula who put it on a chain. Paula held it over Samantha's stomach. Now she held it over her hand and said, "If it swings it's a girl, if it circles, it's a boy. The ring started swinging back and forth. "Marcus, it's a girl. You're going to have another girl." Marcus smiled, "I hope she looks just like her mother."

✳ ✳ ✳

I smiled. I knew that she would be special to me. "I cannot wait, darling, our first biological girl."

"Now, if you have cravings for salt, which you will, that will be a little girl. Did you notice how you ate the potato salad and the pickles I put in your lunches?" I laughed, "I noticed that I was hungrier than I had been in a long time, and I was thinking that I was going to have to double up on the exercise when we get back home."

"Well, I am sorry to tell you, in your first trimester, you are going to experience tremendous morning sickness."

"Oh God, that is something I will not look forward to."

"Just drink plenty of water and keep saltine crackers around. You need to eat, and you will be okay. Do you want to see what the cards say?"

"Yes," I responded. "I've never had a tarot reading."

"Well, just remember that they do not predict sad things. It's your choice. How you choose to take their suggestions is how it will affect your life. The cards do make suggestions; it's how you take those suggestions that will impact your life. Do you understand, Samantha?"

"Yes, I am not afraid. Please, deal them." Paula dealt cards to me first and said, "The High Priestess, and the Sun card, then the Empress. These symbolize that you are pregnant; the Empress is the mother card. The sun card means new life and new growth. The High Priestess means your family comes before work. Now Marcus, the cancer card is the love card which you just told us how you felt about your wife. Capricorn means you live your life true to yourself. You also have a deep connection within a relationship or a forever partner. Now the hanged man means that there is coming a major end in something in your life.

It means you're closing one door before you open another one. It is the sign of change and transition. It means a clearing out of something old. Now remember, cards only predict. It's your judgment and your actions that determine the outcome of the cards."

"Jake, let's see what's going on with you," Paula continued. "Capricorn, looks like a deep love connection is coming your way." Paula turned over the Sun card, "New growth and new life. Looks like you are going to have a baby come into your life and you will know yourself and what to do."

"Paula," Jake said. "I hope that card is right. But do you think you could hurry it up? I am not getting any younger."

"Maybe you need to get out more. Your actions determine your choices and staying up here with the bears can't help you find human companionship." Jim said, "Well, I think it's past time we all went to bed. I know you want to get an early start tomorrow and its midnight. Seven will come early for breakfast. Then Jake will drive you down to the helicopter to take you back to town." We left their cabin; I was growing tired. Marcus opened the door to our cabin and sat down to pull his boots off. "I am too tired for a shower. And they are right about the beer, I'm so wasted that getting undressed and into bed is about all I'm capable of tonight."

"I am so full. And to think we may be having a baby girl."

"Maybe" Marcus said, "We certainly have had enough sex to overcome the percentages of the birth control you're taking. That puts you in the one percent range. And the Matthew's have strong swimmers. Look at dad—he had my sisters in his sixties."

"Darling, I am not Isabella. I hope that when I get the age she was when she had your twin sisters, that we are slowing down on the baby department." Marcus pulled his sleep pants on, I put a t-shirt on, and we got into bed. "Well, the good thing about having money, Sam, is that if we want more children, which I hope you do, we can hire someone to carry a fertilized egg. If they are ours, I do not care who delivers them. I do not want to keep putting your body through childbirth. If I lost, you…" I smothered his mouth with a kiss.

"Sweetheart, let's take it one baby at a time." He pulled me into his arms, and we went to sleep immediately.

The next morning, we both woke up at six and Marcus reached over and pulled me into his arms and wanted to talk. "Now sweets, tell me how you feel about children and me wanting more? I know we discussed it before we got married, and I was excited about the twins, then Lisa dies and we get two more, not really your choice, but left to me. Before they were born, she had asked me to be their guardian because she had no one else. Lisa had been a foster child and her circumstance were not pretty. As soon as she was sixteen, she left home and worked, put herself through school, lived, and paid for her life. Sometimes she said it was a choice of school supplies or eating. Often, she would eat the free crackers and condiments in restaurants. She said she'd go on dates with men so she could have a meal and have sex with them, so she'd have a wonderful place to sleep. Then she met me in a restaurant one day, where I was having lunch and I asked her about herself. She mistook that I wanted a date, and well, you know, sex for money. She was eighteen, and she was hard already, she had negotiated her life and knew who I was, and really wanted to drive a hard bargain. She wanted a job that paid enough for her to live in a decent place, and she wanted me to help with college. I asked her to meet me at my office and I said she had misunderstood. I told her 'Here's what I am going to do. I want you to start out as my receptionist and I want you to enroll full time in business management and move into one of my apartments, free of charge. I will pay for everything: schooling, living expenses, a car, food, clothing—whatever you need. You will get a company credit card and the only condition is you learn my business and figure out ways to better organize the business.' She went to work for me at eighteen and never missed a day of work. She worked all the time and went to school. For six years she devoted herself to our agreement, and even got her MBA. She moved up very quickly and as soon as an opening came up in the office, she took it, until she was running my office and stayed on top of every job site. She'd even go out to the sites and check on the workers. If she found out someone was goofing off, she'd confront them on the spot. Everyone knew that she worked directly for me and she had the say so on so many aspects of the business. She learned to read contracts and blueprints. She was good at her job. I even offered to send her to law school, but she said that that would be too much. All she wanted to do was learn how every department worked and look for ways to make it better. She was happy and we became close. There was talk that she was sleeping with the boss, but that never happened. I never dated my employees. But because she was being sponsored by me, that's how she got away with taking over each job and bossing others around. But, of course, I felt like we were friends, and like family, but that was it."

"She started dating her husband when she was about twenty-five. He was a supervisor on a competitor's job. He worked hard and liked Lisa, but was devoted to his company. Lisa finally talked him in to coming to work for the Matthew's Group. He went through one of our training programs and was loyal to me. He asked her to marry him about a year after they met. She had this neat, orderly plan on how her life was going to be. She needed to plug in a husband who held the same work ethic she did. She asked me to give her away at her wedding. By that time, she was making over a hundred thousand dollars a year. For a brief time, her and Mike dated, but that never worked out. Lisa was all business and did not like to play. Everything had to be about the company and pleasing me and getting ahead. I could never convince her that she was doing an excellent job. She had job security with me, and more than that, I thought of her as family."

"She never lightened up and enjoyed her life, no matter how much she achieved. Her marriage seemed, on the surface, alright. They both worked long hours, and both made good money. She bought some land from me in one of our up-and-coming subdivisions, and together they built their house. What she didn't know, he did. Or she'd contract with one of my workers on their own time to do some construction work on their house. The house was finished, and Lisa got pregnant. Everything had to fit into her plan, then Matilda was born, and she enrolled her into the daycare immediately. The child had to be eighteen weeks old before they would take her. That's the only reason she took family leave, but every so often, she'd be at the office with the baby, just to make sure the temp she hired was handling things well enough. After she put Matilda in daycare, she still worked the long hours, and her husband, who was a good father, began to complain about Matilda being raised by daycare workers and not her mother. Even Mike got involved and was really the only friend Lisa had. He became the doting uncle and helped when he could. He was already head of security and had to travel a lot. So, his time was limited, but he got to know Lisa and would try to get her to relax and enjoy motherhood. Then right on schedule, as soon as Matilda turned one, she got pregnant with Ester. And the same thing, daycare then preschool. She was hard on the girls. They never really had what I would call a 'carefree' childhood. It was always about working hard, learning, and getting ahead of their school mates. There was never much time for fun."

"After a few years of this, I guess her husband, who knew how headstrong she was, turned to gambling. Dad was still the head of the company, so I traveled a lot, and of course, Mike was normally with me. Neither one of us knew that there was trouble in their marriage. One day, she came into my office with papers of guardianship that she had had Robert draw up and asked me if anything happened to her or her husband together, if would I be the girl's guardian. She knew neither one of them had family. He was raised by his grandmother, who they helped financially. She had a mother who was into drugs and men, and she would never allow the girls to know who she was. Her mom had given Lisa to the system and was in and out of her life so that she was never adopted, but remained in foster care."

"Lisa never talked much about her growing up, but she was

tough and street smart. So that's how I ended up with the girls, and then you wanted to adopt them, and now we have four incredibly young children. And if Paula and the stick is right, a fifth one, which will be born just after the boys' first birthday. Sam, I am putting you under a lot with kids and your work."

"I'm just thinking, Marcus, that I want this life." I kissed him passionately, and immediately, I could feel the effects by the hardness of his cock. "I have everything I want. You treat me like a queen. We both have the same parenting styles. I want a big family, full of love, surrounded by curiosity and adventure. You said, 'barefoot and pregnant'? Well, bring it on. I love our family, and unless we both go broke, and cannot afford the help, then we are more fortunate than most couples. We both have so much support from our families and friends. Darling, I would not change things. A little better timing, but we will talk to Dr. McCullough about that. I get pregnant very easily, so she will figure out the best prevention."

"So, what are we talking? Ten or more children?"

"I will say I really want to make sure my body recovers after each baby. You know I am vain about my looks and always want you to desire me."

"Well, sweetheart, I desire you right now." And with that, he moved over me, parted my legs, and plunged his hard cock into already wet core. I began to moan, and his breath quickened. We matched each thrust until I could feel Marcus quicken, and he brought me to my peak. The release ran down my legs and I was so wet. He kissed me again, "I promised you a good life and you will have it. Now, if it is truly a girl..."

"And I said if I am truly pregnant, you mean?"

"Yes, how about naming our daughter Isabella, after my mother? I've always adored that name and it stays with our Spanish culture."

"Isabella it is." I rubbed my stomach and then a violent wave of nausea came over me. "Marcus, get a trash can. I cannot make it to the bathroom." He leapt across the bed and gave the nearest trash can and everything I had eaten came up. He held my hair back and brought a cold cloth. "Should I get you something?"

"Water, please." I rinsed my mouth out. There was a knock at the door. It was 7:30. "Tell whoever it is, I will have to have more time." Marcus opened the door and Paula was there with water and green tea. "You go on and get dressed," she said to Marcus. "Jim will have breakfast for you. I am going to take care of our new mom. You are going to have to push back your departure plans until noon. She will be okay, but right now she needs rest, and a lot of water. This tea will help settle her stomach. No more rich foods for this little one. Now go, she does not want you to see her puking her guts out."

Marcus headed for the shower and came out in jeans and a t-shirt. "Are you sure Sam?"

"Yes, this is a different feeling. I never got this way with the boys. I don't want to move." And about that time, another wave of nausea moved across my stomach. I picked up the bucket and more of last night's dinner came up. I felt like I was heaving my stomach out. "Go, Marcus. Please," I spoke. He kissed my forehead and Paula pushed him out the door.

"Honey, I told you if it were a girl this would happen. But I will get you through this first morning." It was about three when I felt well enough to shower and dress. Paula had been giving me cups of ginger tea and crackers. Finally, the nausea went away, and I had thrown up nothing in the last hour. I had drank a lot of water and could hardly get up to pee, but Paula stayed with me and helped me get to the bathroom and evened cleaned up my vomit. She was a good woman and I hoped to see her again and stay in touch with her. She said it could have been all the rich food I had eaten, but she suggested I check with my doctor as soon as I get back.

"We are about two weeks; I really can only guess."

"I know I am late two weeks, but I am never on time with my period. And well, it has been two weeks since I partied at the Cowboy Cafe, where Marcus and I got a little crazy, and well, we were supposed to make sure we waited thirty days before we stopped using extra protection. And I was in no shape to resist him,"

"And he's a man," she said, "And when the call of the wild hits them, they think with only one head. He loves you though, that's apparent. So, he's a good man there. He will take care of his family and love you to death. I'm sure he's outside beating himself up because he took advantage. You have probably just stopped using protection since that night, right?"

"Yes, what the hell? I already took the risk and well, I do get pregnant easily, so I just went along with him. Truthfully, I love feeling him raw inside me."

"I know what you mean, nothing better than riding bare back. Jim and I have enjoyed us being pregnant, no need to worry about getting pregnant or am I late or whatever."

"Men just have it too easy," I spoke.

"That's why I hold them responsible for always doing the right thing. This baby seems important to you two. I know you said the girls were adopted, but you have twin boys."

"Yes, that's another story." I felt like I could tell her anything, "Well, Marcus is not the biological father of the boys. The man who is their father was the love of my life, and to shorten the story, he had a one-night stand with an old girlfriend, even though he had always said we would be together. I thought he should have chosen me over the woman he married. He chose her because he believed it was the honorable thing to do. He married her and four months later I discovered I was pregnant. Neither one of us put our relationship ahead of our careers or had pledged that we would not sleep with anyone else. We say sex is different from love. He slept with Emily, his wife, and I had slept with Marcus the day before Joseph and I took off on a trip, where I was expecting a ring. Instead, he told me about his situation. I lost it completely, and when I found out I was pregnant, I refused to tell him. Out of spite, I guess, but I did not want him to choose me because I was pregnant. He would have too, but I thought about Emily and how that left her. Her family felt disgraced, and his parents had never wanted us to marry because he is black, and they are expecting important things from him in politics. Then Marcus, from the first time we were together, said he knew I was the one for him. So, when he got back from his trip to Spain, his mother is Spanish, he came by my office and saw what shape I was in. He just rescued me from myself. He pursued me, but never made any demands on me. He is so different from Joseph. He has always known who he was and what he wants in life. His father owns a major construction company that he turned over to Marcus, who has become the head of the Matthew family. He is super responsible and…"

Paula interjected, "And super rich."

"Yes, but you'd never know it. He is generous and kind and a hard worker. So, when I was going to tell him about the twins and tell him it was not fair to him that I was carrying another man's child, he proposed. He said if they were not biologically his, they were a part of me, and he loved me. No matter whose they were. I said yes, and now I am surer every day that he is the right man for me. And the real father, Joseph, is a good man and he knows I am no politician's wife. He knows now we would have had issues because he still puts his career ahead of his wife and child, and she is ok with that."

"So, fate took care of you, or nature, whatever you want to call it. Both of you ended up with the right man."

"Yes, and Marcus, being who he is, said someday the boys will have to know the truth, so he made Joseph a part of our family."

"Like I said," Paula said, "You got a good one. Now let's get you on your way to the helicopter pad. Here is a copy of my book and I know we will stay in touch."

I opened the door and Marcus, Jake, and Jim were waiting

patiently. Marcus walked toward me, "Baby, are you feeling better?" I kissed his cheek. "Yes, Paula got me back on my feet." He took my suitcase and put it in the jeep.

"I called Rosie and said we would see her tomorrow, that you were not feeling well. But she checked us out of our suite and is insisting we stay with her. She owns the hotel, as well as most things in Dubois, I found out from Jim and Jake."

"Yep, she is something. Her husband passed about five years ago, and she been busy doubling his fortune. She's a smart woman, but wild as a buck. She has a daughter that her husband, Tom, raised like a boy. Then Rosie sent her off to college. I hear she's back. Let's get going." I hugged Paula and Jim. "We will be seeing you again."

"Good luck with your baby, Paula. Call and let me know everything is ok."

"I will and you do the same." Marcus handed a check to Jim for twenty thousand dollars.

"Hope that covers everything."

"Man, you know our price was seven thousand dollars."

"I know, but I want to invest in what you're doing here. I want my kids to see what a clean environment looks like. There will be more. When I get back, I'll make those calls." He shook Marcus' hand and kissed my cheek, then we headed toward the helicopter.

Once aboard, it was less than forty minutes before we were sitting down on Rosie's pasture. She was there in a jeep with a beautiful redhead. Marcus got out and helped me out. The girl got out and Rosie said, "This is my daughter, Dee. She's back from college and hopefully here to help her old maw with the ranch." We all shook hands and Rosie said, "And who is this?" Dee said, "That's Jake Terry. We went to school together."

"How are you, Dee?" Jake asked.

"A better rider than you are still."

Jake said, "Is that so? Well, I accept your challenge anytime." Rosie said, "Well, Jake, how about tomorrow? It's too late for you to fly back tonight and supper's on the table. You know that big old house has plenty of room."

"Well, Miss Rosie, if Dee does not mind, I'll take you up on it." Jake was interested in more than riding. You could tell from the expression on his face. We made it back to the ranch. Miss Rosie had Chad show us our rooms. They were lovely and had many antiques. There was a large king size bed in each room with an adjoining bathroom. Chad placed our suitcases in the room, then a house cleaner named Lynn showed up and asked us if she could unpack for us. She placed a cheese tray along with wine and water on a table. I picked up a piece of a cheese and cracker. I was hungry. I told Lynn that we would unpack; we are only staying a couple of days.

"Miss Rosie likes everyone to dress for dinner. She likes to set a formal table. Then after that, she has entertainment in the music room. So, dinner is in an hour, and please call me on the intercom if there anything you need," Lynn said.

"Wow, Miss Rosie really does it all the old fashion way. Good thing the herd is not with us."

Marcus said, "Sam, I think it's important to dress up once a week for dinner. May be a good thing to instruct our children. I want manners to be implemented with our kids. I do not want them ever feeling awkward because they do not know how to handle a situation."

"Sweetheart, I think that's a good idea. The boys will have to be older before that they understand how they are supposed to act." I laid down on the bed and said, "Will you wake me in thirty minutes? Just need a little rest."

"Sweetheart, that's a good idea. I'm going to unpack our suitcases. I hope we brought something formal enough. I'm fairly sure I did."

"You always bring a suit for meetings. You probably have that black linen suit in there," I pointed out.

"You're right. I brought that just in case we did something formal together, which I had planned to the night we went to the Cowboy Café. But you were having so much fun riding the mechanical bull and line dancing, then we left for our wilderness excursion and there wasn't time."

"What do you think about Jake's reaction to Dee?" I asked.

"I think Jake's in trouble. She's a handful—a stallion—but he is so hot for her. And she for him. If they get through their egos, then maybe there might be something there," Marcus replied.

"The sexual tension is there. I think that's going to be the first hurdle. Then maybe they may have a relationship, remember how stubborn you were when we first met?"

"Let's see, you thought I was so arrogant and a spoiled rich playboy. And now you know you are the love of my life, and I am pussy whipped, some would say."

"Pussy whipped, never. Smart, you know how to handle your wife. That makes you smart." I yawned and Marcus took the throw and covered me up.

Marcus finished putting the clothes away and ate some cheese and had two glasses of wine. He went into the bathroom, so not to wake Samantha, and dialed Mike. He answered right away. "You're right, giving them some stability and showing that you are a good guy has loosened his wife's tongue. She said the man who called her husband had something to do with the development. He felt that he was forced into a deal that was not favorable to him. He felt that the bank was in collusion with you and never gave him a chance to catch up his loans. He said he could have found the money to catch up on the loans, so he feels he lost 50 million dollars, and was offered pennies.

Marcus said, "That the builder?"

"Yeah, I'm tracking him down. His wife left him, and I talked with her, and she said all he did was drink and bitch about a conspiracy. She said he is bipolar, went off his medications, and had a fierce temper. She said he moved out of state but does not know where. She has custody of their three boys, and of course, she got their house and five million. He agreed to complete custody; she asked for nothing else. He filed for bankruptcy after the divorce and does not have money now. So, I told the police, and they are trying to track him down. I have a lead on him in New Jersey. The hired guy's name is Dave, and his wife's name is Sherry. Dave's in rehab. I really hope it works out for them; she would take him back if he straightened out his life. She is doing well, is working in our New Jersey office, and using our tuition program to go back to school. She has always wanted to be a nurse." Marcus said, "That sounds great. Just keep security tight on all members of my family, including Sam's parents."

"Man, have fun. You have five days to come back to this mayhem. Joseph's a good guy. He's good with the kids, just a little overindulgent. Ester has him wrapped around her finger. She made him attend a tea party and did his makeup. He's a good sport. He spends a lot of time with the boys, who are crawling all over the house, so we have child-proofed the house. Jacob will always find something to explore. Jared would rather be picked up, rocked, and be read to. His Sophia is a baby doll, so cute and happy. She and Ester play a lot together. Matilda would rather hang out with the nannies and is always on the computer. Either Joseph or I take them to school. Matilda got her report card today and made straight A's. Ester just gets a report, and her area of concern is she so social and talks constantly. Other than that, her report is good."

"Thanks, Mike. When you find the man, let me know. Sounds like he's unstable and is looking for someone to blame for his poor business decisions. Most of his workers stayed on and are working for us. And everything the supervisor says about them is that they are good workers and are grateful not to have lost their jobs. Sam worked out a great deal for all participants and was very generous. So, I am happy with what she did. I'm not concerned about us taking over the development. Have you seen the progress on my house?"

"Yep. Drywall is going up now and will be finished in about six months. The designers have started working on sketches. Denise is on it; she knows you need to get the kids settled."

"And how are you and Denise?" Marcus asked.

"I like her. She and I have a lot in common, I can see it going forward. For the first time in years, I can see me in a relationship. Great in bed."

"Okay, man too much information. Just handle everything until I get back. We needed this. Thanks, man."

"Marcus, you know I always got your back."

"Yep, I know. I am grateful for your friendship. Got to get ready for dinner." Marcus hung up and sat down on the bed and rubbed Samantha's hair, which was spread all over the pillow. "Sweetheart, time to get ready." She stretched out her arms. "I needed that nap. You go to the shower; I'm going to take a bath." By the time they were supposed to be ready, they were downstairs and dressed to the tee. Sam had on a beautiful black dress that showed her figure-off. Her hair was up and she wore the diamonds Marcus had given her as a gift when they got married. He had on my linen suit and white shirt. Sam had picked out a gray silk tie. Jake joined in a blue suit.

He seemed more prepared than Marcus would have thought for an impromptu invitation. Sam said, "You look great."

"Oh. Miss Rosie makes sure that she has clothes ready just in case you are not prepared. She owns the local clothing store. Chad asked my size and I now have two days of clothes, free of charge." Dee came down the stairs in a red silk dress. Her red hair pulled back with a diamond hair clasp and long, dangling diamond earrings. Marcus looked at Jake, "Play it cool. Let her have her way. Treat her like a princess."

"You know, her dad spoiled her rotten," he

spoke. "So, you need to relax and let her win."

"But man, she is so demanding."

"Then rule her in bed. Let her have her way everywhere else. Unless you are not interested in developing a relationship." Jake said, "Well, I have always had a crush on her."

"Then use that. Man, be smart."

✳✳✳

"I agree," I spoke. "The tactics Marcus uses on me, well I never say no." Dee came forward, "We will join Mom in the dining room."

"By the way," Jake said, "You look beautiful."

"Well," Dee said, "You clean up well also." We entered the dining room gleaming with silver, crystal, and fine China.

Miss Rosie had name placards for everyone. She was at the head of the table, dressed in green satin with green aquamarine jewels. She asked everyone to be seated, and waiters started to pour wine and water. I only drank water and ate only small portions. Mostly vegetables and a small portion of the beef Wellington. She had the cherries jubilee, and its flame was the highlight of the dinner. I only took a small bit of that. After the dinner, she asked everyone to join her in the music room. She pulled me aside, "So, what's up, darling? You barely ate and no liquor. That's not what I remember at the Cowboy Café."

"Miss Rosie, I think I may be pregnant."

"Well darling, let's find out for sure tonight. I will call my friend and he can come over to take your blood. Tonight, he will have the lab run the test."

"You do not have to do that."

"It's no problem. And Dr. James will do anything to get an invite to my ranch to see me. I just invite him for drinks. He is in love with me and wants to marry me. I want to marry him. I just need to make sure he's not controlling, like Dee's father was. I cannot be controlled or dictated. He might like that, but I need more time to live my life- like I am in my twenties. I got married so young. I want some time to live life before I say 'I do' again."

"Chase, call Dr. James, tell him to bring his doctor's bag and come for drinks." Making a face, Chase said, "Yes."

"Honey," she said, "Never sleep with the help. Gives them false hope. Chase has nothing in common with me except he's good in bed and I have a weakness for young, good-looking men."

"I got you, Miss Rosie. And thank you." We went into the music room and drinks were already being served. Miss Rosie said, "Bring Mrs. Matthew a glass of sparkling water. That man of yours is gorgeous."

I smiled. "Yes, he is."

"He's devoted to you, not a player. Now help me get Jake and Dee past their little standoff. They've been in love since high school, but my daughter has been spoiled rotten and is headstrong. She wants to be the best at everything. She graduated in business and wants to get her MBA and a law degree. Which is fine. I just want some grandkids before I die." We joined the others in the music room, Dee was already at the microphone singing *These Boots Were Made for Walking*. She was clearly enjoying herself and Jake had not taken his eyes off her. Marcus was sitting in a chair drinking a bourbon. "Miss Rosie, this is some music room. I mean your own stage, and all."

"We are a family of singers, even if it is karaoke. Have you ever tried it?"

"No ma'am. Just choir singing."

"Well, if you ever get my daughter off the stage, you need to try it." Marcus went up to the stage, took the mic, and whispered something in her ear. She went straight to Jake and straddled his lap. He placed his hand on her back and began to caress it. Marcus spoke through the microphone, "This is for the only woman, except for those related to me, I have ever loved." Marcus was different under the influence of Miss Rosie's bourbon, but he did not miss a beat of the song by his good friend Elton, *Your Song*. Miss Rosie said, "Choir, my ass. Boy, where'd you learn to sing like that?"

"Where's your piano?" Marcus went over to the piano and began to play *The Piano Man*. "I can play drums, bass, or harmonica. I had an ear for music, so my mom, being who she is, gave me every lesson she could squeeze in a week. My parents believed in keeping us busy through education, challenging work, or volunteering. She even visited me in Europe when they had asked her to MC a fashion event and had me model. I was twenty-one. As soon as college came around, I headed for Europe. Thought I might be a musician. But not my parents, if I wanted my trust fund check, I had to go to school. That's how I met so many famous musicians. I stayed on for graduate school, stretched it out as long as I could with my good friend, Mike. Sam, you know Mike. Head of security? Then my dad had his first heart attack, and I went home. Went to helping him in the business. Then when he was better, I went back and finished graduate school. Then left Europe and went back home. My mom had already given birth to my sisters, and my dad had his hands full. So, at thirty-one, I took over the Matthew's Construction Group. Loved it, had sown my wild oats, was looking for the one. And her name is Samantha Amanda Weinstein Matthew, and she is giving me my fifth child."

The butler came and said, "Dr. James is here, Miss Rosie."

"Send him in please." Dr. James came in and kissed Miss Rosie on the cheek.

"Well, for starters, let me get you a glass of bourbon and

introduce you to the young woman who needs to know for sure she is pregnant. She has not touched a drink and has eaten like a mouse for fear she will throw it back up." Miss Rosie said.

"Okay." He downed his brandy and said,

"Mrs....?" "Matthe,w," I said back.

"Step here into the bathroom and let me draw your blood. If Chad will run it over to the hospital lab, we will have the results in an hour." I went into the bathroom and Marcus walked across the room. "What's going on, sweetheart?" Miss Rosie said, "He is my doctor friend and I asked him over to take her blood to find out for sure if she is pregnant."

"I want to know, and I think you do to," I spoke.

"Sure, if you're good with it, I am too." So, the doctor removed a needle and a syringe, used an alcohol rub on my arm, stuck the needle in, and withdrew one vial. "That's all we need." He rubbed the needle mark on my arm and placed a Band-Aid on it. Miss Rosie called Chad over and said, "Be a dear and run this over to the hospital lab. Tell them to call Dr. James as soon as they have the results."

"Sure, thing Miss Rosie. Then can I retire for the night?"

"Sure, Chad. And take the Beamer if you want to go to the club tonight. Just bring it back in the morning. Samantha, you have to give them some perks when you use them for your pleasure." Dee was doing *Islands in the Stream* and she had Jake singing with her. They made a cute couple. So, Paula's cards are right. Only the cards said a baby first, then love. I went and sat on the chair arm next to Marcus. He had had his second bourbon, which was unlike him. He had something on his mind. Dr. James' phone rang. "This is Dr. James. Yes, Peggy. Shows patient is pregnant, about three weeks and she has a high amount of the hormone that causes hyperemesis gravidarum. Thank you, Peggy." Dr. James walked over to where Marcus and I was sitting and said, "Congratulations, you are pregnant, but it may not be a smooth sailing pregnancy. So, I'm going to give you my opinion and then follow up with your OB/GYN when you get back home. Have you found that you're nauseous a lot? Certain foods just make you vomit until there is nothing left but dry heaves?"

"Well, just yesterday," I said. "I had a lot of fish and spicy food. It took me at least two hours to stop throwing up, and then I just wanted to sleep." Dr. James explained the condition to me and said it's rare that I had it this early in my pregnancy. He said to eat bland food and drink plenty of water. "Do you remember, Catharine, the Duchess of Cambridge had to be hospitalized for excessive nausea and vomiting? Well, you have the same thing. There is a web site that you should go to and research what your body can go through, and how you can protect yourself and your baby."

"You mean our baby is at risk?"

"Well, could be if you and the baby do not get enough nutrients. You could end up on a feeding tube or an IV. But all of this is worst case scenario. You are early in your pregnancy, so eat five small meals a day. Drink plenty of fluid, and ginger tea has been known to help. It also has a section on how a father feels to see his wife go through the worse of it, so read that part Marcus. It's not your fault, just genetics. Your next one could be different all together."

"Well, that does not help. It makes me feel like shit," Marcus said. I could tell he was agitated, as he was drinking his third bourbon.

"Honey, let's go to bed. Sleep always helps," I spoke. Miss Rosie said, "Clever idea. I'll leave those two to themselves, and Dr. James, I'll walk you out."

Marcus and I went to our room. He hugged me and said, "I am sorry. You know I'd die for you. Do not have this baby just for me."

"Marcus," I said, "This is our baby, and we will get through this. I want Isabella, and if she is already causing this much trouble? Just think what she will be like." He hugged me, "She will be beautiful, like her mother."

We undressed and made love. He was very gentle; he kissed me for a long time and held me to him. He unbuttoned my gown, and I held my arms up so he could pull the gown over my head. He kissed my breasts one at a time, then he began to roll my nipples. He was a little tipsy, but he was not in the mood for rough sex tonight. He pulled his cock out of his pajama pants and pulled me up on him so that I was in a seated position. I slid down on his penis. I was always wet when he was aroused. It just felt good to have him in me. Then he turned me over on my back and propped himself up on his arms and began to thrust up and down. "This is for you, darling. You just got your body back in shape and now you will start all over."

"Marcus, darling, fuck me harder. I'm almost there." He reached down and adjusted his penis so that it scraped against my clitoris. That's all it took, and I orgasmed. I could not stand the situation anymore. "Please, darling. I cannot handle your thrusting anymore."

"Well, darling, I am there also, so one more thrust. Meet me with your body and let's come together." I moved my body to meet his and I could feel the hot stickiness between my legs. He tensed for a moment and his breathing was shallow. He rolled over on his back, "After tomorrow, I want to fly home. I miss the kids. I have enjoyed every minute of our honeymoon, but I want to see my kids and hold them and tell them I love them. I want to see my mom and dad and Saul and Margaret and my sisters. Let's have a big Matthews party. It's Thanksgiving, and I'd love to have my aunts and uncles and cousins and my half-brother. Life is short and moves so fast. The house will be finished in four months, but I am going to put every worker on it, and some subs, and have it finished sooner so we can move in. We need the space and housing for the extra help. I want you comfortable while you go through this pregnancy. Hell, let's fly up Paula and Jim and their baby and Miss Rosie and Jake. We can leave tomorrow evening after the competition between Dee and Jake. Then leave for our ranch, meet with the caregivers of the ranch, and let them know the changes I want to make. See the trainer and outline what my plans are on developing a racehorse and studding his father out. I'll send a supervisor down, along with an architect, to design a house here for our family." He talked until the alcohol put him to sleep. I got up and took a quick shower and put on a fresh gown. Marcus was out; he never snored, but tonight he was laying on his back. I got him to turn over and he mentioned something like, "I will take care of you." I pulled the covers over both of us and went to sleep. This man would walk through hot coals for his family. But something was worrying him. I would have to remind him of our vow of no secrets tomorrow.

Breakfast was at seven—buffet style—outside. Miss Rosie had to put tables up outside and had the servers put the food out on the tables. Dr. James was there, which meant that Miss Rosie had company last night. Jake and Dee were especially close. Everyone had sex last night. Miss Rosie was not judgmental, so staying over was not an issue.

After breakfast, the game between Dee and Jake was who could break the new wild stallion that they had caught last week. Dee was going first, then Jake, until one of them tamed the horse. They would take thirty minutes each time until the horse was broken. This was dangerous, but both were good riders. Dee mounted the horse first and the handlers let loose the ropes and open the gates. Out came the horse, bucking, and trying to throw her off. She was doing well, and everyone was cheering her on. She was signaling that something was wrong. Before the handlers could catch the horse, Dee fell to the ground. Miss Rosie and Jake were the first to get to her. She was knocked out, and her leg was folded under her. The handlers checked the saddle, one of her stirrups had come loose and she could not stay on the horse. Dr. James ran over with his bag and said, "Do not move her. Call an ambulance." She was coming to, but she could not speak. "My leg," was all she could whisper. The paramedics got there quickly and moved her on a body-board. She has a concussion and a broken leg. "Let's get her to the hospital and see what else could be wrong." Miss Rosie and Jake rode in the ambulance with her. We followed in our jeep with Dr. James.

"Rosie was going to announce our engagement today," he spoke. "Dee will be fine. She is a tough one, like her mother." Dr. James looked worried. He was a good man and wanted to protect both of them. He had no children and had never been married. He had waited since they were kids for Rosie to agree to marry him. "I hope Rosie does not see this as an omen. She can be that way," he said.

They took Dee right into X-ray and her spleen was ruptured. She had a broken leg and a concussion. She went right into surgery to remove the spleen. They set her leg and they wrapped her head. Dr. James was in the operating room with her, but because of his closeness to Rosie and Dee, the hospital would not let him perform the surgery. He did come out and tell us all she would be fine.

She was in recovery and would be waking up soon. Rosie and Jake were the first to be admitted. "My sweet girl, I'll fire the person who did not check that saddle and almost got my daughter killed," Rosie said. "Mom, I've had tumbles before."

Jake reached for her hand, "So, I guess when you are well, we will have a rematch?"

"Yea, well this did not count," Dee smiled.

"Darling, I was going to announce this today. Dr. James asked me to marry him, and I said yes. Thought we'd have a spring wedding."

"That's great, mom. I am happy for you," Dee said. Marcus and I wanted to see her to tell her we were leaving but hoped to have her and her mom up for Thanksgiving. "I'd love that. Have not spent much time in New York, count us in," Rosie said. Marcus leaned over and kissed her and said, "Life is short and if you find true love, go for it." I kissed her cheek, "But let no man change you. They have to accept you for who you are."

As we were telling Miss Rosie bye, a call came in from Chase. "This was not accident. Rosie, the stirrups were cut halfway through. I called the sheriff to investigate." Marcus stepped away from the rest of us and dialed Mike. "Have you found him yet?"

"No, he's not in New Jersey and he must be flying under a fictitious name. Why?" Mike asked.

"Something happened. It was unusual, a stirrup was cut, and a rider was injured," Marcus responded.

"I am on my way," Mike said. "And I'll send a local security company back with you, just in case."

"Mike, I want you handle things here with the sheriff. I want to head home."

Mike said, "I understand. I'll take the other jet. Just be careful."

"I will," Marcus said.

"I'm setting you up with a security guy. His name is Zachary

Hunt. He will meet you at the plane."

"Mike, Sam is pregnant and very sick."

"Well, hell, you really meant it when you said you were going to keep your wife barefoot and pregnant."

"Just find a nurse to fly with her. She was sick with the boys, but there is a name for it this time. Hey, keep it to yourself, I'd like to tell the kids."

"Gotcha, those boys are really growing and getting so verbal. Joseph left today, said he'd like to stay until you and Samantha got back, but his wife called and asked him to come home with their daughter. Someday maybe, I will get it, this marriage thing. But right now, me and Denise are having fun borrowing yours and going home to our own fun."

"Mike, just find this guy before someone gets really hurt."

✷✷✷

We boarded the jet, and everyone got strapped in for takeoff. The pilot was going over the checklist with the co-pilot. Marcus was not flying this time but was on the telephone with Mike. He had Zachary next to him and I was in the bedroom with the nurse. The nurse had decided, because flying might cause me to be more nauseous, that she would hook me up to an IV and give me something to help me sleep through the flight. Marcus was tense and worried, but he said he'd take care of it, whatever it is, and he'd talk to me when we got back to New York.

This was late September, and he had called his decorator to call a party planner and plan a big Halloween party inside the building, primarily in the lobby and the penthouse. He was excited for the holidays to come. "Yes, Mike, no sign of him?"

"No, Marcus, he is letting us know he's around and he can get to people who are around you. I've got so much security on all your family."

"Great, I called Dad and let him know under no circumstances was anyone to travel without security. I told him as much as he needed to know for now. Make sure the office is covered, and the development."

"He will slip up," Mike said, "We will catch him."

"I know, but I have this feeling that he's going to get too close to someone. Like you or Samantha or the kids."

"Yea, I think I'm going to hang out at the development so he can target me."

Mike said, "Motherfucker. Marcus, not without

me." "I am on the other jet headed back."

There was a gentle nudging, "Sam, sweetheart, it's time to wake up." The nurse had removed the IV. I was very groggy. Marcus helped me down the stairs and got me to my seat in the limo that was waiting for our arrival. He got in beside me and told the driver to go straight to the penthouse. It was late, and the kids would be in bed. He sent Zachery and the nurse back on his jet and said let him know if anything arose concerning Dee. When we got home, we went in and looked at all the kids and kissed them goodnight. The nannies had all retired, and the night nurse was on duty. Ester woke up and said, "Daddy," and threw her arms around his neck. "You're back. I'm so glad. I missed you so much." He kissed her chubby little hands and then tucked them under the covers. "Sleep, baby. Mommy and I will see you at breakfast."

"Daddy, did you bring presents?"

"Yes, pumpkin, I always do. But you are to choose one of yours to give away."

"Daddy, you always bring good presents."

"Ester, mommy brought a special present."

"Do I have to give it back?" she asked.

"No, sweetheart. We will keep this present." I kissed her goodnight; Matilda did not wake up. She was a heavy sleeper. The boys were in their cribs and had grown so much since we had left. They were both on their stomachs, butts up. Marcus covered them up. He said, "Samantha, I love my family and I am going to love this new baby."

"Marcus, I am so tired. Let's go to bed, then we are going to have that serious talk about what's going on."

"Yes, Sam. Tomorrow I will tell you. My plan is to get the house finished by Thanksgiving. I'd like a more secure area. Someone is stalking us, you and me." He kissed my head and said, "I am going to take a quick shower."

"I'm not, darling. I still feel drugged, so I'm going to bed."

"Sit down on the chaise. Sam, let me help you get your boots off." I sat down and he pulled my boots off and socks. He rubbed my feet and then pulled me up to stand. I unbuttoned my jeans and removed my shirt.

"I think I'm just going to sleep in my bra and panties. I'm just too tired to get fully undressed." "Honey, turn around." And he unhooked my bra and cupped my breasts. He then turned me around and kissed each breast, "I thought I had these back to myself. I better enjoy them while I can." He pulled out one of my gowns and I held my arms up and he slipped over my head. He then turned the covers down and I slid in. He kissed me on the forehead, and I went to sleep. I do not remember him coming to bed.

I woke up in his arms, he was still asleep. I traced his face and the cleft in his chin with my fingers. Then there was a knock and the door burst open, Ester was leading Matilda.

"I told you I was not dreaming. See, daddy and mommy are home." Marcus turned over and said, "Sam, I take it back, sleeping late and making love in the morning was heavenly."

"You wanted a house full of kids."

"Yep, I do." He grabbed the girls and tickled them until Ester said, "Daddy, you are going to make me wet my pants."

"Then go get dressed and we will see you at the breakfast table." He turned to me, "How do you feel?"

"Tired, but glad to be back to all this chaos."

"Sam, after breakfast, meet me in my office and let's talk.

Mike will be over this morning." He pulled on a pair of jeans and a t-shirt. He headed to the bathroom.

"No way, I get it first. I have to pee really bad."

Marcus said, "That's one thing I'm going to like about the new house. My own bathroom." I kissed him, took off to the bathroom, then jumped in the shower. Marcus came in, brushed his teeth, and ran a brush through his hair. He looked at his face and said, "I'm not shaving today." He went downstairs. I finished dressing and went to breakfast.

Pancakes, the girl's favorite. The nannies had the boys in their highchairs and had given them teething biscuits. Jacob had already cut a tooth. The nannies had made them cereal for breakfast. Everyone was seated, and with a pancake in her mouth, Ester asked, "Daddy, tell us mommy's special gift."

"Mommy, you want to tell everyone?" I looked at the girls, "You are going to have another baby brother or sister."

"What? There are too many babies here already!" Marcus laughed, "I told you sweetheart, we are keeping this present. Now here's the thing, mommy gets sick a lot and needs rest, so can I count on you girls?" Matilda kicked Ester, "Yes, Daddy." Ester stuck her tongue out at Matilda. I looked to Marcus, "Ester, apologize to your sister."

"She kicked me."

"Girls, those presents are going to be earned. So, eat your breakfast and go write me a report or a drawing of our family getting along." The babies were ready to be wiped off and

Taken to the playroom. Marcus thanked the nannies and said, "Will you excuse us? We are having a meeting today and later, when the twins are napping, I'd liked to talk to both of you."

"Yes, sir." They wiped the faces of the boys and removed them from their high chairs. Both girls asked to be excused. I smiled at Marcus. "Good, daddy. Want another girl?"

"As long as the baby is healthy, I do not care."

"Those two are giving me good practice."

"I now know why my dad had a heart attack when he was blessed with twin girls." Peter came in and said, "Mr. Matthew. Mr. Mike is here."

"Tell him to meet us in my office. And bring coffee and muffins, please."

"Yes, sir," Peter said.

"Let's go, sweetie. I want to talk to you, then the staff." We left the breakfast table where Mike was eating a muffin and having coffee.

"Samantha, remember the man we bought the development from?"

"Yes," I said.

"He was not happy and never called about working with us. Right, well he's gone off the deep end and has caused some issues at the job site."

Mike said, "Like he hired someone to torch your home and

I'm fairly sure he cut Dee's stirrups. So, we have doubled the security until he is caught. Everyone needs to be extra careful. I want everyone to adhere to the rules I typed out. Then, we need to talk to the staff."

"So far, we've been unable to catch him. He left his wife and disappeared. Has not contacted his kids. He'll slip up and we'll will catch him," Mike added.

"So that is why I want Halloween contained to this building and the lobby and the penthouse. I planned to have the living areas of the house finished, as well as the bedrooms we need. I will then finish the rest of this house. The grounds and amenities are finished. Anyway, I feel that we will be safer there."

"Please, Marcus, you too adhere to Mike's protocol."

"Sweetheart, I plan to catch this guy. Mike, let's go to the staff." He grabbed another muffin and they headed to the playroom.

"Call your dad, sweetheart, and talk to him. I talked to my parents, so my aunts and cousins are covered. Mike, get a hold of Philippe. Make sure he is aware and has plenty of security."

I picked up the telephone and said, "Dad, first let me tell you, I'm pregnant again."

"Daughter, you may need to slow down," Saul responded.

"It was not planned, but we are excited. Marcus wanted me to tell you about this nutcase that has been causing serious problems. So, he assigned extra security to you and Margaret."

"I noticed a van outside the mansion on the road. Marcus

will get him; I know how important it is to him to keep his family safe."

"Dad, I'm really tired, so I am going back to bed. Plus, I'm having severe nausea early in this pregnancy. I'm going to call Rick, fill him in, and take one day to recuperate from our trip."

"So, by the time the twins are walking you are going to be giving birth to another baby?" Saul said.

"Give me that telephone, you old man. Samantha, darling, rest, eat lots of crackers and ginger ale. When you are ready, I'll come over and help out," Margaret said.

"Thank you. I love you both."

Marcus had the lobby and the penthouse decorated for Halloween. He had invited all the neighbors in the building and hired all types of kid's entertainment. He took the girls to get their costumes. Of course, both girls wanted to be princesses. We got lamb costumes for the boys, and since I was not really showing, I wanted to be a sexy witch. Marcus dressed as a pirate. Security was tight, and each person had to be checked out that entered the building or the penthouse. Mike was there. He and Denise came as Count and Mrs. Dracula. Saul dropped in with Margaret. Margaret played the part of a nun and Saul was a priest, which went against his Jewish faith.

It's Halloween, and everyone was having fun. Marcus' sisters came as sexy devils. The immodesty of the costume gave Marcus concern. Isabella and John Marcus came as Henry VIII and Anne Boleyn. Marcus had hired a reputable party planner, and Mike had run security on each staff member. I was back up at the penthouse with some of the kids from the girls' school and their parents. I knew that there was security everywhere. The boys were getting tired, and I had told Marcus that I'd help the nannies put them to bed. I was not feeling too well. He kissed me passionately and said he'd be up as the party was starting to wind down. We expected it to end no later than ten.

A man approached me in a waiter's outfit and said, "Mrs. Matthew, your husband asked if you'd come down and get the girls." I did not think anything of the request; the girls were tired. It was past their bedtime. So, I took the elevator down. It did seem strange that their nanny did not bring them up. There was Marcus, talking to the parents of one of the kids in the building. Matilda and Ester were not in sight; neither was their nanny.

"Darling," I said, "Did you want me to take the girls up?"

"What are you talking about, Sam? The girls are bobbing for apples in the next room. Who told you this?" He looked alarmed. He shouted to Mike, "He's in the building!" As quick as light, all the security personnel and Mike went into action. They did not want to scare the children, so they moved quickly and quietly. Marcus made the announcement that the party would be ending, as it was lat, and tomorrow was a school day. The parents began to gather their children and take them to their various condominiums.

Since the penthouse was eight stories up, the elevators were kept busy. Mike had men on the elevators dressed as attendants and on every floor. The building was surround by security. Mike quickly said, "Sam, what did this person look like?"

"He had red hair and a mustache. Regular waiter clothes, 6 feet tall. I assumed he was with the staff of the party planner. He knew who I was and used Marcus' name." Marcus called the owner of the party planning company and asked if she deviated from the list she had given his head of security. She said she had one waiter cancel at the last minute and she had called a staffing company, who was reliable and ran background checks on all their staff.

"Give me the name of the staffing company," said Mike. You could see the anger flash on Marcus' face. Mike said, "Look, man, you knew we had strict protocol. Who is a redheaded man with a mustache that's about 6 feet tall?"

"We do not have anyone that meets that description." Mike went out into the ally over from the building and found a man in his underwear tied up in his car. Mike untied him and called the police. "What happened?" asked Mike.

"I was getting out of my car when a man put a gun to my head and said, 'Give me your clothes and you will not get hurt.' So, I gave him my clothes and he tied me up. Thank God, you found me." The police arrived and provided the man with a blanket and took him downtown for questioning. Mike went back to the penthouse and the kids had gone to bed. The caterers were cleaning up.

"Well, Marcus," said Mike. "I found a man, two streets over, tied up and in his underwear. He said a man stuck a gun in his face as he was getting out of his car and told him he would not get hurt if he gave him his clothes. So, he did. The man tied him up and left."

"It has to be our man. But Samantha would have recognized him."

"It was a plant, Marcus. It was not him. He is showing us how he can get close to you, no matter how much security you have. So, no one leaves until I question everyone." I was so shaken that I had to excuse myself to our bedroom to throw up. Marcus was right behind me. "I'm just so sorry, Sam. He will slip up."

"He could have hurt someone."

"But he didn't."

"Marcus, he was in our home. Or his man was. I do not feel safe here. Maybe I should take the kids and stay somewhere else," I spoke.

"I cannot protect you anywhere else. The house has three weeks and then we can move in. It will have the major rooms finished, and the bedrooms we need. Sam, I need to be with you. Mike is staying with us. I'm locking access to the lobby and the penthouse elevator. I told you I'd protect my family with my life."

"I do not want it to come to that."

"This man, this *beast*, is sick. He feels like I took it all from him. He will surface, we will find him."

Marcus went back downstairs and said to Mike, "I know, man, call in the goon squad. That's right, have them do whatever it takes. Call the papers, offer a million dollars for information leading to his arrest. Find him. Samantha wants to leave and hide out."

"You told her that's not a good idea."

"Of course. I'm going to check on my kids and see to Sam."

"I'll be here buddy, all night. I have men all around this building, on every floor. All elevators are locked down. Try to comfort Sam."

Marcus went to the nursery; the twins were asleep. Then he peeked in on the girls. Fast asleep. "Call dad," Marcus said to Mike. "And Saul. Make sure all my family is okay. Let dad and Saul know what happen."

"I got you, man. This guy is whacked, but he's taking chances. With that kind of reward on the street, he will turn up. I give it about 2 days."

"The house will be ready for us in three weeks. I'm moving my family in. I feel like, even though it's not completely complete, we have a better chance of taking care of my wife and kids safely."

Marcus went up to Sam. She was trembling and had her pajamas on all ready for bed. She was white as a ghost.

"Sweetheart, do I need to call the doctor over?"

"No, just hold me and our child." Marcus took off his costume, washed his face, laid down beside Samantha, and held her. "I promised I'd take care of you. He wants me, Sam. I am going to make sure that he stays away from my family."

✻ ✻ ✻

Next morning, I awoke to violent heaving. I finally got to where there was nothing else to throw up. Marcus was frantic and called the doctor. Dr. McCullough said, "Take her straight to the hospital. Marcus, this is early. She needs to stay at the hospital and let us hook her up to an IV, with nutrients and fluids."

"I am on my way," he said. I was too sick to change clothes, so he scooped me up, wrapped a blanket round me, called Mike to call the limo and be ready to leave as soon as it got there. Mike called the limo driver and an extra security van to follow. Marcus came down the elevator, the door attendant opened the door of the car. Mike got in the front seat. "Take us to the hospital," Mike said. Marcus called back and said, "Talk to the children's nurse and explain what was going on. But do not tell the children, just their nannies. Tell them to keep them home from school today, but tell them to keep them busy with projects. They know the drill. Keep their music appointments, but no outside activities, not even on the balcony. I'll call as soon as I know something about Sam."

I was too weak to move, other than to snuggle against Marcus. I was eight weeks pregnant, and at this time, I did not know if I could survive this. "Sweetheart," he said. "We will get through this."

"Marcus, I want this baby. It's ours, this child is you and me. We deserve this child; you deserve this child."

"Sam, I love you and I cannot stand your suffering." He kissed my forehead. The driver pulled up in front of the emergency room. The attendants were there with a gurney and immediately took me from Marcus. Matthews do not wait, and they took me straight up to the Matthew's suite. Dr. McCullough was there, along with two nurses. The nurse hooked up the IV and had an ultrasound to see the progression of the baby. She rubbed the gel on my stomach; it was cold and wet. She placed the monitor on my stomach and turned the monitor toward us. The screen showed a tiny fetus, and we could hear the heartbeat.

"Okay, the baby's good. Small, but seems strong. So, tell me what started this bout?" Marcus explained the Halloween party and how we had intense security around the penthouse and the building. "So," Dr. McCullough said, "This is Samantha's nerves which brought about this severe nausea. We need to keep her here for a few days so we can monitor her closely. Marcus, you know we have talked about her panic attacks. I say this is a combo of the baby and a panic attack. Samantha, did you get any sleep last night?"

"No, not really. Spent most of the time in the bathroom."

"Let's get you a sedative. This IV will give you the nutrients and the fluids you need. Once you wake up, we will reassess. Marcus, can you arrange for security while she is here?"

"Of course." He called Mike who was outside the door waiting. "Arrange security on the suite and in the hallway and the elevator up to the suite."

"Marcus, I'll stay myself. Everything is buttoned down for all the family, even the extended family."

"Thanks, man." The phone rang. It was John Marcus, "Son, what's going on?"

"Dad, I'm at the hospital with Sam. I am up to my neck with this stalker."

"We've had things like this before. We'll get through it."

"I offered a million-dollar reward, so it will bring someone forward."

"Take care of Samantha. Let me help you son."

"Dad, I welcome your help. You know this is the first time I had something like this happen."

"I know, son, and you are a fair man, so I know this guy is a nut. So, I'm going to start making calls. Have Mike call me please. Marcus, take care of Samantha. Saul said Margaret is on the way to the penthouse to distract the children."

"Dad, I did not tell the kids anything yet. I did not want to scare them."

"That's what you should do. As little information until utterly necessary. I'll be in contact later with you. Thanks, dad." He hung up.

The drugs were working; I could feel myself falling asleep. Marcus pulled a chair close to my bed and held my hand. "Sam, I love you so much. There is no family without you being a part of it." He kissed me on the lips just as I fell asleep.

It was after three when I woke up. Marcus was stretched out on the couch in the room; he looked like hell. He sensed I was awake and said, "Darling, how are you feeling?"

"Better." The nurse rang for Dr. McCullough. Dr. McCullough came up immediately.

"Samantha, let's start you on a very bland diet. Eat what you can. Do not worry, we have the baby being fed through the IV. Your color is better, so I say unless there is a change, I'd like to keep you for three days."

Marcus said, "I have around-the-clock security. I want all people entering to be screened by Mike."

"I do not blame you, Marcus. But what I'd like to see you do is go home and shower. Get some rest, a good meal, and see your children. Samantha will be fine. We've got her, but she needs you to be okay, also."

"Go, sweetheart. I feel better, and safe. I want to sleep some more. Our kids need their father, and you need to answer their questions about where mommy is."

"If you're sure."

"I'm sure. There is no family without their daddy." He gave me a long, passionate kiss. "If that's what you want. I'll leave Mike here with you."

"No, take Mike with you. His men know how to handle the security. I'd rather Mike be with you and the children."

The phone rang. It was Saul. "Sweetheart, do not worry about the office. I talked to Rick. He's got everything under control. I told him I'd be in later to help him out."

"Dad, I'd hate for you to do that."

"Samantha Amanda Weinstein Matthew. I would not consider myself a good father or grandfather if I did not pitch in. And you have forgotten, but I'm still a hell of an attorney."

"Thanks, dad."

"Sweetie, take care of you and my new grandchild. Margaret's over at the penthouse, and John Marcus is on the problem. Isabella is going over tomorrow to have a tea party with the girls and help with their lessons. Let the grandparents do their part. I told you you'd make my life interesting, full of adventure. I love you, little girl."

He hung up. I was so blessed to have so many people who cared for me. Marcus left with Mike. The nurse brought me some mashed potatoes, toast, and ginger ale. Surprisingly, I was able to keep it down. She gave me another sedative to sleep. I was fast asleep.

9 781956 876901